MW00653349

ALICE'S WAR

ALICE'S
WAR

WILLIAM
MCCLAIN

Alice's War

All rights reserved. No part of this book may be reproduced or transmitted in any form or by any means, print, electronic or otherwise, including photocopying, without express written consent.

This is a work of fiction. All incidents, dialogue, and characters, with the exception of well-known historical figures, are products of the author's imagination and are not to be construed as real. Where real-life historical figures are mentioned, the situations, incidents, and dialogues concerning those persons are entirely fictional and are not intended to depict actual events or to change the entirely fictional nature of the work. In all other respects, any resemblance to actual persons, living or dead, events, or locales is entirely coincidental.

Copyright © 2023 William McClain
WilliamMcClainWriter@gmail.com

green
planet
books

Published by:
Green Planet Books
williammcclainwriter.com

Book Design: Design for Writers
Printed in the United States of America
Publisher's Cataloging-in-Publication data:
McClain, William
Alice's War
ISBN: 978-1-7351598-2-9

Go out into the sunlight and be happy with what you see.
Winston Churchill, *Painting as a Pastime*

CHAPTER 1

Weymouth, April 1939

THE DAY WAS TOO perfect for anything as dreary as a funeral. Even along the south of England, weather this warm was rare in April—so warm that the Channel breezes abandoned their usual role of intensifying the damp coastal chill, and were that day a welcome intrusion. Their cool fingers slipped through the high neck and long sleeves of Alice's black dress, breathing life into her suffocating skin. Their onshore flow brought a hint of salt and seaweed, luring her thoughts away from the solemn proceedings.

A cough nearby brought Alice back. She reset her face to what she hoped was an appropriately mournful expression and tried to focus on the words of the well-meaning vicar. But the service felt heavy and dark, blanketing her soul just as the thick fabric of her dress weighed down her body. Her eyes drifted upwards and outwards to the bluebells just beginning to flood the small woods beyond the churchyard with their soft waves of colour. Even the ancient elms and oaks that stood over the gravestones and should have lent gravity to the service, drew her away instead. The wrens she could hear but not see in the branches overhead had more pertinent things to tell her than the vicar.

A man caught Alice's attention. Although he was standing towards the back of the group of mourners directly across from her, the intensity of his gaze drew her in. Their eyes met briefly before he redirected his attention towards the vicar. His face brought to mind a younger version of her son Henry, although she felt sure she had never met him. It wasn't the presence of a stranger that disquieted her. She didn't expect to know everyone who had crossed paths with her husband. Rather, it was the sense that she was being studied surreptitiously. His fleeting glances in her direction seemed furtive and his focus on the vicar a bit too determined.

She put him out of her mind and tried to concentrate on the service. She noticed Elizabeth Chambers staring at her with her fixed smile, her wool coat securely belted and buttoned to the neck, despite the warm weather. She clasped her black-gloved hands primly in front of her. Elizabeth was a member of their local parish and the wife of a wealthy town councillor. Behind the smile, Alice felt the condescension in her cold measuring eyes. Or was it pity? A pity that savoured her own superiority.

Again, Alice tried to turn her attention to the vicar. She had never been one for ceremonies. She wondered if it was obvious to everyone that her heart was not part of the proceedings. They would think she hadn't loved Edgar, but she had. For almost forty years she had done her best to fulfill Edgar's expectations, centred her own life around his. She would miss him, yet she was not distraught. She knew now that eighteen had been too young to understand her own heart, let alone the heart of a stranger to whom she had pledged to devote her life.

Now Edgar was gone. After decades together, it was difficult to imagine a life separate from him. Was she too old to start over? Did she have the energy to create something of her own?

The cancer had emptied Edgar. Drained away his vigour and his commanding presence, until the shell that remained was unrecognizable from the man who, for almost three decades, ruled unchallenged over the district courthouse. But the cancer had emptied her as well. Throughout his long decline she had nursed and watched over him. Her reserves were spent. She was eager for all this to be done—the service, the endless stream of well-intentioned visitors, the expectations of mourning and grief. More than anything, she wanted space for herself, to assess what remained.

Alice was momentarily startled by Henry's hand, gently taking her arm. She became aware of the silence. The vicar had stopped talking, and all eyes were on her. It was time to finally bury her husband. With a sense of decorum that he'd inherited from Edgar, her tall, handsome son led her to the graveside. There she tossed the sprig of lily-of-the-valley she had been holding, followed by the obligatory handful of soil.

Henry, Kathleen, and Alice's three grandchildren made the trip down from London four days ago. Kathleen, as usual, assumed control from the moment of her arrival, commanding poor Rosa around the kitchen as if, after forty years of domestic service in the Standfield home, she didn't know her own craft. Kathleen's physical presence made it hard to resist her. She was tall and confident, with the athletic frame of someone you would think had been raised to ride horses and chase hounds through her country estate, when in fact, she had grown up in the outskirts of London.

Alice knew her daughter-in-law's actions were well-intended. Besides, she had no energy for deciding details around the service or the subsequent wake to be held at her home. She had that still to endure. Then Henry and family would return to London, her loss would slowly recede from the consciousness of her Weymouth neighbours, and she would, for the first time in her life, be free.

The vicar finished his last words of benediction. Alice felt herself again being led by her son, this time to his motorcar. It was fortunate that Alice was physically small and adept at taking up as little space as possible. Kathleen and Alice had to share the front passenger seat, with the three grandchildren filling up the back seat.

"Such a beautiful service. And the vicar's remarks were lovely—so appropriate," Kathleen remarked. Alice couldn't disagree, as she hadn't registered anything the vicar said.

"Stop it!" little Irene demanded from the back seat, interrupting her mother's commentary.

Kathleen twisted her body to face the children, the rim of her expansive black hat knocking Alice's askew. "Martin, leave your sister alone!"

"I didn't do anything," Martin insisted. His older brother, Leo, looked over and smirked.

"Just keep your hands to yourself. And sit up straight, like your brother."

Alice felt solidarity with Martin, squeezed between his younger sister and his older brother, just as Alice was now trapped between her son and daughter-in-law. She knew it was natural for parents to bestow less attention to their second born, each milestone carrying the slight tarnish of familiarity. And then Irene, their only daughter, arrived. The six years between her and Martin confined her in perpetuity as the baby of the family. Yet from Alice's perspective, Martin was the one who was overlooked in the push and shove of family life.

As Henry steered the motorcar down Alice's drive, she surveyed Elm House with a new perspective. It had a stately presence, with its Portland-stone walls, tall, white-framed windows, and expansive wood-beam gables. Strange to think that the place now belonged to her. It didn't feel that way, despite the fact that she had by now spent most of her life there. But Edgar had been privileged to call Elm House his home through the entirety of his well-ordered lifetime. And it had belonged to the Standfield family for multiple generations.

Alice led the way into the wide entry hall with its high corniced ceilings. Large, black-and-white chessboard tiles, set at a diagonal, ran the length of the hall, bordered on both sides by a black-and-white interlocking tiled pattern. A doorway on the right opened onto a generous sitting room, which connected to the formal dining room in the far-right corner.

Kathleen marched past Alice to the far end of the entry hall, where a side door led to the kitchen. After putting away her coat, Alice followed.

"Mind that you set the smaller dishes towards the front." Kathleen was already supervising Rosa as she trekked back and forth placing the food on the extra serving table they had set up in a corner of the sitting room. Alice noticed Rosa's face redden. She anticipated hearing an earful from her, once Kathleen and family returned to London.

Soon the table was covered with cakes and tarts, slices of ham and roast, sardines, baked eggs, a giant aspic salad, breads and local cheeses, pickled vegetables, and apple cake. It was a wonder to Alice why wakes required such quantities of food.

The day had not placed any physical demands on her, yet Alice felt eager to be off her feet. Besides, she knew that Kathleen would not allow her to help in the kitchen. She made her way into the sitting room and lowered her small frame into her favourite high-backed chair with its rich midnight-blue upholstery. She would play her part, sitting politely and smiling up at the faces of the arriving visitors as they trailed past, offering their awkward condolences.

Without warning, Elizabeth Chambers' face was hovering over Alice, her china-doll eyes and nose hardened by her grim, thin-lipped smile. She patted the top of Alice's hand. "Alice, dear, you look tired. It's to be expected. Edgar's illness has been a burden. He was a remarkable man. But we can't have you thinking your life no longer holds purpose. I'm here to help. We must talk soon." Elizabeth was gone before Alice could muster any response to her remarkable speech.

To Alice's relief, the next to offer condolences was Helen Bascome. Helen lived next door. Alice wished that she could spend time alone with just Helen, with her simple honesty and lack of agenda, but there were others waiting to pay their respects. Helen leaned down to give Alice a hug and then moved on.

Eventually, her guests gravitated into small conversational groups. Left in peace, Alice was content to sip her tea, tuning in or out of the conversations circling nearby. Alice had been watching for the mysterious man she had observed at the graveside service. Apparently, he chose not to attend the wake.

A discussion was playing out just behind where she was sitting. "Hitler completely ignored the Munich Agreement. Anyone taking the trouble to listen to what he's telling the German people must know he won't be satisfied with Czechoslovakia." She recognised the voice of Helen's husband, Thomas. He taught history at their local secondary school.

It was her son, Henry, who responded. "This isn't the time to provoke a conflict. France is in no position to serve as a proper ally, and we've no guarantee that the Commonwealth would do any better. Chamberlain's being cool-headed on this. The Germans can no more afford a major conflict than can we. I say they won't risk it."

Alice had heard enough. She quietly rose from her comfortable chair and made her way back to the kitchen. She should stay up-to-date on what was taking place on the Continent, but she couldn't bear to listen in. She knew where those events were heading. The Great War had been a monumental waste. She couldn't fathom that it might happen again. War threatened everything—her family, her country, her community. And, although it felt selfish to be worried about it, it also threatened her vision of a chapter in her life where her role would not be so tightly conscribed, where she might hope to make her own mark, no matter how small.

Alice found Rosa in the kitchen. "How can I help?" she asked, anxious for something to keep herself occupied. Kathleen swooped into the room before Rosa could answer.

"Alice, my dear, what are you doing in here? It's all been taken care of, and you needn't worry yourself. Come sit down." For the third time that day, she was being led by the arm. *Patience*, she told herself, *soon this will all be behind you.*

As she dutifully returned to her chair, Alice noticed her cat. Oscar was slinking under her best white linen tablecloth, draped like a tent over the main serving table. The plan had been that Oscar would remain outside for the duration of the wake, but someone must have let him in. Now her grandson, Martin, was reaching under the serving table, through the folds of tablecloth, trying to retrieve the cat. Alice knew Martin to be a fellow cat lover.

She had tried to get Edgar to fix the leg on that table. She realised that it, like so many other things, would now be left to her to figure out. As she watched the leg collapsing inward, her initial thought was that perhaps this was Edgar's last contribution from the grave, a way to liven up his own wake. Behind her, Edgar's old grandfather clock began to chime the hour just as the table started tilting precariously to starboard.

It was the meat platter, being the heaviest item, that got things started. It collided mercilessly with the three-tiered china cake stand that had belonged to her mother-in-law, sending tarts and petite fours pelting like missiles in an all-out attack on the quivering aspic salad, which finally gave way as the entire tablecloth began its descent to the floor. The aspic salad took centre stage as it merged with bread, cheese, pickled asparagus, apple cake, china plates, and teacups. Their race to the floor generated an enormous, prolonged crash which caused all conversations to freeze and all heads to turn in their direction. The cat, unscathed, shot off through the dining room in the direction of the kitchen.

Red-faced, Martin got to his feet and then slumped when he caught his mother's glare. Alice quickly intervened, reaching across to take Kathleen's hand. "This is my doing. I should have warned you that the table has a bad leg." Kathleen hesitated and then, with her long, martyr's sigh, turned to survey the shambles. Martin retreated to the kitchen where he pulled a spooked Oscar from under the kitchen table and took him outside.

Alice stood near the wall as Kathleen and Rosa began extracting those food dishes that were still salvageable. Some guests joined in, offering their assistance and advice. It was the distraction Alice needed. She slipped out the kitchen door and sat down on the steps of her back porch beside Martin who was still holding Oscar, stroking his fur and trying to calm him down.

She surveyed her grandson. His cherub-like features were fading under the transformation to adulthood. It occurred to her how little she knew of the young man that was beginning to take form. The family had come to Weymouth for a week's holiday every summer, but with trips to the beach and carnivals and sweet shops and paddle boats, their visits were always a whirlwind of activity and distractions. The family also came down every Christmas, and Edgar's sister's family would join them in Weymouth as well. At those times, her full household left little opportunity for individual connections. She felt she could never really get to know someone in a room full of people.

After a few moments of silence, she leaned over and said solemnly, "Thank you, Martin." Martin looked up from petting Oscar. His mouth hung open, his light blue eyes widening slightly beneath his sandy mop of hair. Alice continued, "Between you and me, these social obligations have never been my cup of tea. I think you may have landed on the best device for bringing an early close to the dreary event."

Martin said nothing. He seemed to be trying to decide if he was being teased. "Did you and Oscar plan this out together, or was this all your idea?" she asked him.

Realising she was not going to get a response from her grandson, Alice looked out to her vegetable patch with its lettuce and radishes already showing promise. "If not for the distraction you and Oscar created, I wouldn't have escaped outdoors for a few minutes. Splendid spring days like this are too rare to be wasted inside."

Martin followed her gaze out towards the garden and then turned his attention back to the cat. After a few moments of stroking Oscar, he looked back at his grandmother. "How are you going to get on without grandfather about?"

It was one of the things that Alice found refreshing about young people—they could get right to the point, without preambles or disclaimers. She thought for a moment before responding, taking in the male greenfinch on a lower branch of the great London plane tree at the back edge of her garden. The bird flew from branch to branch, showing flashes of yellow and green as it searched for insects. "Your grandfather was an important and loved person, both in our family and in Weymouth. He died knowing that he had led a full life and contributed to the lives of the people around him. You can't hope for more than that."

Alice paused as the greenfinch swooped off, disappearing into the stand of trees behind her garden. "When you lose someone, it's important to take time to embrace the loss. Yet it's equally important to move on. Anyone who truly loved you, would want you to move on."

The back door swung open behind them. "Oh, there you are." Kathleen sounded exasperated. "People were wondering where you'd gone." Then, looking over at Martin, "After the trouble you've caused, young man, I should think you'd be making yourself useful in the kitchen." The door slammed shut again.

Alice rose from the porch and reached down to pull Martin to his feet. "Shall we face it together?" she asked with a smile.

CHAPTER 2

Weymouth, July 1939

I T WAS ANOTHER PERFECT July morning, and the breezes off the Channel felt deliciously cool as Alice sat under her broad Panama hat with her sketchbook and binoculars. She wished her summer could stretch on indefinitely. To avoid the holiday crowds, she had set out early with a picnic lunch, a jar of iced tea, and her ever-present, tattered copy of *The Birds of the British Isles* by T. A. Coward. Her route took her past the late-Georgian terraces, over the Town Bridge, which spanned their narrow harbour crowded with fishing trawlers and pleasure craft, and then out past the edge of town to where the beach transitioned to limestone cliffs.

For the first time in her life, she was making her own decisions. She had quickly established a routine built around mornings. It was in the early hours that her creatures were out and going about their business, mostly in search of breakfast. The summer holiday-goers and many of the townsfolk would still be waking up. Their distraction and noise would come later. And then there was that quality of light to be found just after dawn. Alice always felt mornings offered the best light for viewing the world.

Mornings also offered the best chance to avoid the disapproving frowns of her Weymouth neighbours as she rode her bicycle through town. She tried to tell herself that she was no longer the wife of a district judge, so her conformity no longer mattered. But it had mattered for too many years. She still found herself trying to avoid scrutiny. And crossing paths with Elizabeth Chambers that morning was the last thing she wanted.

Elizabeth was out doing her early-morning shopping, her modestly groomed daughter Lydia in tow. Lydia had inherited her mother's fine features, but they were softer, more delicate.

Elizabeth hailed Alice to a stop. "My, this is energetic of you. I do hope it's safe for someone your age to be out on a bicycle."

"Thanks for your concern, but I'm quite used to riding," Alice responded.

"Well, anyway this is most convenient. I've been wanting to extend to you an invitation to join the women's auxiliary for our parish. I should not want you worrying about how you're to fill the empty hours now that you're alone." Standing slightly behind her mother, Lydia stared at the pavement. Her expression hid whatever thoughts she might have about her mother's social agendas.

"That's extremely kind of you. The truth is, I do have some projects that I'm keen to move forward, and there is still so much to sort through of Edgar's things. I will definitely keep your offer in mind though."

Elizabeth forced a smile in response to Alice's refusal. "Well, I don't want to keep you from your… projects. Good day." She glanced over her shoulder. "Come along, Lydia."

Early on, Alice had recognised Elizabeth as a keeper of societal lists and had assumed that her own name was penciled in on the wrong list. After that morning's exchange and given that her status was no longer that of a judge's wife, she was quite certain that her name would now be firmly inked onto the list of those "found wanting". However, she didn't see how it could be avoided. She had no interest in joining Elizabeth's little society for debating Sunday flower arrangements, or in pouring tea at the annual fête.

She put the morning's interaction out of her mind. A steady south wind was driving the waves to shore, filling the air with salt spray and the muffled distant churning of breakers on the shingle beach and stone outcroppings. Alice was welcoming back a small flock of curlews, recently returned from their inland breeding grounds. Her grassy perch just off the footpath and only twenty feet above a narrow cove provided the perfect viewpoint as the stilt-legged birds darted between waves, probing with their exceptionally long, downcurved beaks.

Alice concentrated on sketching the details of their smart, brown, tartan-tweed coats. She had studied art as a youth. Her instructor emphasised aesthetics and favoured classical subjects, vilifying anything modern, especially the French decadence movement. None of that seemed important. Alice was drawn to the beauty she found in living things—the closely viewed anatomy of the bee orchid, the handsome jacket worn by the green tiger beetle, or the sleek arrangement of tail and legs on a sand lizard. By observing and accurately recording their smallest details, she felt a closeness, an understanding of nature that she could never adequately explain to Edgar.

And Alice had a gift for observation, for rendering her subjects with both scientific accuracy and beauty. Her dream was to complete a book containing her drawings and observations of the birds of the coastal regions of Dorset. She couldn't imagine that such a book would attract a large readership. But that was of little importance. To be able to translate her appreciation for the world around her into something of beauty that others might enjoy—that felt to her to be the talent she was born to express.

All those years with Edgar, her fear had been that her life would slip past her without the opportunity to express this part of herself. Like Elizabeth in the Bible, who in her old age was finally granted a child, Alice felt her time had, at last, come. But for how long? As she looked out across the water, she felt a foreboding. She worried that the Channel was neither wide enough nor deep enough to keep the turmoil that was spreading through the Continent from reaching their island.

She tried to focus her thoughts on her drawings. As she looked up from her sketchpad and raised her binoculars, a gust of wind snatched her hat before she could reach up to secure it. Laying down her binoculars and pad, she turned to retrieve it. But a man was already bending to pluck it from the patch of cow parsley where it had landed a few yards behind her. He was close to her age and wearing a brown tweed jacket, grey pants, and a sturdy pair of wellingtons.

He walked over to offer Alice her hat. "It's a battle to keep the sheep from blowing away, let alone hats and sketchbooks."

"Thank you," Alice replied. She did not recognise the stranger.

The man seemed to sense her reserve, and he offered his hand. "Nathan Stone, sheep herder and veterinarian."

Alice had heard of Mr. Stone, but as her household had never raised livestock, she had not had reason to cross paths with him. "Alice Standfield."

"Yes, I know who you are."

Alice recoiled inwardly. She hated being a public figure, and that role persisted, even with Edgar dead.

Mr. Stone looked down at the sketchpad on the grass behind Alice. "Do you mind my asking what you've been sketching?"

Alice did mind but thought it too impolite to refuse. "Curlews."

"I thought perhaps so. Nice to have them back for the season. I heard reports of a red-necked phalarope blown off course in these parts and was hoping to spot it."

It was then that Alice noticed the pair of binoculars around Mr. Stone's neck. "Are you a bird enthusiast?"

"Whenever I can snatch the spare minutes." He paused. "You've become a regular out here this summer." Alice's eyes widened in slight alarm, and he quickly clarified, "My farm is just over the rise, so I catch most of what goes on along the footpath."

Alice weighed her desire for privacy against the discovery of someone who appeared to share similar interests. She hadn't known of any other bird enthusiasts in the area. "Have you seen a red-necked phalarope before?" she finally asked.

"Nope, was hoping to add it to my list."

"Your list?"

"Yes, the list of birds I've identified during my lifetime."

"I see." Alice bent to pick up her sketchbook. "And how did you hear about the phalarope?"

"The Dorchester Ornithological Society. Our July meeting was just yesterday."

Alice's hat threatened to take flight again, so she raised one hand to hold it down. "I hadn't realised such a group existed."

Mr. Stone gave a self-deprecating smile that caused the corners of his gentle blue eyes to crease in well-worn lines. "Well, there's just the four of us. We meet monthly to compare notes on what we're seeing. We also share our sightings with the British Trust for Ornithology."

Alice had not heard of that organisation either. Her passion always seemed freakishly peculiar, and she'd become used to being viewed as the odd duck. That there might be others like her in and around Weymouth—she felt her world shifting slightly.

Mr. Stone watched her for a moment before continuing, "Would you care to join our August meeting? We're a welcoming group."

Alice hesitated. Mr. Stone was not a complete stranger but close to it. Yet she felt a definite affinity to him as a fellow bird enthusiast, and she was curious about his birding society. "Yes, I think I would, if I wouldn't be intruding."

They made arrangements, and then Mr. Stone continued on his way. Alice turned to resume her sketching, but the curlews had moved on. She decided it was time to head back.

As she pedalled back through town and up the hill towards home in the hot July sun, sweat pooled on her forehead and across her back. When she reached her drive, she paused to listen. It sounded like someone crying, and it was coming from the direction of Walbridge Manor. The manor bordered Elm House to the west and was easily the grandest residence in the area. At the time Alice married Edgar, there had been an active family and full staff. Now, the elderly Lady Walbridge lived alone with just one maid and a manservant.

Following the sound, Alice walked her bicycle up the drive towards the manor. A young lady was sitting on a stone bench sheltered by a curved line of yew trees. Alice realised it was Sonja, the Jewish refugee that Lady Walbridge had recently sponsored. The decision to take in a refugee had caught Alice by surprise. Lady Walbridge's charitable actions were always distant and detached in the manner that was expected of someone of her standing. Alice never sensed any hint of sentimentality from her distinguished neighbour.

Alice set down her bicycle and walked the gravel path towards the alcove created by the line of trees. Hearing the crunch of gravel, Sonja's head jerked up, and her deep, dark eyes—now lined in red—widened with alarm at being discovered.

"Sonja, my dear, whatever is the matter?" Alice asked her. Even in tears, she was a beautiful young lady with her dark hair, wide-set eyes and flawless complexion.

"Sorry, Mrs. Standfield. It is no matter," she responded in her strong German accent. Despite her distress, there was an intensity to her gaze. Alice sensed a maturity and gravity that you would not expect in someone only fifteen years old.

"It looks as though something has upset you. Is there anything I can do to help?"

Sonja rose from the bench. "No, it is no matter. Please not to tell Lady Walbridge." She turned and hurried back towards the manor.

Alice stood and watched Sonja as she crossed the grand front lawn to the side door of the manor. She wondered at the level of menace that had driven Sonja's parents to send such a beautiful child to England despite being forbidden from accompanying her.

As she wheeled her bicycle home and stored it in her back shed, she pictured what it must be like for Sonja to be living with Lady Walbridge. Six months had passed since her arrival, yet this was the first time Alice had seen her outside the house on her own. In fact, she seldom seemed to leave the house. The poor young lady didn't appear to have any social life, and she had not been enrolled in school. She was past the age for which school was compulsory. Still, Alice was surprised that Lady Walbridge kept her at home.

To be forced to leave family and community behind and then to be confined to that dusty manor with the coldly aloof Lady Walbridge—that was a kind of despair to which Alice could relate. She made a mental note to invite Sonja and Lady Walbridge over for tea sometime in the not-too-distant future. That was at least something she could do for the poor girl.

CHAPTER 3

London, Early September 1939

I T HADN'T BEEN A proper holiday, and Martin felt cheated. All summer, his father put in long days at the Ministry of Transport office, just on the off-chance there might be war. Martin thought this was the main reason both his parents were in sour moods. It was also why they hadn't gone anywhere that summer. Added to that, Martin, along with his brother and sister, were assigned additional chores on top of all their regular chores.

The summer started with his fourteenth birthday, celebrated with a small cake his mother baked that day and not much else. Martin suspected that his birthday might have been forgotten altogether, had he not happened to mention something to her that morning.

Then, a few days later, Martin had to help his father and his older brother, Leo, set up their government-issued Anderson shelter in their tiny back garden. This involved digging a four-foot-deep rectangular hole, constructing the shelter from corrugated steel panels, and then covering the top of the shelter with the dirt from their hole. Chester, their cocker spaniel, was equal parts confused and excited by all the digging, a responsibility that normally fell to him.

When it came to erecting the shelter, Martin could tell his father was unsure of how to go about it, and this contributed generously to his sour mood. He made no effort to include Leo or Martin in working things out. Their role was to do as they were told. Martin sat on the back steps scratching Chester's belly while his father puzzled over the directions, and Leo kept making unsolicited and unwelcome suggestions. Martin was happy to stay clear of the tensions between his father and brother. He preferred being an observer.

A train passed along the tracks that ran within five blocks of their home. Martin expected his father to comment on the type of engine they were hearing, or note with derision that it was running behind schedule. But he was wholly absorbed by the task, which took much longer than Martin thought it should have done.

The small amount of ground left over from the shelter was dug up for vegetables. Besides having to help with weeding, it became Martin's job to drag their shovel around the neighbourhood in search of manure piles left from any horse-drawn delivery carts.

Once his father, on his walk home from the tube station, noticed a pile left sitting out in their street. "Martin! Were you not responsible for collecting fertiliser for the garden? I hope you're not expecting me to haul it home in my briefcase."

"Sorry. I'll go find it."

"Too right, you will. We're depending on you for this one task. Do you feel that's asking too much from you?"

Martin felt he had practically been accused of dereliction of duty. He knew his father was stressed at his work, but he didn't think that was reason to make their lives stressed as well. Never mind that, by the time he went out to look for the manure pile, someone else had already snatched the precious commodity. He couldn't see how it mattered. With brick, two-storey homes both in front and in back of their garden, their plot didn't receive enough sunlight to produce much of a harvest. If war did break out, hopefully they would not be relying on their back garden to feed them.

Then they were required to attend the most tedious class imaginable on the proper use of gas masks. He preferred not to think about actually needing to wear the awful device. At least he was old enough to wear an adult mask—not one of the eerie Mickey Mouse masks that his sister, Irene, was forced to wear. Irene was just concerned that there wasn't a mask for Chester.

As a complement to the nationwide campaign to eliminate fun over the summer holiday, his favourite wireless programmes kept being overtaken by news bulletins. In fact, that was why they were missing church on the last day of the summer holiday. Some news broadcast related to Poland. Martin doubted whether he could even locate Poland in the large atlas that anchored the bottom rung of their small sitting room bookshelf.

Their neighbours, the Millers, who didn't have a wireless set of their own, joined Martin's family waiting for Prime Minister Chamberlain's address to begin. All eyes were on the wireless as it sat squeezed between the sewing machine and the upright piano that used to belong to Martin's maternal grandmother. The opposite wall was taken up by two wing-backed chairs that flanked their small fireplace. This was where Martin's mother and father usually sat, but they insisted that Mr. and Mrs. Miller should have the two best chairs, leaving barely enough space to accommodate Martin's family plus the Miller's two children.

Finally, the Prime Minister was speaking in his slow, measured voice that reminded Martin of his history teacher patiently and disappointedly explaining why most of the class had failed their most recent exam. Large stretches of the speech were lost on

Martin. In particular, why Germany's invasion of Poland should involve them. But the statement, "consequently, this country is at war with Germany", was abundantly clear. The other fragment that would lodge in Martin's memory of that day, "I know that you will all play your part with calmness and courage."

Calmness was, perhaps, to be achieved at a later date. Martin was trying to take in the fact that they were at war. He had no prior experience from his short life that prepared him for this. He knew in a vague way that it threatened to make a dog's dinner of his life but couldn't imagine the specifics on how it would impact him. Almost as shocking as being at war, was the sight of his mother, the one who always maintained tight control, sobbing openly onto his father's shoulder.

Martin wondered whether Germany would invade England the same way it had invaded Poland and Czechoslovakia, or would the English Channel protect them. Would his father join up or was he too old? More than once, he had carefully explained to Martin and Leo how he had narrowly missed serving in the Great War, having turned eighteen the year it ended.

His brother, Leo, was probably too young at seventeen but that might change should the war drag on. When they were younger, Leo and his friends often played war out on the street in front of their house. It was the one activity for which they would include Martin but only because they wanted him to play the Hun.

Martin's mother was just starting to settle down, and the Millers were about to head home, when the air raid sirens started their eerie, chilling wail. Chester began to howl while everyone else froze, staring at each other. Surely the Germans were not attacking already. That's when Martin noticed what was wrong. "Where's Irene?" he asked his parents.

Martin's mother shrieked as the sirens, and Chester, continued to howl. His father finally took command. "Leo, you and Martin to the shelter!" Mr. Miller offered to help with the search for Irene, as the rest of the Miller family headed home to their shelter. Martin offered to help look for Irene as well, but his mother turned on him, "To the shelter, now!"

Leo and Martin took Chester to the backgarden, and there, sitting on their back steps with her blond curls and blue eyes, was Irene. She was playing with her stuffed rabbit, Matilda. "I didn't like listening to that man," she told Martin, as Leo raced back to let their parents know that she was safe.

The entire family then crowded into the Anderson shelter and waited on the hard wooden benches Martin's father had installed. Nothing was happening outside. Martin's father had laid down wooden planks for flooring, but mud had seeped in from the recent heavy rain giving the shelter a damp, earthy smell. They continued to wait. A single sheet of corrugated metal—could that really protect them from high explosives falling from the sky? No matter. Martin didn't really believe that could happen—planes flying all the way from Germany to drop bombs on a big city like London. The Great War had been fought in France, and that's probably where this war would take place as well.

The sirens finally stopped, but there was no all-clear signal. They hadn't yet placed supplies in the shelter, not expecting to be using it so soon. All they could do was sit in silence. Everyone avoided eye contact, which was difficult as there was not much else to look at. Martin watched a millipede tracking across the floor, unaware and uncaring that the country above it was now at war. Chester broke free from Irene's lap and started pawing at the door and whining. Martin thought they should peek outside to see if it was okay to leave, but he dared not say anything that might set off his mother again.

Finally, the all-clear sounded, and they were allowed back in their house. Martin sincerely hoped that it would be a short war. It was less than a day old, and already he was sick of it.

He later heard from Leo that the false alarm was down to one of the spotters at a look-out station on the Thames delta. He had misidentified British fighters returning from France and panicked, thinking that the invasion had already begun.

The next day Martin was supposed to start school, but that didn't happen. Over breakfast, his mother announced that he and Irene were going to live for a time with his grandmother in Weymouth. She shared the news in the same matter-of-fact way she might have told them they were having shepherd's pie for dinner that night. Martin couldn't believe his parents would do that to him. "Why do we have to go there?"

"In case there are bombing raids on the city." It was the tone she used with Irene when having to explain something rather simple. "They're evacuating all the children as a precaution. You're fortunate to be staying with your grandmother and not with strangers."

This was not Martin's idea of fortunate. "How long do we have to stay there? Why isn't Leo going?"

"We don't know how long. I'm sorry, but things are going to be unsettled now that we're at war. We all need to get used to that."

Martin put down his knife and fork, completely forgetting his kippers and fried tomatoes. "But why isn't Leo coming with us?" he repeated.

"Leo is seventeen, dear. He's old enough to make his own decisions about staying in London and helping with the war effort."

Martin felt mutinous. He would be stuck with his little sister and his grandmother in the middle of nowhere, while everything exciting would be happening in London. "I want to help with the war effort too."

"Yes, I'm sure there will be many ways for you to help, even in Weymouth. Now, I need you two to finish your breakfasts so you can get packed." She started clearing away her own breakfast dishes.

"What? Are we leaving today?"

"Yes, of course," Martin's mother answered from the kitchen. "We don't know what will happen, or when it will happen, but we need to be ready. Your father went into work quite early this morning so that he can leave early and drive you two down this afternoon." As usual, his father had not been bothered to explain any of this to Martin.

"What about Chester," Irene asked.

"He'll need to stay in London for now." Irene started to protest, but her mother reminded them that their grandmother had a cat.

Martin went upstairs to his room. Chester followed him and settled onto his unmade bed. As he looked around the small space he shared with Leo, he wondered what he should take with him. Was he packing for days, weeks or months? He decided he should assume it might be months, although he couldn't imagine being away from his friends and everyone for that long. Would he have to start at a new school in Weymouth, or was this an extension of his summer holiday?

Leo sauntered into the room, pitched himself onto his top bunk and watched with detached enjoyment as Martin packed. "You'll have a great time with Grammy," he said with his usual smirk. Martin tried to ignored him. With Leo watching, it was harder to think about what to pack. Even though Martin thought it was unfair that Leo was allowed to stay in London, he was a little excited by the idea of being the oldest sibling in the household for a change and not having Leo around to laugh at him.

Martin could not picture moving to Weymouth to live with his grandmother. His entire life up till now had been spent in the same home in London. He liked his grandmother, even if she was a bit odd. She wasn't as strict as his mother. Of course, that might change with his living there long-term. They couldn't be expecting him to live in Weymouth long term, could they? No one seemed bothered to explain anything to him. Why couldn't his life simply go back to the way things were?

CHAPTER 4

Weymouth, Early September 1939

THE WEATHER WAS MAGNIFICENT, the trees just starting their transition towards autumn, their leaves and branches turned golden by the slanting sunlight. Alice spotted siskins out her window that morning, their canary-yellow markings illuminated to their best advantage by the soft light. Autumn was her favourite time of year.

Unfortunately, she would have no opportunity to be outside that day. Rosa had Mondays off. Alice had checked on whether her housekeeper could switch days, but she had already made arrangements to visit her mother in Tolpuddle. Alice stopped by the local school to find out what was needed to register her grandchildren, then continued on into town to visit the green-grocer and the butcher. Rosa usually handled the shopping, but there hadn't been time yesterday following the telephone call from Henry asking if Martin and Irene could come to stay.

Alice had just left the greengrocer and was heading towards her motorcar when she saw him. He was walking towards her, along the path. Their eyes met, and he quickly turned his gaze downward and quickened his pace. But Alice stood in front of him.

"Excuse me, I believe you were at my husband's graveside service. Did you know Edgar?"

His eyes widened. "No. I'm sorry. You must have me confused with someone else." He rushed past her, and Alice turned to watch him continue down the path. She felt sure it was the same man. But she had not been expecting to run into anyone that morning, so maybe she was mistaken.

Alice spent the afternoon making space in the spare bedrooms and changing linens. Nothing had changed in Henry's room since the day he moved out to attend university. It felt strange to be clearing out his old things to make room for his son to take up residence. At the bottom of a large chest, she discovered his old school tie, a scattering of school papers, rowing medals, and other memorabilia. She took some satisfaction from his having left all these school mementos behind. Had it been up to her, they would never have sent him away to boarding school. But in Edgar's family, Winchester had been an immutable assumption, like the existence of God. It had been far too soon to lose her son. Not that she had much say over his upbringing, even when he was living at home. Her mother-in-law, Cora, had seen to that.

She thought back to her son packing for his first year at Winchester. He had included the large sketchbook and pencils that had been Alice's gift to him on his twelfth birthday. But nothing in that household escaped Cora's silent scrutiny. Alice assumed she must have said something to Edgar, because that evening, he had a serious discussion with his son about what was and was not acceptable to take with one to Winchester if one was to avoid unwanted attention from his more senior Wykehamist classmates.

She was glad Henry had decided against boarding schools for his children. Alice saw Martin on a divide. The man he was to become had not yet been determined.

After carrying the last of the boxes to the attic, Alice felt the strain in her lower back. By this time, Rosa had returned. The two lingered over a light tea. Since Edgar's passing, they had started taking meals together. With just the two of them in that big old house, it seemed silly to do otherwise.

She inquired about Rosa's mother's health but wasn't giving full attention to what Rosa was saying. She couldn't help wondering how her role would play out with the two grandchildren under her care. This time she would be free from set expectations and judgmental eyes. She felt equal parts excited and nervous.

Her friend and neighbour Helen Bascome stopped by after tea. Helen came from a humble background and had been a primary school teacher before marrying Thomas. Alice felt a freedom in their relationship that she could not find among the society that her husband kept, the society that she had been expected to adhere to. Helen was the only person, other than Edgar, to whom she had confided her dream of creating a book, or even a series of books on the natural history of Dorset. Helen didn't just tolerate Alice's unusual interests; she encouraged them in her typical down-to-earth fashion. "Way I see it, you don't have to worry about putting bread on the table, and you no longer have a man to please, you'd be daft not to do as you fancy," she had told Alice.

Helen stopped by because she had just heard an announcement on the wireless—conscription had been expanded to include all men between the ages of 18 and 41. Her son Sidney had recently welcomed their first child—a healthy girl.

"How'd they expect a family to cope without their pa?" she asked. "I suppose I'll be needed to stay with them for a bit. But then Thomas is useless in the kitchen, so I can't fathom how he'll manage without me."

Helen's situation helped Alice put her worries into perspective. "Please let Thomas know that he is welcome to take his tea here while you're away. It won't do to have him starving." *They would have to find a way through this together*, Alice told herself.

"I'd be grateful. That way I have just one family to fret about."

"No trouble at all." Alice paused and smiled. "An unusual household we'll make, Rosa, your Thomas, my grandchildren, and me."

Helen laughed at that. She paused and then turned more serious. "I've been quarrelling with myself on whether to speak or keep quiet on this. But I think it's best that you know."

"What's on your mind?" She had Alice's attention.

"There's a rumour out about your Edgar. I thought you ought to know."

"What sort of rumour?"

"It's daft, but there's folk saying he was a secret supporter of the Blackshirts."

Alice almost dropped her teacup. "Edgar? Who's saying this?"

"I overheard it at the last Women's Voluntary Services meeting. Complete speculation, I know. It's on account of a trial from a year ago where a Blackshirt was accused of attacking anti-Nazi protestors. I guess Edgar ruled in the bloke's favour."

"Yes, I remember the trial. Edgar found the man repellent, but there was a lack of evidence, so his hands were tied."

"Yeah, well I told them it was nonsense, but you know how people are."

Alice thought for a minute. "Just out of curiosity, is Elizabeth Chambers a member of your group?"

It was Helen's turn to look surprised. "Now, how'd you work that out?"

Alice was puzzling over how to explain to Helen her reasons for suspecting Elizabeth. Thankfully, she was spared by the crunch of gravel announcing the arrival of Henry's motorcar. Helen slipped home via the side door.

So, this was the price she would pay for not doing Elizabeth's bidding, she thought as she headed outside to greet the new arrivals. She guessed that Elizabeth's venom was not just a result of Alice's lack of interest in joining the women's auxiliary. She sensed that everything about her, her general inability to conform, was offensive in Elizabeth's eyes.

Alice was determined to escape from living under the expectations of others. She was prepared to accept what people might say about her behind her back, but it was another thing to sully Edgar's reputation—a reputation he had carefully cultivated and was no longer here to defend. And the matter took on a greater importance with the grandchildren arriving to live in Weymouth. Would they be hearing nasty rumours about their grandfather, or worse, become targets? Then Alice realised that she was perhaps blowing the incident out of proportion—giving Elizabeth more power than she actually possessed. It was just a single episode of gossip.

Henry was already pulling suitcases from the boot of his motorcar. Alice was taken aback by the change in his appearance compared to when she'd last seen him at Edgar's service. He hadn't shaved that morning, and his sandy, brown hair was uncharacteristically untidy. As she got closer, she noticed the baggy eyes and sallow skin. This was a man clearly in need of a holiday and some time outdoors.

Irene ran to her grandmother and gave her a big hug, while Martin slowly emerged from the motorcar and went to help his father with the cases. "Hello, Martin," she called over to her grandson.

"Hi," he responded without looking up.

"Have you eaten?" Alice asked Henry.

"Kathleen packed a supper to eat on the way, but some tea would be welcome," he replied as he carried cases up her front stairs.

Rosa brewed tea and set out biscuits while Alice and Henry helped the children get settled into their rooms. Alice felt excitement at being, once more, in the centre of the activity and life that children bring to a home. At the same time, she felt her short chapter of independence slipping through her fingers, swept away by the coming tide of war. She knew that, given a choice, her family would always come first. It didn't do to fuss about the things she couldn't control.

Even so, she found her mind revisiting the August meeting of the Dorchester Ornithological Society. Nathan Stone had given her a lift to the meeting, and they picked up another member along the way, the three of them packed into the front seat of his lorry. The talk remained lively the whole way to Dorchester and back, filled with stories of owls, raptors, song birds, and geese. She had worried that the others would be much more knowledgeable than she and felt some intimidation at being the only woman at the meeting. Yet she surprised herself with how much ornithology she had accumulated during her stolen moments outdoors over the many years of her marriage. She thought back wistfully to the meeting, the gentle enthusiasm of the others, their interest in hearing of her experiences and observations, and their readiness to share their own discoveries and the locations of their favourite observation posts. Now, with a war on, she wasn't sure if they would continue meeting, let alone whether she would be free to attend.

Gathered around Alice's large dining table for a late tea, Martin remained silent and withdrawn. Henry, after his early start to the day and long drive from London, kept slumping onto his elbow, his eyes drooping, while Irene acted as if she had siphoned off all the energy from the other two. She had countless questions as she bounced in her chair, top of which was, "Can we go to the beach tomorrow?"

"Tomorrow is a school day," her father reminded her.

"True, but we may not be able to get you registered right away, so we'll see," Alice added.

From the sitting room, the grandfather clock chimed nine times, which Henry took as the signal to head for bed. He was planning a very early start back to London the next day, intending to head straight into work. Alice helped with getting the grandkids to bed.

Sitting on the side of Irene's bed, she told her, "Be sure to give your father an extra hug tonight. He needs to be up quite early tomorrow to return to London, and it's likely you'll still be asleep when he leaves." Irene bravely nodded but appeared on the verge of tears as it sunk in that she would be away from her parents.

Alice gave Irene a final hug and went down the hall to Martin's room. She hesitated outside his door, not wanting to intrude on father and son.

"You'll be the man about the house now. We're depending on you to watch out for Irene and to be a help to your grandmother," she heard Henry saying.

"Yeah, okay."

There was a pause, and Alice thought Henry was going to say something more to his son, but all he said in the end was "Well, goodnight, Martin."

"'Night"

Henry came out into the hall and stopped short when he discovered Alice waiting near the door. She thought she saw moist eyes reflecting the light coming from Martin's bedside lamp, but the hallway was dark, and it might have been her imagination. She went in to say her goodnights to Martin and then went downstairs.

Henry and Rosa both retired for the night, and Alice made her way into the sitting room to her favourite chair. She looked across the room to the grandfather clock. She resented its chimes, cutting short the fragment of time she had been allowed with her son, free from Kathleen's distracting energy. That clock had measured time in the Standfield family across two centuries. It carried little adornment aside from its burr-walnut veneer and three round giltwood finials along its crown. Its square base, square top, and long, thin case had always struck Alice as stern and confining. It reminded her of Cora, who, along with the house, had turned out to be part of their marriage contract. Tall, thin, and unadorned, she had never relinquished control of the household. That was probably why Elm House had never felt like it was hers. By the time her mother-in-law passed, three years before Edgar's passing, her presence had permeated the walls and furniture—permeated Alice even, as if she were part of the furnishings.

She had thought that, being on her own, she would be free from having her life measured and constrained. But the clock continued to tick, unyielding across the many decades. It had allotted her a few months of freedom but no more.

CHAPTER 5

Weymouth, Early September 1939

MARTIN HAD NEVER THOUGHT of his grandmother's house as silent and empty. Always their visits included the entire family and then only during summer holiday or at Christmas—or for a funeral. You could depend on there being plenty of people and activity. He wasn't sure he could stand it with just his grandmother and his little sister. There was no one else he knew within a hundred miles. Did people ever die from boredom? He wasn't sure.

He spent the entire drive to Weymouth staring out the window, angry at his parents for having engineered all this. His father made some pathetic attempts at conversation which were easily deflected.

After unpacking, they had tea and biscuits accompanied by Irene's endless chattering about the beach and how exciting it all was. Martin was starting to think he might be less miserable without her there. But that would have seemed completely unjust if he were the only one serving this sentence.

They did make it to the beach the next day. But instead of Weymouth beach where Martin's family always went, his grandmother took them to a tiny beach, bordered at each end by rocky outcrops. It was just a beach—no sweet shops, booths, or anything.

But he didn't feel he could complain. His mother had gone on at length about what a big undertaking this was for his grandmother, that he should be grateful, and that as the older sibling, he needed to set an example for Irene.

As it turned out, there was a low tide that morning, so the rocky pools were full of starfish, anemones, crabs, and a miniature transparent jellyfish, shaped like an umbrella. Irene loved the tidepools, and even Martin had to admit the tiny jellyfish was fascinating to watch.

They made two more trips, each to a different beach, including one where they collected fossils that had eroded from the cliffside. His grandmother told him the fossils were ammonites, and that they had lived millions of years ago.

Martin's attitude about staying with his grandmother improved when he discovered his father's old bicycle in the back shed and was told that he could use it to explore Weymouth on his own. Back in London, he was never allowed to wander around on his own.

Martin thought his luck was continuing to improve when the following Saturday turned out sunny and warm. He set off to explore Weymouth's town centre, crossing the Town Bridge, and heading towards the beach. He was a few hundred yards away when he first detected something was wrong. As he drew closer, he found his way blocked by a tall metal barricade stretching off in both directions. Soldiers were unrolling huge bails of barbed wire. Just his luck. What was the best thing about Weymouth? It was the beach. He was stuck here with his grandmother and his little sister, and now they'd closed the beach.

He stepped off his bicycle to join a group of bystanders, mostly boys, catching glimpses of activity in the restricted area beyond the barricade. Some soldiers marched past, while others worked on the beginnings of the defensive structures that were replacing the beach shelters, candy floss stands, and Punch & Judy tents. It was a hot day for so late in September, and Martin was standing in full sun. Now that the beach was off-limits, the water looked all the more inviting.

"My pa's gonna be taken on as a carpenter for the army," said the boy standing next to Martin. Martin looked over his shoulder, trying to determine whether the boy was talking to him or to someone else nearby, but the boy continued staring out through the fence. He was taller and skinnier than Martin, and looked older. His trousers were dusty and worn, and his dark hair was overdue for a haircut. He turned to face Martin. "Means I'll be working here with him."

"My father just works in an office all day," Martin replied, and then looking back out at the beach, "Shame we can't jump in the water to cool off."

"I can fix that. Follow me." The boy didn't wait for a response. He picked up his bicycle and started pedalling. Martin hesitated for just a moment, before following the stranger. He seemed very sure of himself, and Martin had not yet made any friends in Weymouth.

He pedaled hard to keep up as they followed a road uphill, away from the beach. Suddenly the boy swerved unto a dirt path, careening over bumps and dips until he came out on a narrow lane. A short way down the lane, he veered once more onto another narrower path, leading further uphill. The boy raced up the path, unfazed by the rocks and ruts, and again Martin struggled to keep up.

When they passed alongside a stand of trees, the boy braked. A trail branched off into the trees, but you wouldn't notice it unless you were watching for it. They walked their bicycles down into a small hollow and emerged at the edge of a pond, disturbing a pair of ducks who protested loudly as they took flight. A two-foot-wide, sluggish stream entered the pond at one end and exited at the other end over a narrow spillway. Trees enclosed the pond on all sides, their dry leaves giving off the faint scent of decay that warned of the end of summer.

The boy dumped his bicycle and began taking off all his clothes while Martin stood and watched, wondering whether the pond was sufficiently secluded. Ignoring Martin, the boy dived into the pond and then turned around and looked up. "Well, you swimming or just watching?" Martin felt a daring with this boy that he hadn't experienced with any of his friends back in London. Despite feeling self-conscious, he stripped off his clothes, waded a few paces into the pond. Reaching out with his arms, he launched himself into the water.

After the uphill bicycle ride in the hot September sun, the coolness of the pond felt fantastic, refreshing beyond anything Martin could remember. There was a boldness in being out in the woods and jumping in and out of the water completely naked. This was not something he would be allowed to do back home.

The boy climbed the bank and demonstrated a perfect cannonball. Martin gave it a try, and they took turns until things devolved into a splash fight, leaving Martin slightly out of breath. The boy climbed up on the grass along the edge of the pond, lay on his back in the sun, and closed his eyes. He seemed unconcerned about being naked and exposed. Martin did the only thing that made sense and lay down a short distance from him.

Having cooled off in the pond, he now welcomed the warm embrace of the sun. He closed his eyes and breathed in the scents of pond water evaporating off his skin, the damp grass beneath him, and the decaying leaves from just beyond the grass bank. It was quiet but for the occasional buzz of insect and the background of bird calls from the woods behind them. Martin felt he could lie there on the bank all afternoon.

"I'm Ellis," the boy said without opening his eyes.

"Martin."

"You're not from around here." It wasn't a question but neither was it an accusation—simply a statement.

"Down from London. My sister and I are stuck here with my grandmother on account of the war."

Ellis propped himself up on one elbow. "You're not stuck here. Weymouth is the place to be, now there's a war on."

"My older brother got to stay on in London. That's were all the action will be."

"Don't be so sure. Portland and Weymouth have their harbours. That's why they've brought the boys down in a hurry—to secure the beach. Those harbours are going to see some action."

Martin didn't know what to say. Ellis seemed better informed than he was.

Ellis sprung to his feet and started pulling on clothes. "Come on. Let's scram before the landowner kicks us out."

Once more they were racing down pathways and back alleys. Martin had no idea where they were going, or how he would find his way back to his grandmother's house. Ellis pulled into a large vacant lot and steered his bicycle through tall dry grass and scattered empty bottles to a stand of trees at the back of the lot. Without breaking stride, he hopped off his bicycle and wheeled it through a gap in the trees and brambles. Martin followed him to find a small abandoned shed that had not been visible from the alley. It had a cracked four-frame window in front and was missing its door. Any paint it might have once carried was long gone, but the inside was dry, and a heavy, worn blanket was spread on the floor along with a scattering of tattered cushions.

"Mi casa." Ellis answered Martin's questioning stare, then clarified, "I live with me dad. This is my hangout. Make yourself comfy." Martin continued to stand as Ellis went over to a corner shelf and pulled out a large wooden box hidden under some old flour sacks. He brought the box over to the blanket and sat on one of the cushions. Pulling out a pack of cigarettes from the box, he held it out to Martin.

"No thanks," Martin responded, feeling embarrassed that he wasn't brave enough to try smoking. No one in his family smoked, and he didn't want to look foolish not knowing how to go about it. Ellis shrugged and lit up his own cigarette with practiced ease. Martin found another cushion and sat a short distance from him.

Cigarette in one hand, Ellis used his free hand to pull a stack of magazines from the box and spread them out on the blanket. "Take your pick," he said, looking over with a grin to watch Martin's reaction. They were unlike any magazines Martin had ever seen. All the front covers featured beautiful young women with large amounts of breasts and buttocks, and small amounts of clothing.

Martin immediately thought of what his mother would do to him if she knew what he was up to right now. No matter— she was miles away back in London, and he was curious about what was in these magazines. He picked up the closest one and started flipping through it. There were pictures of women with their breasts entirely exposed. Martin stared in amazement. So, this is what a woman's nipples looked like. He felt a sense of euphoria that Ellis, clearly older and much more worldly, had chosen to be friends with him, and that he was at last gaining some of the experiences that he thought one should have in this world on their way to becoming a man.

Ellis put down his magazine to watch Martin's reaction. "You like those strawberry creams?" he asked with a grin.

"Where'd you get these?"

Ellis reclined sideways on his pillow, propped up by his elbow. "Nicked 'em from me dad—and the fags." He seemed to notice Martin's reaction and added, "Easy peasy. The trick is to make them disappear in ones or twos so he don't notice."

Martin had the impression that Ellis had looked at these magazines many times. But this was Martin's first time. He turned the pages in fascination.

"How old are you?" Ellis asked.

Martin considered lying but then said, "Fourteen. What about you?"

"Seventeen this month."

Martin looked up from his magazine. "My brother's seventeen. He wants to join up next year when he turns eighteen."

"Not me." Ellis snapped his magazine shut.

Martin put down his magazine in surprise. Ellis had impressed him as fearless. Most of Leo's friends talked about how they couldn't wait to be fighting the Jerries. "Why not?"

"Who decides to go to war? The toffs in London, that's who. Who ends up getting killed? Not the bloody toffs. It's the poor working blokes, and they don't care shit about them." Martin was taken aback by the swift change in Ellis's mood. "Going to war is for fools who want to get blown to bits." After a pause, he sprung to his feet. "So, where's this grandma's house of yours?"

As it turned out, Ellis lived a quarter mile down the road from Elm House and closer in to town. This was fortunate, because otherwise Martin might have had a challenge finding his way back. "You can come in. Pa's out this afternoon," Ellis said as they reached a single-storey cottage, set back from the road.

A dirt path led through weeds and high brown grass, past overgrown willow trees to a front door with grimy white paint.

The paint was flaking from the lower half of the door which was exposed to the sun. In place of a porch, there was a single narrow wooden step, with cigarette butts scattered about.

The door was unlocked, and Martin followed Ellis inside. While his eyes adjusted to the gloom of the sitting room, his first impressions were the musty smell and the silence. It was a small room, with a single front window covered in curtains that might at one time have been bright and cheery but were now faded and limp. A sofa and side chair in matching worn, brown upholstery stood in the far corner, opposite a brick fireplace. Stuffing was escaping from the corner of the chair, and several dark bottles sat among the clumps of dust at its side. There were no pictures hanging from the walls. Through a narrow doorway into the kitchen Martin caught a glimpse of dishes and cartons filling a sink and spilling onto an adjacent free-standing cabinet.

Martin decided that he would be in no hurry to introduce Ellis to his grandmother. He wasn't sure how she might react to his having a friend who lived in such a place. Ellis was watching Martin's reaction. "Mum died when I was 'bout five. Don't really remember her. It's just me and dad, but he's pissed drunk most times. That's what war did for him."

Martin didn't know what to say in response. He glanced around the room but couldn't find anything to take the conversation in a different direction. He told Ellis he was due back at his grandmother's. But before he left, he checked on whether Ellis would be around the next week.

CHAPTER 6

Weymouth, Early October 1939

MARTIN'S SISTER WOULDN'T STOP talking about the Sunday afternoon tea his grandmother was hosting for Lady Walbridge and Sonja. She was annoyingly excited about the chance to wear her knee-length party dress with puffed sleeves and white dress gloves. Martin, on the other hand, was aware of countless other activities he would have chosen over sitting politely in his uncomfortable three-piece wool suit and answering questions fired at him by the intimidating Lady Walbridge. He wondered what mischief Ellis was up to while he was stuck inside.

Lady Walbridge, seated at one end of his grandmother's dark, carved-mahogany dining table, asked about the work Martin's father did back in London. "He works for the Ministry of Transport," his grandmother replied.

Lady Walbridge nodded. "Well then, he must know Captain Wallace. My nephew was friends with him at Harrow. I've heard he has a proper sense of government, despite being a Scottish industrialist." His grandmother seemed to at least know who Captain Wallace was, but Martin was quite certain that anyone in Lady Walbridge's circle would not be on familiar terms with his father.

While Lady Walbridge droned on, Sonja, seated across the table, kept drawing Martin's attention with her wide dark eyes and heart-shaped cheeks. He had heard that Germans all had blond hair, except Hitler, of course. But Sonja didn't look at all German. Maybe that was because she was Jewish. The only other Jewish person Martin knew was a boy in the class ahead of him at school back in London. Martin had seen this boy being teased occasionally, but he wasn't sure why. He knew very little about the Jewish religion other than that they didn't believe in Jesus and had a different set of rules they were supposed to follow.

Martin had never known someone from another country, nor had he traveled beyond the borders of England. He was curious about her former life back in Germany. Had she seen Nazi soldiers? Why did she come to England without her parents? According to his grandmother, they were still in Germany.

Sonja caught Martin watching her, and she smiled briefly before looking back down at her plate of sandwiches. Lady Walbridge took notice of the interchange. "Sit straight, Sonja," she commanded. Sonja tightened her posture, and all emotion left her face. Lady Walbridge turned her attention to Irene. "This young lady acts quite grown up. How old are you, Irene?"

"Eight," she replied, showing a self-conscious smile at receiving a compliment from this lady who seemed so important. Martin noticed Sonja's eyes shift over to Irene, even as she continued to hold her head perfectly straight.

Martin was relieved when Lady Walbridge swept off to her manor with Sonja in tow. His grandmother told Irene and Martin that, with having just finished afternoon tea, they would be having a lighter supper that evening. By then it was too late to catch up with Ellis. Martin felt his afternoon was wasted.

He slowly climbed the stairs and headed to his room near the far end of the upstairs hallway. His eyes fell on the door at the end of the hall, opposite the stairway. Before, when Martin's family visited, this door had always remained locked. He had meant to ask his grandmother what was in that room. Trying the doorknob, he found it unlocked. As he slowly pulled it open, he felt a draft of stale, musty air. A bare, wall-mounted light bulb was located just inside the door. He pulled on the slender chain hanging from the bulb, and its light revealed a wooden stairway spiraling tightly upward into darkness. Climbing up one floor, he found a small landing with a single door, which turned out to be the access to the attic. But the stairway continued. He closed the attic door and climbed one more flight. This led to another, even smaller landing, also with a single door.

Martin opened the door to find himself squinting in bright daylight. He was at the apex of the roof line, and the door opened to a rooftop platform about five feet square. The platform was enclosed by a stone wall that came just past his waist. But what caught his attention was the view. He was facing south towards the Channel. To the east was the town of Weymouth, clustered around the River Wey. A beach continued off in the distance beyond the mouth of the river, and he could just make out what he thought were construction projects and clusters of soldiers. Directly in front of him the shoreline curved south to the Island of Portland which formed the southern horizon. Ellis had informed Martin that everyone called Portland an island, even though it was connected by a narrow strip of land. A flat transport ship, some naval vessels, and a number of smaller boats sat in the bay that lay between Weymouth and Portland.

When Martin finished surveying the territory to the east and south, he turned his attention to the west, where he had a clear view of Walbridge Manor. It was built of the same Portland stone as his grandmother's house but was several times larger. He counted eight chimneys. A long gravel drive connected the road to the front of the house, meandering past ancient oaks and elms. Most of the expansive front lawn had been dug up to form a giant vegetable garden.

A delivery van pulled up the drive and parked on the side of the manor closest to Martin. A man jumped out of the van and went down some steps to a side door. It took Lady Walbridge's maid, Margaret, a minute to answer the door, after which the delivery man carried in several boxes and then left. Martin could see no sign of Sonja.

He turned his attention back to the activity taking place around the harbour. Then, an idea occurred to him. He raced down three flights to ask his grandmother if he could borrow her binoculars and then raced back to the lookout. Out of breath, he rested his elbows on the stone wall and focused in on the activity on Weymouth beach. The binoculars opened a world of detail as he watched the soldiers marching and drilling across the sand. Turning towards the bay, he could see details on the ships, including the numbers and letters painted on their hulls and individuals moving about on deck. There were also soldiers out on the breakwater, but he couldn't tell what they were doing there. Further down on the Island of Portland, military vehicles and large delivery vans clustered around some piers.

At last, Martin had something that would impress Ellis, instead of it always being the other way around. He turned to survey Walbridge Manor, but the windows were dark in contrast with the bright daylight, and he could see none of the goings-on.

He had just decided to head back downstairs when some motion by the side of the manor drew his attention. Sonja was coming up from the delivery entrance. She had exchanged the outfit she had worn to tea for a grey dress which was covered with a white bib apron similar to the one that Margaret wore. As he watched, she walked briskly out to the vegetable garden and began harvesting the last of the green beans into a basket she carried at her side. When she finished the row, she picked two large orange-red tomatoes which she placed on top of the beans and headed back inside.

At supper that evening, Martin asked his grandmother if she had been inside Walbridge Manor. "Yes, from time to time," she replied.

"Does she ever give tours? I've never been inside a proper manor house."

His grandmother set down her cup of tea before replying. "I'm quite sure she'd be willing to have you two over for a look around. I'll speak with her. The manor has a past, and Lady Walbridge is never parsimonious about sharing its history."

The next day, Martin couldn't wait for school to finish. One of the few good things to come out of the war was that the large influx of children from London forced the school to divide its students into three groups, with each group attending reduced, partial-day schedules. Martin and Irene were lucky enough to be attending the morning session which left their afternoons free. As soon as their shift was excused, he collected Irene and they headed back to their grandmother's house. Halfway home, Irene wanted to stop and inspect a caterpillar crawling steadfastly across the road, but Martin hurried her along.

Martin and Irene's contribution to the household was to prepare lunch each day after they arrived home from school. Martin wanted to dispatch with lunch as quickly as possible, but his grandmother seemed to consider mealtimes as opportunities for deep discussion.

As they munched on cheese sandwiches and sliced apples from his grandmother's tree, Martin's thoughts returned to an incident from school.

"We didn't study science today. Our teacher's been called up, but someone said he's angling to be a conscientious objector." As soon as the words left Martin's mouth, he realised his misstep. He had provided his grandmother with a perfect subject around which to build a full-length discussion.

"What did your classmates have to say about that?" his grandmother asked.

Martin finished chewing his bite of sandwich before responding. "They say he's a coward. One boy said that he should be shot as an example to others."

"What are your thoughts?"

Martin didn't know what he thought. He was still getting used to being asked that sort of question. His parents would have shared their own views on the matter, and that would be the end of it.

On the one hand, it didn't seem fair that some people risked their lives to defend their country, while others got a pass just because they didn't agree with going to war. On the other hand, the thought that he might one day be asked to kill other people frightened him. While other boys at school boasted that they couldn't wait to be shooting Jerries, Martin was in no hurry to be shooting at anyone. Nor did he want anyone to be shooting at him. Ellis talked about the common folk being sent to the trenches to fight wars that just helped rich people. He wasn't sure if that was true or not.

"I don't know," he finally replied. "We need to defend our country. It's not right if some folk get out of serving just because they're not keen."

"Do you think it matters if they don't want to fight because of their religious beliefs—for example, if they're a Quaker?"

"I suppose. But couldn't someone just say that they're a Quaker, even though they're not?" Martin had forgotten, momentarily, that he was in a hurry to be done with lunch.

"You're right. They could. Is there any way the government could determine whether someone truly was a member of the Quaker religion?"

"I suppose they could check to see if they've been members all along, or just signed up when it looked like war was coming."

Martin suddenly remembered that he was planning to see Ellis today. He figured they had conversed enough to satisfy his grandmother and asked to be excused. He hurried outside, hopped on his bicycle and headed down the street, hoping to find Ellis at home.

Ellis recently started work as an assistant for his father who had finally secured employment on a military construction project. Martin didn't know if they were working today. The project had been subject to delays. He knocked on their door, and thankfully, Ellis answered. As it turned out, work had been interrupted once again due to a holdup in the transport of building materials.

Martin stepped inside and then noticed an unshaven man sitting slumped in the chair with the empty bottles. He figured this must be Ellis's father. He reminded Martin of the men he had seen in London hanging around the train yard, men they were instructed to stay well clear of. Ellis's father had the disoriented look of someone who had just awakened.

"Who's this chap?" he demanded of Ellis. Martin could smell the alcohol on his breath.

"Martin. He's down from London. Lives with his grandma."

"City boy, huh?" Ellis's father gave Martin a bleary-eyed stare. Martin didn't know how to respond, and there was an uncomfortable silence.

"We're heading out. See ya later." Ellis grabbed Martin's arm and ushered him towards the door. Ellis's father started calling out, but Ellis closed the door behind them.

Martin didn't know what to make of Ellis's father. His own father never had time for him, but at least he was never drunk in the middle of the day. As Ellis retrieved his bicycle from around the side of the house, Martin thought about what it must have been like growing up with that man for a father and having no mother around at all. He knew what his mother would think of his having a friend with this background. How would his grandmother react? He had told her about Ellis—that his father worked on military construction but left out the part about his not having a mother at home. As it turned out she was already aware of Ellis's home situation.

Ellis interrupted his introspection. "What'll it be? Fancy some blackjack?"

"I want to show you something over at my grandmother's."

Ellis hopped onto his bicycle. "Grandma's it is," he called over his shoulder. Martin hopped onto his bicycle, hurrying once more to catch up.

The two boys walked their bicycles up the front walkway and left them resting against the double pillars supporting the elegant portico that extended over the front porch. Martin worried that Ellis would think him posh for living in a place that was so much bigger and grander than Ellis's rundown cottage. But there was no hesitation from him as he marched in alongside Martin.

They found Martin's grandmother working at her Art Nouveau mahogany desk. The desk had been his grandfather's, but after Edgar's death, his grandmother had moved it from the study to the sitting room, so she could enjoy the view of the magnificent elm tree in their side garden.

As Martin's grandmother set down her manuscript, Ellis stepped confidently forward to shake her hand. "Nice to meet you, Mrs. Standfield. You have a lovely home. Sorry to hear of your husband's passing." Martin's mouth hung open. He had never seen Ellis act polite and cultured, and had not expected him capable of it.

"Nice to meet you, Ellis." Martin couldn't tell if his grandmother was buying it. "I hear your father will be helping with the military construction."

"Yes, ma'am. And I'll be his assistant, just as soon as our supplies come through."

"So, you've left school already?"

"Yes, ma'am. I'm seventeen, and my father needs the help." Martin knew that his grandmother thought seventeen year olds should still be in school, but she kept that to herself.

"Well, there're a few biscuits in the pantry, so why don't you two have a spot of tea before you head off to whatever mischief you have planned. Mind you, leave some biscuits for Irene."

"It was nice to meet you, ma'am."

His grandmother returned to her manuscript, while the boys gulped down tea and biscuits before heading up to the rooftop.

"Brilliant!" Ellis approved of the sweeping view. But to Martin's surprise, he seemed more interested in Walbridge Manor than the goings on at the beach and harbour. "Now that's posh. Just Lady Walbridge that lives there?"

"Just her and Sonja, the refugee. She's pretty, Sonja, and nice— shame she's Jewish."

Ellis put down the binoculars and looked straight over at Martin. "Nothing wrong with Jews. Just different, that's all." Martin felt a twinge of shame. Truth was, he made the remark because he was worried Ellis would look down on him for being too friendly with a Jew. He had not expected the gentle rebuke.

But he didn't think he had said anything too awful. He overheard much worse about Jews from other students at school.

Ellis was already back to peering through the binoculars at the manor house. "Seems a waste, all that for two people, while most blokes hardly have room to fart." He continued staring for a minute before asking, "You been inside?"

"No, but my grandmother's going to ask Lady Walbridge about having Irene and me over to see the place."

"Your grandmother won't want me joining your tour," Ellis said as he continued surveying the manor.

"What do you mean by that?"

Ellis lowered the binoculars and turned once more to face Martin. "You bloody well know what I mean. My lot's not the sort Lady Walbridge wants trotting through her manor."

Once more, Martin felt uncomfortable. He knew that he and Ellis came from very different backgrounds, but this was the first time either had specifically acknowledged it. "Nonsense. You should join us. I'll talk to my grandmother."

A bare flicker of a smile started across Ellis's face and disappeared. "It's gotta be a Sunday. I'll be working full-time soon."

The following Monday, Martin and Irene were sent to Walbridge Manor after school to help Sonja and Margaret with the harvest. The majority of the giant vegetable garden that had replaced most of the manor's front lawn was devoted to potatoes. Margaret showed them how to use a garden fork to gently lift the tubers without damaging them.

Irene's enthusiasm quickly wilted under the heavy work of extracting potatoes from the dense, wet soil, and her pace grew steadily slower. She impressed the others with her creativity in finding excuses for laying down her garden fork, quickly running through the obvious ones—bathroom breaks, untied shoelaces, and minor abrasions, and moving on to more advanced stuff, such as fear of big black beetles, being allergic to potatoes, and claiming to have spotted a German spy among the trees that bordered the property. Eventually, she achieved her objective of being more distraction than help and was sent home. A short while later, Margaret also left to clean up so she could start preparing supper for Lady Walbridge.

Warm from the digging, Martin stopped to throw off his jacket. He was impressed with Sonja's steady progress down the row next to him, finding it difficult to keep up with her. "You're good at this. Were you raised on a farm?"

Sonja straightened up and wiped her brow with her sleeve. "No, I grew up city of Dortmund. But I had summers with my grandparents' farm." She paused for a moment before adding, "You never worked in farm, did you?"

Martin looked back at Sonja, trying to interpret her remark. Her relaxed smile told him there was no ridicule intended. "Am I that bad at it?"

"No. I think you have future of farmer in you."

Encouraged by Sonja's openness, Martin broached the subject he was curious about but had avoided as being too personal. "Why'd you have to leave Dortmund?"

As if part of a magic act, Sonja's smile vanished. She turned to her row of potatoes. "They say for me is too dangerous in Germany. My parents not permitted to come with me."

Sonja's curt response only raised more questions. What danger drove her to leave her parents and her homeland? And why was Sonja allowed to leave while her parents were not? But he sensed her reluctance to discuss the topic further.

They worked on in silence. It started raining—not hard—just a coastal drizzle. Martin wished he could go back to the easy conversation they were enjoying before he ruined things with his question. Finally, he stopped and turned to Sonja with both hands resting on the handle of his garden fork. "Sonja, sorry if my question bothered you."

She looked over and smiled once more. "Is okay. For me is painful. I hear no news of parents. But that is no fault from you."

Martin tried to think of another topic. "I haven't seen you at our school. Are you attending a different school?"

Again, Sonja's smile disappeared. "Lady Walbridge says school not needed."

Martin was surprised to hear this. He knew of classmates whose families removed them from school when they reached the leaving age of fourteen, but that was usually because the families needed them to work and provide financial support. Surely Lady Walbridge could afford to keep Sonja in school. "Don't you want to attend school?"

Sonja turned back to her row of potatoes. "Lady Walbridge says work needed to pay for food and home."

Again, Martin sensed the conversation was closed. They worked on in silence until the beginnings of dusk provided an excuse to quit for the day. After storing the day's harvest and putting away their tools, Sonja looked over at Martin. "Thank you for the help." There was the smile again. He felt he would do almost anything for that smile.

CHAPTER 7

Weymouth, November 1939

THE HARSH JANGLE OF the telephone destroyed a rare moment of tranquility. Mornings with no demands on her time had become rare for Alice. Rosa was getting older, and Alice found herself helping more with household duties. She didn't mind. It wasn't that she thought the work was beneath her. It just made her more protective of the few times she could work uninterrupted. She regretted Edgar's decision two years ago to install a telephone. Setting down her manuscript, she made a conscious decision not to let the intrusion upset her composure.

"Yes. Mrs. Standfield speaking."

"Mrs. Standfield? Nathan Stone here. Can you spare a few minutes?"

"Yes. How can I help you?"

"I assume you know of the Observer Corps?"

Alice's forehead creased. "Yes, of course. I confess I'm not well informed regarding their operations. Why are you asking?"

"You're undoubtably aware that they play an important—actually critical—role in our civil defence. The reason I'm calling, we've so many called up or helping with war production, we need volunteers. You've been spotting wildlife all these years. You'd be a natural at spotting aircraft. Of course, we'd provide training. Is this something you'd consider?"

Alice's thoughts went immediately to protecting her time. All those years with Edgar she had waited and waited, kept her talent and creativity buried. Had she escaped the cage of marriage only to fall captive to the demands and deprivations of war?

"Were you aware that my two grandchildren are in my care, having evacuated from London?" As she stood in the entrance hall, she looked through the open sitting room door to the window on the far side of the room. A sudden burst of wind scattered the last of her elm tree's golden leaves. They flashed luminously as they joined the others on the ground, beginning their decay back into the earth.

She reminded herself that young men everywhere were putting their lives and ambitions for the future at risk. In comparison, this seemed a small price to pay. Besides, it was her intention to look into some way she could contribute to the war effort, beyond looking after her grandchildren. She just hoped to keep from having her life completely disrupted. This sounded like a major commitment.

"Yes, I was aware. Seeing how the Germans don't stick to schedules, we need shifts at all times of day, and I believe we can accommodate your schedule. Is this something you might consider? We could meet somewhere to chat about how the Corps operates and what would be required of you."

She did want to do something to help out, and this sounded more interesting than making sandwiches, although she was skeptical about her ability to identify aircraft. "Alright. Where would you like to meet?"

After ending the call, Alice sat back down at her desk and stared out her window. The words were neutral, but Alice detected a note of anticipation in the voice from the other end of the telephone line. She thought back to their conversations traveling to and from the Ornithological Society meeting. She had been so focused on her birds. Had she missed something? She would need to make sure their relationship remained that of co-volunteers and friends. She was determined to remain a widow.

Her thoughts were interrupted by the arrival of Martin's friend, Ellis. Today was the date set by Lady Walbridge for the tour of the manor. She called for Martin and Irene, then sent Martin back upstairs to put on a clean shirt. Ellis had outgrown the pair of pants he was wearing, and his entire outfit showed considerable wear. The tie he wore was faded and slightly frayed—probably borrowed from his father. But she could see that he had made an effort to wash his face and comb his hair.

It was a sunny afternoon but windy and cold as the foursome walked up the gravel drive towards the manor. They detoured around a giant gnarled branch that had fallen from one of the estate's ancient oaks, blocking the front walkway. Alice guessed that the branch came down during the windstorm that swept through several weeks earlier. They passed a large bed of unpruned rose vines, tangling and fighting each other as they spilled out over the overgrown boxwood hedge that was intended as their border. At the front entrance, Alice noted that the trim around doors and windows had gone yet another summer without a much-needed repainting.

Samuel greeted them at the front door. At the time that Alice and Edgar were married, the Walbridge family employed a staff of six. Now it was left to Samuel, who filled in as both butler and groundskeeper, and Margaret, who served as a combined housemaid and cook, to keep the place running. The overgrown gardens and the dusty chandeliers hanging high above the entry hall attested to the fact that this was too big an undertaking for just two people.

Nonetheless, Samuel maintained the demeanor of a butler for a great house with his understated greeting and efficient gathering of hats and coats—not working too hard to hide his disdain for the worn cap and jacket he took from Ellis. The entry was larger than that of the Standfield home, with a high, barrel-arched ceiling. An enormous burgundy Persian carpet ran the length of the hall.

"Please wait in the parlour," Samuel said and then left to retrieve Lady Walbridge. Irene almost ran to place herself in the largest, most overstuffed chair, while Ellis wandered over to the mahogany and glass cabinets that stood the length of two of the parlour walls. These housed an eclectic display of artifacts that appeared to be loosely grouped according to origin: Africa, China, the Indian sub-continent, and the Americas. No fire had been set in the large stone fireplace, and Alice wondered if it would be impolite to ask for her coat back.

As Irene sat taking in the room's extensive collection of furnishings and relics, a frown materialised. She got up from her chair and stared upwards, nose-to-nose with one of the hunting trophies mounted on the far wall. "That poor deer," she said.

"That's an elk," Martin replied.

Irene was about to fire back at her brother, but he was spared when Lady Walbridge made her entrance. She wore a full-length emerald-green gown, with elaborate black trim and a diamond necklace. Alice couldn't help noticing that, like the manor, the gown showed signs of wear. Ellis backed away from the cabinets.

Sonja followed in Lady Walbridge's wake, wearing a plain cotton dress patterned in muted greys and browns. Despite the best efforts of the dress to marginalise Sonja's appearance, it's plainness only served to heighten one's focus on her deep, dark eyes and flawless complexion. Ellis caught Martin's eye and gave an approving wink and slight nod. This did not escape Lady Walbridge, who scowled in Ellis's direction.

Alice stepped in. "This is Martin's friend, Ellis. He has today off from his work helping with the construction of coastal defensive structures."

The subtle reference to Ellis's patriotic employment had little effect on Lady Walbridge, who acknowledged him with the smallest of nods and an undiminished scowl. She then turned to face the rest of the group and launched into her narrative. "Walbridge Manor was built in 1680, with the east and west wings added in 1748. It has been home to nine generations of Walbridges. The artifacts in this room attest to services to the Crown rendered by this family ranging across Shanghai, India, Afghanistan, the Boer War, the American Colonies, the defeat of Napoleon, and the Great War, to name a few."

Alice noticed Irene starting to fidget, while Martin's attention had diverted across the room to Sonja. Ellis, in contrast, appeared to be studying Lady Walbridge. She felt a need to liven up the tour. "Is it true that the manor played a role in the smuggling operations during the eighteenth century?"

Alice was fairly certain the stories were true but still thought she was taking a small risk in inquiring about this aspect of the Manor's history. To her relief, Lady Walbridge appeared to relish the question. "Yes, the Walbridges did not support the extreme taxation rates levied by Parliament to the detriment of local commerce." Looking over to Samuel, she said, "Very well. We'll tour the basement next. You have with you the key to the burrow?"

"I have it here, my lady."

The group returned to the entry hall. Lady Walbridge led them to the far end of the hall under the watchful eyes of her Walbridge ancestors who looked down disdainfully on the unlikely party from their oversized gilt frames. They descended a cramped staircase that opened onto a low, narrow hallway made all the more claustrophobic by comparison to the spacious one they had just left upstairs. The hallway ran past several closed doorways and one open one that led to the kitchen. Margaret looked up at the passing group and immediately looked back down at the vegetables she was preparing.

The hall ended at a heavy door, which Samuel unlocked with one of the keys he kept on a large metal ring. The temperature dropped as they entered an ancient-smelling room with stone walls and floor. The entirety of the far wall was taken up with tall wooden wine racks, mostly empty. Samuel slid one of the racks to the side, revealing a door built of aged timbers.

While Samuel wrestled with the antique lock on the door to the burrow, Lady Walbridge explained how the respect held for the Walbridge name made the manor a relatively safe place to temporarily hide contraband awaiting transport inland. "It was the local vicar, being above suspicion, who drove his wagon on the cross-town trip from the coves to the manor." Despite what Lady Walbridge believed, Alice suspected that the townsfolk knew full well what the Vicar was up to. But smuggling had widespread support from the general population. She pictured the townsfolk smiling knowingly as they exchanged greetings with their vicar, his wagon creaking under its load.

As Martin and Irene peered into the dark recesses of the burrow, Alice became aware of a side conversation between Ellis and Samuel. Samuel looked over to Lady Walbridge. "Excuse us, my Lady. Ellis needs to use the facilities."

Lady Walbridge frowned and then waved them off.

Ellis turned back to Samuel, and said in a hushed voice, "I can make my way if you could point me in the right direction."

Samuel hesitated a moment before provided directions, while Lady Walbridge resumed her monologue.

It was a while later that Ellis caught up with them in the library, a large room covered floor to ceiling in books. There were two comfortable sofas gathered around a fireplace but no fire burning. The opposite corner was taken up with a broad, claw-footed desk on which stood an enormous antique globe. Lady Walbridge was describing in fine detail the rare and historic collection of books and manuscripts. As Ellis entered the room, heads turned, as if hoping he might bring relief from the monologue. Lady Walbridge paused momentarily to glare at Ellis as he slipped into the room, but he took no notice.

At the conclusion of the tour, they returned to the parlour for tea. Lady Walbridge declined to serve scones or bread, which Alice attributed to the shortages. Ellis quickly drained his tea and thanked Lady Walbridge for the tour.

"Sorry I can't stay. Pa needs my help getting the equipment set for tomorrow." Lady Walbridge scowled while Samuel retrieved Ellis's cap and jacket, and he was gone.

A short time later, as Alice and her two grandchildren walked home, she wondered to herself whether it was a mistake to allow Martin to bring his friend on the tour.

"Why did Sonja leave Germany without her parents?" Martin's sudden question interrupted her musings, and she took a moment to respond.

"I don't know the specifics, but I understand that they weren't allowed to leave. Apparently, they felt the danger was sufficient that they needed to get Sonja out of the country, even if they couldn't accompany her."

"So, her parents sent her to a foreign country all by herself?"

They reached Elm House, and began removing hats and coats. "Yes. A horrible dilemma for a parent, wouldn't you agree? If you were in her parent's position, how do you think you would respond? Suppose you had a child whose life was in danger, and the only way to save your child's life was to give him or her up?"

Martin didn't answer right away. "You'd have to give the child up. If your love for your child means the child dies, then that's not really love, is it?"

"No, Martin, I don't think it is. But it's a brave parent who is able to face that."

Martin was quiet for a bit. "I think it would have to be a brave child as well."

"Yes. Sonja is a brave young lady."

CHAPTER 8

Weymouth, December 1939

T HE WEATHER WAS COLDER than any Martin could remember back in London. He thought winters would be warmer on the south coast. No matter—he didn't mind the bitter cold. Unlike his old neighbourhood, Weymouth's hills seemed made for sledding, and he and Ellis had tested the limits of his father's old sled.

It felt strange to be in Weymouth in the days leading up to Christmas with just Irene and his grandmother. Most Christmases, his family would make the trek to Weymouth and stay for the week. They established a tradition of celebrating with his grandfather's sister's side of the family. At those times, Elm House was filled with cousins racing up and down the staircase, while wonderful smells kept drifting in from the kitchen. Snowball fights were followed by hot chocolate around the fireplace and charades in the evenings.

This year looked far less promising. Over the past several weeks, meals were even more spartan as Rosa saved up on sugar, suet, and butter so she would have something with which to try to replicate the traditional Christmas pudding, mince pies, and other treats. Martin's family would not be joining them until Christmas Eve and would be returning early on Boxing Day, all due to his father's workload at the Ministry of Transport.

"I wish they could stay longer than two days," Martin told his grandmother as they walked over to the woods behind Walbridge Manor. Lady Walbridge had offered that they could cut one of her trees, since they couldn't waste petrol on driving into the country.

"I wish they could as well. Your father shoulders some important responsibilities. Transport of troops and supplies is vital to the war," his grandmother explained, "especially with shipping disrupted by U-boats." They stopped to appraise some promising candidates. "I'm sorry to say your cousins won't be joining us either—they've all been evacuated to the countryside. Your aunts and uncles are staying in London with Home Guard duties and God knows what else."

They selected a modestly sized tree, and Martin tied it to his sled. Snow began falling just as they reached Elm House. Martin nailed the tree to a stand and carried it into the sitting room. He sat on the sofa, staring into the tree, thinking about past Christmases at Elm House as the scent of pine filled the room.

His grandmother brought out her gramophone. While the sounds of Sibelius, Mozart, and Handel performed their magic, the three of them decorated the tree with traditional ornaments as well as chains, stars, and snowflakes cut from coloured paper.

On the day before Christmas, Martin and Irene waited at home while his grandmother drove to the train station to pick up their family. They had taken the train because their petrol ration wouldn't cover the trip by motorcar. Irene talked Martin into playing snakes and ladders, and then she complained because he kept looking out the window instead of watching the game. He was going to see his parents. It had only been a bit over three months, but that was the longest he'd been separated from them.

Finally, there was the sound of tires crunching frozen snow. They threw on coats and went out to greet their family. Irene ran to give her mother a hug which was briefly returned. Leo and Martin's father were unloading luggage.

"Let's get inside," Martin's mother said. "There was almost no heat on that train, and we're all freezing." She walked briskly up the front walk. "Hello Martin." She passed him standing on the front porch, stopping just long enough to peck a kiss on his cheek.

The group moved into the front hall. Martin thought his parents would want to know about what he'd been up to during his time in Weymouth, but his mother was still complaining about their train trip. "I've never seen the train so crowded, and I lost count of all the delays."

"You have to expect delays—the military takes priority," his father responded.

"But there were so many military on board…"

Irene interrupted her mother. "Where's Chester?"

Her mother spun around to locate Irene. "Oh, honey, don't you remember? We had to put Chester down. Most families have had to do that. The food needs to go to people. There's not going to be enough for all our dogs."

Martin froze. He slowly looked up at his mother, not believing what he'd just heard. His parents had killed Chester? There had been no mention of this. He saw Irene's face crumple before she turned to run upstairs.

Martin's mother turned to his father. "Can you try talking to her? She might be more accepting of it coming from you." Turning to Martin's grandmother, she said, "I brought down some cranberry sauce for tomorrow's lunch. I'll make sure Rosa knows about it." She walked off towards the kitchen. Martin dropped into the nearest chair and stared into the room. On top of everything else, Chester was gone.

A short time later, his father returned downstairs, but Irene was not with him. He sat in Martin's grandmother's favourite armchair and buried his nose in a newspaper, periodically throwing out commentary on the rife incompetence of Britain's military leadership. Martin noticed his grandmother slip upstairs.

Martin's mother was still in the kitchen, presumably trying to direct Rosa on every detail of the upcoming Christmas lunch, ignoring the fact that Rosa had been fixing Christmas lunches for as many years as Kathleen had been alive.

Martin wanted to get out of the house. He turned to Leo. "You fancy some sledding? We found the perfect hill."

"Nah, I'm still cold from that train." He pulled out a paperback from his jacket pocket and started reading.

Eventually Martin's grandmother returned with a red-eyed Irene, and they settled onto the sitting room sofa. Irene picked out the book *Black Beauty* for her grandmother to read to her.

Martin sat down next to his grandmother to listen to the story. But he wasn't really listening. He thought about Chester. If only his parents had let Chester come to Weymouth—he was sure his grandmother would have found a way to feed him.

He had missed his family and couldn't wait for them to arrive. Now that they were here, he found himself wishing they would go back to London. Having spent time away, he viewed his family from a new perspective, as if seeing them up on stage at a play while he was in the audience. Martin's mother came back into the sitting room and told the kids to get changed for Christmas Eve service.

On Christmas Day, Martin received a winter coat from his parents. It felt warm and fit him much better than his old one which he had outgrown. Eager to try it out, he finally convinced his brother to go sledding. By the time they returned, Rosa had conjured up something resembling hot chocolate for the family. The day had come off alright, after all.

Martin had never been keen on the family tradition of gathering around the wireless for the Christmas message. He hadn't been bothered last year when King George VI choose not to deliver one. His speeches reminded Martin of sitting in church listening to deadly dull sermons. But when their monarch began this year's message, the family became quiet and sombre.

"I speak now from my home and from my heart to you all; to men and women so cut off by the snows, the desert, or the sea, that only voices out of the air can reach them."

Martin thought of Leo. By next Christmas he would probably be posted who-knew-where, unable to be with the family. Leo was mostly annoying, but even so, Martin found it difficult to imagine him away at war, with just himself and Irene left at home. Who could tell what the next year had waiting for them? The normal rules of life, rules he had naïvely mistaken as immutable laws of nature, no longer seemed to apply.

Early the next morning, Martin's grandmother took his parents and brother back to the train station. Though Martin still missed his parents, he was also relieved to have them gone. It was as if the version of his parents that he missed never really existed. But he wasn't too bothered about all that. It was snowing again, and Ellis wouldn't be working on Boxing Day. Hopefully there would be more sledding.

CHAPTER 9

Weymouth, Late December 1939

THE OBSERVER POST WAS perched like an aerie, sitting atop a local high point almost directly above the spot where Alice first met Nathan the previous summer. The views extended inland as well as both directions along the coast, west towards the long Weymouth beach and east towards the rugged cliffs and Jurassic rock outcroppings. Alice felt she could be content to spend the entire day staring at these views, although she could do without the Observer Corps helmet.

Alice completed her training the week before Christmas. The Corps manned their local observer posts in pairs, and Nathan, as regional coordinator, had paired the two of them together. He seemed determined that her introduction should go smoothly.

"You seem to be off in your own thoughts today." Nathan had observed Alice's preoccupation. "Is everything okay?"

"Sorry." Alice set down her binoculars. "Christmas was not a great success at our house." She told Nathan about Chester's demise and the callous lack of concern shown by her son and daughter-in-law.

The veterinarian smiled, knowingly. "Children have a special connection with their pets. Do you think all that city life has dulled Henry's perception on that?"

Alice offered a wry smile. "That's generous of you, but I fear this is part of a larger pattern of passive neglect on their part. I can't help wondering how a son of mine could be so oblivious to his own children. Did I miss something in how I raised him?"

Motherhood. Such a painful memory. Her family under Cora's constant scrutiny, her cold judgmental eyes and silent thin lips. Alice never felt free to be spontaneous or relax her guard. Over time, she grew to resent motherhood as just one more way in which she must conform. She tried to shield Henry from those feelings. But how could they not have impacted him? Did that at least partly explain why he remained distant from his own children?

Nathan resumed scanning the horizons. "I can't picture you as anything other than a terrific mother to your kids. Is Henry your only child?"

Nathan had no way of knowing how painful a question that was. Alice's heart plunged as her mind revisited that bleak December of 1906. Nothing could ever be the same after that horrible time. "Henry's the only surviving sibling," she responded, hoping that would satisfy Nathan. She tried to stay clear of those memories.

Nathan put down his binoculars again. "I'm sorry to hear that. I understand if you're not keen to talk about what happened." He seemed to notice her clipped tone.

"Diphtheria took my youngest two. And, yes, it is a painful topic for me."

"Of course. I'm very sorry for what you've been through." Nathan watched her closely.

"Thank you," Alice said. She resumed her plane spotting.

They continued in silence as Alice's mind churned. How could a six-year-old boy be expected to understand? To lose one sibling would be enough to forever affect a child of that age but to lose two? The diphtheria passed over Henry, but it hadn't spared him. James used to follow his older brother everywhere, and Henry adored his baby sister Lilian. The memories of Henry searching room to room, unable to accept that his brother and sister had vanished—still so painful, even after all these years.

Edgar had been determined that the family would carry on, determined not to acknowledge that the tender affection that should bind together a young family was forever lost to him. He took his lead from his mother. She never openly blamed Alice, but her appraisal of the tragedy was made clear. Much was communicated through all that was left unsaid.

When the time came for Henry to head off to Winchester, Alice was powerless to prevent it. Remove them from their families, especially from their mothers, so that all emotion can be purged from their souls. At least Martin had escaped that fate. Was there still hope for this boy who was so quickly turning into a man?

Whatever baggage Henry carried from his childhood, she could not excuse his or Kathleen's behaviour. She could accept their decision to put Chester down, even if she might have decided differently. With the prospect of sustained food shortages, many families had made that decision. But to forget to tell their own children? No apologies. No comfort. It was as if Irene's question had irritated Kathleen. Both children were devastated, yet there was no allowance. And at Christmas time, on top of everything else. The whole time Henry behaved as if everything was normal. She decided that, whatever her own shortcomings were as a mother, she never allowed her son to be as isolated as Martin and Irene had been.

Alice tried to focus her mind on the task at hand. Despite the weather being slightly warmer than the December they had just endured, their exposed outpost remained under continuous assault from onshore winds. The damp chill infiltrated her layers of coats and jumpers, making her grateful for the steaming cup of tea Nathan brewed for her on the station's portable camp stove. By the time their shift was complete, the morning's drizzle had tapered off, leaving strands of grey cloud clinging to the distant headlands.

As she headed for home, Alice decided that she would do whatever she could to help her grandchildren. She wasn't sure if she was up to the task.

CHAPTER 10

Weymouth, January 1940

ALICE FOUND THAT BEING outdoors, facing wind and sea and broad horizons, her thoughts ran more freely. The quiet stretches between plane sightings provided space for free-ranging conversation. They talked often about war and change. It felt natural to share their hopes and their fears for various family members and for the world at large.

At other times, they left each other to their own thoughts. Alice often turned contemplative. With her expanded household, there were fewer opportunities for reflection at home. Everyone seemed to think the war would be over soon. But she harboured doubts, doubts that she was reluctant to share with her more optimistic neighbours.

They heard a solitary plane heading east, but it was hidden by low clouds. Below them, a flock of several thousand knots caught their attention. Their dense formation pulsed with alternating flashes of white and grey as they made their tight synchronised turns and dives. Shooting out over the water, they suddenly raced back towards land, veering first left, then right, before diving downwards to settle momentarily on the beach.

The skies became quiet again. Alice thought about Nathan's family and the challenges they had faced. A bit of gossip came to mind, disclosed to her years ago by the town councillors's wife, Elizabeth Chambers. She remembered it clearly.

"When my husband, in his business dealings, has need of a veterinarian, he steers clear of Nathan Stone," she had said. "Not to be trusted, I understand. They keep to themselves on that farm, so no telling what they are up to." Elizabeth then leaned in close, as if what came next was scandalous. "He married a German, you've no doubt heard. And she remained on the farm for the duration of the war—watched every ship that came or went. She's dead now, but there were suspicious circumstances surrounding her death."

Alice didn't consider a German wife scandalous. She regretted her failure to stand up to Elizabeth all those years ago. Nathan seemed an undeserving target. She wished she could convey her support to him—that even in this time of war, she didn't consider his German connection cause for suspicion.

"I understand that your wife was originally from Germany," she ventured.

"Indeed, she was." Nathan continued to gaze out across the water, but his voice tensed.

"How did you the two of you meet?"

Nathan glanced over at Alice, as if trying to assess where the line of questioning was leading. "At a college social when I was studying at the Royal Veterinary College. Charlotte's father was a visiting professor, and she came to London with her parents. She found work as a file clerk in the administrative office."

"Did her parents eventually return to Germany?"

Nathan leaned against the corner post and looked back at Alice. "Yes, her father was in London on a two-year secondment. We married just before their return."

"She must have been a brave woman, taking on a new country and culture."

"By the time we married, she was pretty near fluent in English, and it was before the war."

The thick curtain of drizzle that had stalled just off shore finally moved inland, and visibility plummeted. Alice set down her binoculars. With the mention of the Great War, she decided to take a risk and explore further. "How was Charlotte treated during the war?"

Nathan took a fortifying breath before responding. "To be honest, not well."

No surprise to Alice, based on the attitudes she'd witnessed around town. "I'm terribly sorry. What happened?"

"Folks made it clear she wasn't welcome. Anything we needed in town, I made sure to pick up myself. The whole family came under suspicion, but at least none of the shop owners refused to sell to me."

Alice was shocked. "I had no idea."

"Yes, she kept to home after that, especially with what they did to our boy."

"What happened to your son?"

Alice shivered as the wind picked up, and the rain intensified. Nathan pulled out one of the spare blankets from their small cupboard and placed it over Alice's shoulders before answering. "Some boys from his school attacked him on his way home. He was just nine at the time. That's how he lost the hearing in his left ear."

"That's horrible! This was all because of the German connection?"

"Yes. I don't think his being named Emil helped. Had we known when he was born, we would've chosen a proper English name. But we named him after my father-in-law, whom I held in high regard." Nathan hesitated before continuing. "That I wasn't fighting overseas may have contributed. But I was thirty-four when war broke out, and the farm was considered a vital industry. Plus, I didn't think it safe to leave my wife and children here alone. I did join the Voluntary Training Corps, but that didn't go far enough for some folk."

"But you grew up here. Surely people knew your character."

"Yes, not everyone suspected us. But with all that loss, some people seemed in need of targets."

Alice had been unaware of the damage inflicted on this family, even though it occurred in her own town. "What do your children do now?"

The rain stopped abruptly, and Nathan lifted his binoculars to perform a routine scan before responding. "Martha's married with two children and lives in Bristol. Emil never married. Always kept to himself. Stayed on at the farm after finishing school—a shame in some respects seeing he's got a good mind for numbers. The plan is for him take over at some point. That's assuming he returns safe and sound. He joined up straight away when war broke out. His unit's shipping out to France next week."

"And they accepted him, despite his hearing loss? Do you think he enlisted to prove his loyalty?"

"Don't know. I reckon he could've finagled a deferment due to the farm had he wanted. His hearing loss is in just the one ear, and he's adept at covering for it."

"How're you keeping up on the farm work, without your son?"

Nathan gave a wry smile, and looked over at Alice once more. "Struggling. Fortunately, we're not at our busiest just yet. I've applied with the Women's Land Army but no joy so far. Lambing starts late February, so I'll definitely need a hand come spring."

They were interrupted by the sound of an aircraft. A few seconds later it came into view, and they identified it as another British surveillance plane. Alice sighted it through the instrument plotter and tagged its location on the table-top map. Nathan logged the sighting. Once the plane disappeared from view, Alice picked up their conversation. "Do you think there'll be more trouble for your family this time around?"

"I shouldn't think so. Charlotte's passing was near twenty years ago, and we keep to ourselves. I reckon our German connection is mostly forgotten by now."

Alice thought Nathan was underestimating the collective memory of small towns, but she kept that to herself. A shaft of sunlight broke through the clouds, illuminating an excitable flock of oystercatchers on the shingle beach below. Their shrill piping carried all the way to the Observer Corps shelter. There was a comical look to their large orange beaks, but in flight, seen from above, their black and white wing markings flashed handsomely in the narrow band of sunlight. As the birds migrated on, Alice and Nathan realised it was time to wrap up their shift and complete their report for the day.

Alice was grateful that Nathan arranged for her to work mostly morning shifts—she was able to return home each day not too long after her grandchildren returned from school. Martin always eagerly awaited her arrival. It meant he was no longer stuck at home watching Irene. That week Martin and Sonja were collecting scrap metal and newspapers to support the war. Alice suspected that not all of Martin's enthusiasm for this task was down to patriotism.

The previous day the pair combed through the Standfield home and back shed, collecting a pile of items for Alice to review to make sure they truly were nonessentials. That afternoon, they planned to start at Walbridge Manor, working under Samuel's supervision. Martin had been gone only a short while before he returned home. Alice and Rosa were sitting at the kitchen table, working together on the mending. Alice looked up from the pair of trousers she was mending for Martin. "What's happened? Aren't they doing scrap collection today?"

"Walbridge Manor was robbed last night!"

Rosa set down her mending. "The manor robbed? Well, if that don't take the biscuit."

Alice set down her mending as well. Her grandson was leaning against the kitchen doorway, staring into space, his face pale. "What was taken? Was anyone hurt?"

"I don't think anyone was hurt. Samuel came to the door. He didn't say what was stolen—just that Sonja was not at home. She's been taken to the police station for questioning."

"Sonja? Surely, they're not suspecting her." Alice rose from her chair. "Come sit down." She brought over the teapot and pulled out some biscuits. "Tell me everything Samuel told you."

Martin sat at the kitchen table but continued staring straight in front of him, unfocused. "That's all he said—they were robbed, and Sonja's being questioned."

Alice sat back down as Martin slowly chewed on a biscuit and sipped some tea. Once he seemed more settled, she sent him up to his room to complete his schoolwork. She then walked over to the manor to pay a visit with Lady Walbridge.

By the time Alice arrived at Walbridge Manor, Sonja had returned home and was in her room. Alice began the conversation by offering her sympathy and asking if there was any way she could help. Then she got to the real reason for her visit. "Do you really think Sonja could have done this? She didn't strike me as the type to wrong someone who is her benefactor."

Lady Walbridge sat up straight in her chair—more so than usual—her head tilted slightly upward, her face drained of expression. "The police report indicates no sign of forced entry. Also, the perpetrator appears to have known the location of objects of value—Walbridge silver, irreplaceable family heirlooms. Margaret has been with us for a decade and Samuel for three decades. Sonja is the newcomer." She paused for just a moment before continuing. "Also, I'm not sure she views me as her benefactor. She has become withdrawn and sullen, which I can only interpret as a lack of gratitude."

"But what would she do with the stolen items? Did they find anything in her room? Where would she sell them?"

"That is a matter for the police. I have no expertise in the handling of stolen property."

Alice still did not think Sonja was to blame, but she couldn't think of anything additional to say.

***

Martin paced his bedroom. One thing he was sure of—Sonja was not a thief. As soon as he heard his grandmother return, he dashed downstairs. She was in the front hall, hanging up her coat and hat.

"I did speak to Lady Walbridge. The police suspect someone worked the theft from the inside because there was no evidence of a forceable entry. Sonja, Margaret, and Samuel are the only ones with access, and Lady Walbridge is convinced that neither Margaret nor Samuel are thieves."

"Sonja would never steal from her. That's rubbish!"

"Yes, I agree. But Lady Walbridge trusts Margaret and Samuel—they've been members of the household for many years. I'm afraid she doesn't hold much trust for Sonja."

Martin wanted to yell at his grandmother or shake her or something. She was being so calm and matter-of-fact. But he reminded himself that this mess was not her fault. He returned to his bedroom and stood, staring out his window.

There was an additional angle to the robbery, one he couldn't risk sharing with his grandmother. First, Ellis had been keen to tour the manor. Second, he disappeared for a suspiciously long time, claiming he needed the lavatory. Had he joined their tour so he could scope the place? He told Martin that it was unfair to squander so much wealth on Lady Walbridge while others carried on with so little. What if his friend Ellis was the thief, and Martin had been the connection that made the robbery possible? Now Sonja was being blamed, and it was his fault.

But how could he be certain? Was he quick to suspect Ellis because of his lower-class background? He started pacing his father's old bedroom. His eyes fell on the framed photographs from his father's time at Winchester. In every corner of Elm House there were reminders that his background and heritage were far removed from Ellis's humble experience. Although Martin's father was perennially busy with work and home responsibilities and never had time for him, at least he wasn't alcoholic. And his family had never worried about keeping a roof over their heads or having enough to eat.

Ellis had been correct on one point—he predicted that he would not be welcome at Walbridge Manor, and Martin had seen with his own eyes how Lady Walbridge and Samuel treated him. Martin wanted no part of that upper-class snobbery. Was he being too hasty in suspecting his friend?

Martin decided it was best to keep his head down. If Sonja was innocent, and Martin was convinced she was, there would be no proof against her, so she couldn't be convicted. She would come out of this okay. If Martin spoke up, he would lose his friendship with Ellis and in all likelihood, for nothing. Probably some professional thief did this—someone who knew how to break into a house and make it look like an inside job.

The next day, Martin went over to Walbridge Manor to see if Sonja could resume their scrap metal project.

"Sonja will no longer be working on scrap collection." Samuel started to close the door.

"Can I talk to her?" Martin had to speak up quickly, before the door closed.

Samuel paused just long enough to reply. "I'm sorry, Sonja is not available." The door slammed shut.

The next week brought more snow. Ellis was working, so Martin went sledding with Irene, which was not nearly as much fun. He kept thinking about Sonja and decided to make another attempt to talk to her. Walking up the long drive to Walbridge Manor, he left deep tracks in the new snow. The bitterly cold wind burned his exposed nose and cheeks, and the grey-white clouds threatened yet more snow.

Samuel answered the door with a disapproving frown, the door held only partway open. "Sonja no longer resides here," he said before Martin could frame his question.

"Where did she go?"

"She's in detention." Samuel handled the word "detention" as if it were something smelly left by a stray dog on their grand front lawn.

"Has she been arrested?" Martin felt his heartbeat thumping in his chest.

"No, she's been detained as an enemy alien. I'm sorry, we don't know which detention centre she's been taken to." The door closed.

Martin stood on the front step, staring at the closed door. He didn't know what that meant—detained as an enemy alien. Sonja was Jewish. She couldn't possibly be spying for Hitler.

There was nothing left for him but to trudge back home through the snow. He was still trying to make sense of Samuel's news as he shed his boots, coat, and cap. He wandered into the kitchen where his grandmother was helping Rosa, who had just lifted a cheesecloth bag from a pot of boiling water. After letting the bag drain for a minute, she began squeezing it with her hands. She then unfolded the cheesecloth to reveal a misshapen bar of soap newly reformed from the leftover scraps they had all been diligently saving.

Martin's grandmother looked over to say hello. Seeing the expression on Martin's face, she set down her towel.

"What's wrong, Martin?"

"Sonja's in detention."

"Detention?"

"Yes." Martin sank into one of the chairs at the kitchen table. "She's an enemy alien."

His grandmother sat down next to him. "Who told you that?"

"Samuel. He said he didn't know which detention centre they've taken her to. What's a detention centre? Is that a prison?"

"No, it's a camp for people that the government wants to keep from traveling freely about, in case they might be helping the Germans."

"That sounds to me like prison." Martin stood up and started pacing around the kitchen.

"Well, these people haven't broken any laws. But I imagine the conditions in detention centres are not great, and for a young lady on her own—that's really not a good place to be."

Martin slumped back down in his chair. "Why do they think she's an enemy alien? Is this because of the robbery?"

"I'm afraid some people are giving in to hysteria on account of this horrible war." His grandmother placed her hand on Martin's shoulder. "It's nonsense, of course. I'll talk to the police superintendent. We'll see if we can get this sorted."

Martin felt some comfort thinking that perhaps his grandmother could help Sonja. She must have connections in Weymouth, with his grandfather having been a district judge for all those years.

***

The police station was housed in the imposing Weymouth Guildhall, made of the same Portland stone as Walbridge Manor and Elm House. The building was familiar to Alice because it housed the council chamber and the courtroom where Edgar had worked. But the police offices were on the ground floor, below the stately Ionic columns and portico.

After a considerable wait, she was told that the Chief Inspector could see her. She stood in the doorway to his tiny office. "Be with you shortly," the Chief Inspector said without looking up from his writing. After a minute, he set down his pen and rose from his desk. "Mrs. Standfield." He gave her a small smile and removed a stack of papers from the only guest chair so that Alice could sit down. Alice attributed his yellowed complexion to the cigarette butts overflowing his ashtray and to too little opportunity to see daylight. He resettled himself behind his desk and looked up at her expectantly, his hands formed into an inverted 'V'. "How are you faring? We do miss your husband around here."

"Thank you, Chief Inspector. I'm doing as well as can be expected, but I'm hoping you can help straighten out a serious misunderstanding." Alice succinctly described Sonja's background and what took place at Walbridge Manor.

The Chief Inspector sighed. "I do wish I could help you. The problem is, the tribunals that oversee alien detentions are under the War Office. Our department has no say in those matters, other than providing evidence. I can ask around, but I doubt I'll be able to do anything to help her situation."

"I understand." Alice tried not to show her frustration. "It's just that I have no connections with the War Office. It's such a travesty that this poor young woman comes to us as a refugee from our common enemy, and then we send her into detention."

"Yes, I quite agree. There's just not anything our department can do about it. You need to take this up with the War Office. Doesn't your son work at Whitehall?"

"He does but with the Ministry of Transport. I'll try him, none-theless." The Chief Inspector stood up, which Alice understood to be the end of the interview. "Thanks for seeing me. I know how short-handed your department is. If you do hear of anything, you will let me know?"

"Yes, of course. Good to see you." Before Alice could reach the door, the Chief Inspector had returned to his chair and was inspecting the next document from his desk.

As soon as Alice returned home, her grandson came downstairs. "What did the police say?"

"The Chief Inspector would like to help, but apparently, this falls under the War Office. I'll try to follow up with them, but honestly, Martin, this does not make me hopeful."

Martin's face fell with disappointment. "Why not? She escaped the Nazis. She's hardly going to spy for them. Once they know she's a Jewish refugee, they'll have to release her, won't they? She's only fifteen."

"I feel the same way, but with how poorly the war is going, people are fearful. They're not responding rationally. And the War Office has their plate full."

"But this is helping Hitler. Isn't this what he wants? To get rid of Jews?" Martin's face flushed as his voice rose.

"I know this is difficult. I'll do everything I can. But this may be out of our hands." Martin's fists clenched as if he was ready to lash out, but he stormed off to his bedroom instead.

That evening, Alice telephoned Henry. "I don't know whether you recall that Lady Walbridge sponsored a Jewish refugee."

"Yes, a young lady I think you told me."

"She's fifteen, and she's been forced to leave her family and community to escape Nazism. Now there's been a horrible mix-up, and she's been sent on her own to a detention centre."

"I should think Lady Walbridge could obtain her release, with the connections she has."

"She not inclined to help the poor girl. That's part of the mix up. You know how she can be. And the local police are unable to help. Detentions fall under the War Office. I'm hoping you might know someone in that department who might be sympathetic." Alice held her breath. She seldom asked favours from her son. Surely, he would see this as a worthy cause.

"I'm sorry—there's simply no way I could trouble anyone in the War Department. The stress they are under. Twelve-hour days and then weekends too. If I were to go to them over the case of a single German refugee—that would not go down well at all."

"Well, we certainly wouldn't want to let the plight of a young refugee get in the way of your golden reputation!" Alice hung up and immediately felt remorse over her loss of temper. But she wasn't sure whether her anger and sarcasm would even register with her son. Perhaps it was a good thing she was standing up to him.

The next morning, Alice woke up to the coldest weather she could remember over her many years living in Weymouth. As she dressed for the day, she found herself regretting her decision to volunteer with the Observer Corps. Making sandwiches and pouring tea didn't sound quite so stifling in the face of going outside in the frigid weather. She and Nathan kept the small camp stove stoked, but even so, they remained at the mercy of an unrelenting wind. A mug of hot tea helped, and Alice held the mug to her forehead and then to the side of her neck, trying to absorb its warmth.

Visibility was excellent in the crisp morning air, and they were relatively busy recording reconnaissance and transport flights. All were friendly aircraft, except for a German Heinkel reconnaissance plane that followed the coastline a short distance before heading back across the Channel.

During a break in the activity, Alice told Nathan about Sonja. He listened attentively until she finished the entire narrative, including the events leading up to Sonja's detention and her attempts to solicit help, first from the local police and then through her son. "It's proper for you to write to the War Office, but further than that, there's little else to be done. I know it's hard to accept. But you should take care that this doesn't fall back on you."

Alice lowered her binoculars to look over at Nathan. "What do you mean by that?"

"Trust me—you don't want folks questioning your loyalties during wartime."

Alice tried to control her impatience. "A fifteen-year-old girl is on her own in a foreign country and has now been thrown into detention. I'm hardly bothered by any gossip my concern for her might engender."

"No, I'm not suggesting you shouldn't help the poor girl—just that you may find that your hands are tied. Also, I've seen first-hand what gossip and suspicion does. I don't want that happening to you."

"I appreciate your concern, but I rather doubt they'll put me in detention for attempting to help a German refugee." Her son refused to help, Lady Walbridge refused to help, the police chief was unable to help, and now Nathan was suggesting she abandon her efforts on Sonja's behalf. She turned away from Nathan to scan the horizon. She was determined to win Sonja's release, and she didn't need his protection.

CHAPTER 11

Weymouth, Late January 1940

"**I**'M SORRY, SIR. COULD you repeat the question."

It was the second time that day that Martin was called out by his maths instructor. And maths was his best subject. He seldom earned a reprimand at school. He liked to keep a low profile. But today, he couldn't concentrate. Both times he realised too late that he was being called on and hadn't a clue what the teacher had asked. The pair of boys seated directly behind him snickered and whispered taunts in his ear, but Martin ignored them.

When he arrived home from school, he went straight up to his room and sprawled out on his bed. He had no good options. He could try doing nothing. But then he might be responsible for Sonja remaining in the detention centre, and he had no idea what might happen to her there. He had difficulty imagining what detention centres were like. The newspapers talked about the Germans sending people to detention centres. He hadn't realised the British were doing that as well.

The only other option he could see was to go to the police. But that also would not end well. Either he would be responsible for Ellis being thrown in prison, or else he would be falsely accusing him. Either way, his only friend in Weymouth would end up hating him.

His bedroom felt confining. He went downstairs to retrieve his grandmother's binoculars and then climbed the stairs to the lookout. His usual surveillance routine started with the Weymouth Harbour and Beach, then covered the Portland Harbour, and finished with the bay and breakwater. Nothing caught his interest. He returned to his room, but couldn't settle to anything.

His grandmother called him down for tea, but when he sat down to supper, he wasn't interested in it. He took a few bites, and that made him feel slightly nauseous.

"Are you feeling poorly?" It was unusual for Martin to pick at his food, and his grandmother had certainly noticed.

"Yeah, I'm okay. But I want to telephone my father tonight."

"I wish I'd known you wanted to speak to him. I just telephoned him last night. What is it you want to talk about?"

Martin got up from the table. "I just need to talk to him. It's private." Martin thought that maybe he could convince his father to take him back to London. The bombing threat had not materialised. Other children from his school in Weymouth had already returned to London. If he was in London, having Ellis as an enemy wouldn't matter as much.

After supper, his grandmother made the call to Martin's father. She explained that Martin wanted to talk to him, then she handed the telephone to Martin and took Irene with her into the sitting room, closing the door behind her.

"Hello, Father?"

"Hello, Martin. What's this about?" His father sounded curious, but Martin also detected the usual note of impatience.

"I want to know if I can come home. There haven't been any bombings, and lots of my classmates are returning to London."

"Oh, I see. Sorry, no. That's not possible. The government still has good reason to believe that London's not safe, and they're trying to convince parents to keep their children in the country-side. If I allowed my own children to return to London, think how that would appear to my superiors."

Martin sank onto the chair next to the telephone. "But people wouldn't need to know about it. I could keep quiet."

"Martin, I expected better of you. The neighbours would know. Your classmates would know. We need to set an example. I understand you'd rather be in London, but this is your way to contribute. I thought you would like being with your grandmother."

The conversation was not going as Martin hoped it might. But he should have known that his father would not understand. "It's not that. Something's come up. It would be easier to manage if I could return home. It's complicated."

"Sorry, the answer's no. If work allows, we'll try to make it down to Weymouth again soon. We can talk then."

"Can't we talk now? That will probably be too late."

"I'm having difficulty understanding how your return to London is so urgent that it can't wait a few weeks. I can't have you running up a large telephone expense for your grandmother, on top of what she's already doing for you and Irene."

Martin didn't know what else to say. There was a short interval of silence on the telephone.

"Look, I know you're keen to be with your friends in London, but we each need to do our part right now. I need you to watch out for your sister and to help your grandmother. We'll talk soon."

"Okay." Martin had pinned his hopes on his father providing an escape from his predicament.

"You make sure to pitch in to help your grandmother, now."

"Yeah." Martin's response was barely audible.

"Goodnight."

Martin threw the receiver down and remained seated, his frustration in danger of boiling over. He was now completely stuck and could see no way out. As he rose from the chair, he kicked the heavy clawfooted side table in frustration, but that only gained him a sore toe.

He went into the sitting room where his grandmother was on the sofa reading a story to Irene, who was snuggled into the crook of her arm. Oscar the cat was asleep in her lap. With all the attention she received, Irene was content in Weymouth. Martin sat down in the chair opposite them and leaned forward, staring at the large oriental rug, his elbows on his knees and his chin resting on his palms. His grandmother was reading *The Wind in the Willows*, the chapter where Rat and Mole get lost in the woods during a snowstorm. They are saved by discovering the door to Mr. Badger's home, buried under the snow.

His grandmother finished the chapter and turned to Irene. "Time for you to get ready for bed. I'll be up in a bit to tuck you in."

Irene headed upstairs, and Martin's grandmother turned her attention to him. "Did you get the answer you needed from your father?"

Martin sunk back in his chair. "Not really."

"It seems that something's bothering you. Would you like to talk about it?"

Martin didn't answer. He didn't want to tell his grandmother about asking his father if he could move back to London. She might get the wrong idea—that he didn't like staying with her. He also didn't want to tell her about Ellis. She might decide to go straight to the police, and Martin wasn't ready to do that. "I don't know," he finally said.

Martin's grandmother studied him for a moment. "I'm guessing this has to do with Sonja." Martin nodded. "Sometimes bad things happen, and there's nothing we can do about it. That's a difficult place to be."

"No, you don't understand!" It came out more harshly than Martin intended. He hadn't meant to raise his voice with his grandmother, but part of him didn't care. He didn't know what to think or say. He just needed to be alone. He got up and left the room, avoiding eye contact. It was too late to go anywhere, so he headed up to his bedroom.

Martin woke up the following morning with his mind decided. Sonja needed his help, and he needed to be brave, just as Sonja had been brave.

He went to school as usual and then as soon as his grandmother returned from observer duty and they finished lunch, he set out on his bicycle. First, he rode down to the beach where the military defensive works were under construction. Walking the perimeter and peering through the barricade and barbed wire, it took Martin a while to locate the spot where Ellis and his father were working. He needed to be sure that Ellis was indeed at work. He was fairly certain they had not spotted him. Reluctantly, he rode up the hill to Ellis's shed.

It was a dumpy old shack on the verge of collapsing, yet it had been their hangout. Throughout the past three months, it had sheltered many an entertaining afternoon—a place where Martin could experience things he would never be allowed to do at home. He learned to play blackjack and five-card stud. He overcame his self-consciousness and tried smoking. Ellis had not laughed at his coughing fit when he took his first drag too deeply. And then there was the storytelling. Ellis was a master at it. Where he came up with all his yarns was a mystery to Martin. Having a friend who was older and who knew so much more about the world had bolstered his confidence. He was no longer just the kid brother in a family that never did anything exciting.

The place felt strangely empty without Ellis there spinning stories or hatching one of his crazy schemes. It didn't take Martin long to find the stash—items of silver, carvings in jade and ivory, and many other treasures loosely covered by old newspapers. With the evidence staring up at him, he could see no escape from the conclusion that Ellis was a thief. He replaced the newspapers over the items, eager to get away as quickly as possible. He worried that someone might happen along and find him in procession of stolen property.

Jumping on his bicycle, Martin headed straight to the police station. He wanted to be done with the shed and with Ellis. His mate was someone who robbed other people's homes. Was this why his mother didn't want him to be friends with someone from a lower-class background?

The thought of talking to the police made him feel light headed and nauseous. But he wasn't going to allow Sonja to remain in detention, falsely accused. He walked up to the front desk and waited for the receptionist who was listening on the telephone. She ended her call, jotted down some notes onto a writing pad and then looked up.

"How may I help you?"

"I have information related to a robbery."

The receptionist took down Martin's name and asked him to take a seat in the waiting room across the hall. The room had no windows and smelled strongly of stale cigarettes. He slumped into one of the uncomfortable old wooden chairs. In the far corner, a young lady was quietly sobbing into her handkerchief.

Martin resisted the urge to get up from his chair and walk out. What if the police didn't take him seriously? Would they think that he had been in on the robbery? How would Ellis react when he found out his friend had ratted on him?

A detective poked his head into the waiting area, called out Martin's name and then led him back to an interview room. He explained to the detective why he suspected his friend and described what he had found in the shed. The detective took notes, asked a few questions and then asked Martin to wait. A few minutes later, he returned and asked Martin if he would be willing to take him and another detective to the site.

Martin rode ahead on his bicycle, while the two detectives followed in their motorcar. When they arrived at the abandoned shed, one of the detectives pulled away the newspapers that covered the stolen items while the other took detailed notes recording the exact location where the items had been found.

The detective's serious manner made Martin nervous. "Is there a way to keep my involvement quiet? I would rather that my friend not know that I turned him in."

"If it comes up in court, we can't hide your involvement. But don't fret, son. You did right by letting us know."

Martin immediately began to fret. He pictured himself standing before a judge and a packed courtroom while his friend stood on a platform off to the side, caged in by iron bars and staring accusingly at Martin. Just thinking about it made him feel sick again. He asked if it was okay for him to return home.

Upon arriving home, Martin went straight to his room. When his grandmother called him down for tea, he told her he wasn't feeling well. As he lay on his bed, he kept thinking about what might happen if he came face-to-face with his friend Ellis. He also worried about having to testify in court. He didn't know anything about how theft cases were handled. He had never visited his grandfather's courtroom. Would he be cross examined? He also thought about Sonja. At least solving the robbery would get her released. The authorities would know that she was innocent.

After Irene was sent to bed, Martin's grandmother knocked on his door. She set a tray of tea and crackers on his father's old desk and then sat on the edge of the bed. "How are you feeling?"

"Okay." Martin sat up with his back resting against the headboard and took a sip of tea, still avoiding eye contact with his grandmother.

"Are you ready to tell me what's going on?"

Now that he had shared his story with the police, he couldn't see any further harm in telling his grandmother. He explained everything, starting with the day he took Ellis to see the rooftop lookout and his particular interest in Wallbridge Manor.

Martin's grandmother did not interrupt. When he finished, her first words were, "I can imagine that it was extremely difficult to come forward and share that information about your friend."

With the telling of the story and his grandmother's quiet acceptance of how he had handled the situation, Martin felt his arms and fists relax. He took another sip of tea and reached over for a handful of crackers. "Well, at least now they know Sonja is innocent," he said.

CHAPTER 12

Weymouth, January — February 1940

A LICE DECIDED THE SITUATION with Sonja called for another visit to Walbridge Manor. Upon her arrival, Samuel took her hat and coat and asked her to wait in the parlour, as usual. She wondered if his behaviour toward her was more distant, or perhaps she was simply imagining it. Samuel never behaved in a manner she could label as friendly. He left to summon Lady Walbridge but did not summon Margaret to bring them tea as had been customary on past visits.

Lady Walbridge entered the parlour and sat across from Alice. They exchanged remarks about the weather, and then Alice broached the topic of the theft. "I'm relieved that you'll be able to recover your property. Will you be contacting the authorities about Sonja's return?"

Lady Walbridge's head tilted slightly upward, which Alice knew to be an unfavourable omen. "That young lady will not be returning to Walbridge Manor."

Although she sensed this was a losing battle, Alice pressed on. "I don't understand. We know now that she's not responsible for the theft."

"We only know that Martin's friend was holding the stolen property. We don't know who else was involved." Alice noted the emphasis on 'Martin's friend'. Lady Walbridge repositioned her embroidered silk shawl across her shoulder before adding, "You did not witness the look of greed that girl showed for anything that sparkled. I should have known better than to open Walbridge Manor to one of their kind. They will stop at nothing to acquire wealth."

Alice was stunned but tried to keep her voice even. "Am I to take it that you still think she's guilty?"

"We may never know what she is guilty of, or who else was involved." Lady Walbridge paused a moment to let the last bit sink in before continuing. "It no longer matters. The manor has been requisitioned for officer quarters, so we will not be in a position to accommodate additional boarders."

Alice sat up rigidly in her chair. She decided to ignore the veiled accusation against her grandson. But she was not going to let this lady's vilification of Jews go unchallenged. Trying unsuccessfully to keep the anger out of her voice, she asked, "But you think that because she's Jewish, she's inclined to theft? Do you then support Hitler's campaign against the Jews?"

Lady Walbridge, in contrast, kept her voice icily calm. "I don't disagree with his assertion that much of the economic woes they've experienced on the Continent can be traced to their avarice. That does not make me a supporter of Hitler, and I will not be accused of such in my own home. Your family's intrusion has wrought enough damage here." Lady Walbridge rose from her chair, rewrapped her scarf, walked with measured pace to the thick tasseled cord which summoned Samuel, and then, without a backward glance, left the room.

As Alice picked her way back home through the snow, it sunk in that she may have just ended her long-standing friendship with Lady Walbridge. She had always looked past the dowager's vanity and self-superiority as relatively harmless traits of a lonely old lady and had worked hard to remain on good terms. But today a line had been crossed. She also realised that it was now entirely up to her to rescue Sonja.

That evening, she once again telephoned her son. "Is this about that same refugee girl?" he interrupted when Alice started to explain the situation.

Alice had anticipated his reaction. "I realise you have too much on your plate to become involved in this case. All I need from you is some guidance on whom I should contact. Do you have any insights on who within the War Office might be sympathetic?" She did not entirely hide her impatience with her son's apparent lack of concern.

The next day, Alice spent her afternoon on the telephone chasing down referrals but with little to show for her efforts. She also posted letters to the offices she thought might be able to help with resolving Sonja's predicament. While everyone said they were sympathetic to Sonja's situation, the reality was that no one was willing to make time for a single Jewish refugee.

Alice heard Helen call out a loud "Hello" as she let herself in through the side door. "I'm in the sitting room," she replied.

Feeling thoroughly discouraged, Helen's visit came as a welcome distraction. Rosa was busy cooking, so they went into the kitchen to brew their own pot of tea, before returning to the sitting room.

It helped to share her frustrations with Helen, who had always been suspicious of Lady Walbridge. "All that wealth goes to people's heads. They get to thinking they're next best thing to royalty."

Alice laughed. "Yes, I know, but I've made an effort to stay on her better side. She still carries a lot of influence in the community."

"I've never been terribly bothered about the dowager. As my mother would say, 'I live too near a wood to be frightened by an owl'." Helen took a sip of tea before continuing. "But that's not why I stopped by. I know you're not keen on gossip, but this I thought you might want to hear."

"Out with it, Helen. What have you heard?"

Helen smiled, enjoying the suspense. "It involves our very good friend, Elizabeth Chambers." She looked up at Alice. "Yes, I thought that would catch your ear. I'm sure you've heard talk about black markets and war profiteers."

"You're not going to tell me that Elizabeth is dealing on the black market. I'll find that hard to believe."

"No, not that. It's her husband. Markets need inventory and distribution, and he controls plenty of that."

"You mean Mr. Chambers is operating a black market?"

"Not that he runs it, just facilitating things, for a slight fee, of course."

"Has he been charged?" Alice was glad Irene was reading up in her room and not around to hear this.

"No. That sort of thing is hard to prove. You need someone on the inside who's willing to talk."

"It's simply gossip then."

"Yes, of course. I know. But doesn't it just warm your heart to hear that?"

"I dare say it does."

"Yes, I know you're not the kind to spread gossip. And, neither am I, usually. But this I thought you needed to hear. Might even the playing field a bit."

Alice simply smiled.

***

A month following Alice's break with Lady Walbridge, Nathan asked her about developments with Sonja's case. "I've accomplished nothing," she replied with a sigh. "Everyone is stressed and stretched, and no one seems to have time or energy for an individual case such as Sonja's."

Nathan stoked their Observer Corps stove. The exceptionally cold weather had stretched into February with no end in sight. He looked up at Alice. "I've been pondering this. Seeing as I'm in desperate need of assistance with the farm, perhaps we can sort two problems in one."

"How do you mean?"

"Do you think Sonja would be at all keen to help with lambing? We could try flogging the notion to the authorities that her release would support the war effort."

"It's worth a try. But I don't know if Sonja has experience working with farm animals."

"At this point, I'll take whomever I can get. I can train anyone if they've a mind to work. What about that grandson of yours? Might he consider lending a hand after school?"

Alice smiled. "I suspect that if Sonja is in the picture, he'll be quite keen about animal husbandry. I'll check with him."

Despite the clear skies, it had been a slow morning for plane spotting. Alice cast about for another conversation topic. "Any news from your son?"

"Precious little." Nathan turned instinctively to look out across the water towards France. "The post from France is spotty. From what I do hear, he seems in good spirits."

Alice thought of Nathan alone on his farm with his son off at war. "What caused your wife's death?" The question seemed to fall from Alice's lips before she realised what she was asking. She felt her face flush despite the cold temperature. She had always been one to process her thoughts before vocalizing them.

Nathan once more looked over at Alice, this time with a look of surprise. "I thought the entire town knew." But Alice just shook her head. She often remained outside the circle of town gossip. She realised the personal question was a horrible misstep but didn't know how to undo it.

"She took her own life," Nathan finally said.

"I'm so sorry. Forgive me. I should not have intruded."

Nathan shrugged. "It's a long time past. Even with the war ended, she was never welcomed by the townsfolk. I think the isolation did her in. I wish I'd realised how poorly she was. We should've sold out and moved somewhere far away. Too late to change that now."

Another British reconnaissance plane approached from the east, and they paused their discussion so they could track and record its progress down the coast. At their next break, Nathan asked what the news was concerning Ellis's robbery trial.

Alice was grateful for a neutral topic. "Ellis confessed to the theft, so a trial won't be necessary. His sentencing hearing is next week. I certainly don't excuse his behaviour, but I feel that throwing this young man in prison is a terrible waste. He struck me as someone who could make something of his life, given a chance."

"What makes you say that?"

"My understanding is that the father is unemployable on account of his alcoholism. He was hired by the military because they didn't know his history and because they're desperate for manpower. Whether he'll be able to retain that employment remains to be seen. I suspect that the theft was something Ellis felt compelled to do to keep himself and his father from being thrown out into the street."

Nathan didn't immediately respond but continued to sweep the horizon for aircraft. Then he turned to Alice. "You're right—that would be a waste. And our armed forces desperately need recruits.

Is there any way he could obtain a deferred sentence and enlist instead? Does the judge take into account his age and situation?"

Alice thought for a minute. "I'm not sure. The judge in his case was a colleague of Edgar's. We've had him and his wife to our home for dinner. Perhaps I could speak to him."

CHAPTER 13

Weymouth, March 1940

MARTIN KNEW NOTHING ABOUT sheep and to be honest, wasn't all that keen to learn about them. He pictured them as being a bit dim, as far as animals go, and rather smelly. But he might be willing to put up with that. Sonja had been released from detention and had started working on the farm owned by the veterinarian who worked with his grandmother in the Observer Corps.

Even though the farm was out past the far edge of town, he was stuck using his father's old bicycle to get there. Petrol was too precious to waste when a bicycle would serve.

As he set out, his thoughts were of Sonja. He would finally have a chance to talk with her. Would she want to discuss the theft that had subjected her to police interrogation and then sent her into detention? Should he explain why he didn't go straight to the police to alert them about Ellis? If he had, that likely would have kept her out of detention. Maybe she hadn't yet made that connection. He was undecided on what he should do. Perhaps he would just see how the conversation went.

Martin pedalled a bit faster as he rode past Ellis's house. His grandmother had told him that Ellis would not be going to prison. They had arranged for him to join the army under a deferred

sentence, even though he had not yet reached the age of conscription. His grandmother had worked it out with the judge. He
would have a few weeks at home to work with his father while
waiting for his enlistment papers to come through. When they
first met, Ellis had told Martin that war was for fools who wanted
to get themselves blown up. Would war drive him to alcoholism
as it had his father?

He was hoping he would not run into Ellis. Martin wasn't
sure how his former friend would react to seeing him, and he
had no idea what he would say to him. On their way to and from
school, he would hurry Irene along every time they passed Ellis's
tumbledown cottage.

Martin had quit going out to explore on his father's bicycle
after school, preferring to stay at home and read. Sometimes he
would indulge Irene in a game of *sorry*, or *snakes-and-ladders*. His
grandmother had taken them to see *The Little Princess* with Shirley
Temple, which Irene loved but Martin found embarrassing. Then
she made up for it by taking them to see *Stagecoach*. Always, in
the back of his mind, Martin wondered what Ellis thought of him
for going to the police, especially now that he had been forced to
enlist ahead of reaching the age for conscription.

Passing through town, he happened upon Lydia Chambers.
He waved and said hello as he passed her. Martin had not made
many friends at his new school, but Lydia was in his year, and
very friendly.

As he pedalled up the exposed hill on the far side of town,
erratic gusts of wind kept pushing his bicycle sideways. The cal-
endar had finally flipped to March, but no one seemed to have
informed the wind about that. The cold still felt like February. As
he crested the hill, he glanced to his left. He stopped his bicycle to
stare at the view off to the north. On the next hill, across a small

valley, stood an enormous white figure of a man riding a horse. It appeared carved into the hillside. He recalled Ellis describing the carving. At the time Martin had dismissed the tale as an invention of Ellis's, designed to test how gullible his friend was. Now he realised Ellis had been telling the truth. He wondered who had made the giant figure and why.

From his grandmother's directions, Martin recognised the potholed drive that led to the sheep farm. He approached a substantial two-storey farmhouse constructed of soft-tan brick. The well-proportioned, rectangular home had a chimney at each end, which framed a steeply sloping roof. Three twelve-pane, white-framed windows sat evenly spaced across the top level. The ground level had two large, similarly-framed windows set symmetrically on each side of a covered entrance. The front rose garden was neatly pruned and sprouting vigorous, young shoots.

No one answered the door at the farmhouse, so he walked over to the main outbuilding built of the same brick as the house. As he rounded a corner, Mr. Stone and two young ladies came into view. They were bent over a ewe that was lying on her side in one of the chest-high, open stalls that ran along one side of the outbuilding. A border collie came running out to greet Martin, and he crouched down to scratch his neck and ears.

Martin stood up from petting the dog and called out, "Hello". He walked toward the trio as they turned up from their work. Suddenly, Martin stopped. One of the two young ladies he didn't recognise, and the other, of course, was Sonja. But he almost didn't recognise her either. He stared in disbelief. Her face was horribly disfigured. An angry, red burn mark, about the thickness of his finger, ran down the length of her face at a slight angle, starting at her forehead, above her right eye, skipping over her eye socket, then just right of her nose, across her lips and ending at her chin. It looked as if she had been branded by a metal bar.

Martin didn't know what to say. Sonja's face reddened, but she did not turn away. She looked Martin directly in the eye, until Martin averted his gaze. By that time Mr. Stone was introducing himself. "I understand you've already met Sonja. This is Audrey, and this little rascal is Moss," Mr. Stone added, indicating the border collie. Martin simply nodded. His brain seemed to stop working.

Mr. Stone turned back to the ewe, and the other two followed. He called over his shoulder to Martin, "This one's not even born but already managing to turn things cattywampus. His legs are pointing back—should be pointing forward, alongside the head." A little repulsed, Martin watched Mr. Stone reach in to reposition the lamb. As he drew out his gloved hand, covered with mucus and blood, two skinny legs emerged followed closely by a nose, and then the entire lamb ejected all at once. It lay on the straw for a few seconds, before it started to kick it legs. But the ewe was not finished. A few minutes later there were two lambs being licked energetically by their mother. Martin would have been fascinated by the birth, except his mind was on whatever it was that had happened to Sonja.

The two lambs latched on to the ewe's teats, and Mr. Stone stood up. He removed his gloves and brushed the straw and dust off his trousers. "Okay, Martin. Let's do the tour, and then we'll put you straight to work, seeing as that's the one thing these days of which there's no shortage." Turning to Sonja and Audrey, he added, "Would you two be so kind as to replace this soiled straw?"

Mr. Stone insisted that Martin call him Nathan. After showing Martin around, he put him to work mucking out stalls, moving bales of straw, and hauling bags of feed from the lorry to a weathered wooden storage shed. The work was heavy, and Martin's muscles started to complain as the time dragged on. Nathan's dog, Moss, spent most of his energy chasing after his owner but would check in on Martin periodically, demanding attention.

The property sloped towards the Channel, separated from it by the footpath. It was hard not to be distracted by the view out across the bay, with vessels of all descriptions traveling to and from the two harbours. Enormous clouds alternated grey and white as they chased across the Channel in the March wind.

When the sun was close to setting over the hills beyond Weymouth, Martin decided it was time to head home. His body felt like it had been run over by a trolley, with every muscle aching. But he still had the bicycle ride ahead of him. All the way home, he wondered about what had happened to Sonja. He hadn't had a chance to talk to her alone and wasn't sure what he would have said if he had.

Upon arriving home, he dragged his body up the stairs and caught a bath before tea. He was glad to be working only three days a week. He felt he would need a full day off just to recover.

It being Rosa's day off, Martin helped his grandmother clear up after dinner. This provided an opportunity to talk to her without Irene listening in. "Do you know what happened to Sonja?"

"What do you mean?"

"She has this big scar across her face."

His grandmother paused in the middle of drying a large dinner plate. "What type of scar?"

"I don't know. A burn, I think. It's huge. All the way from her forehead to her chin."

"Oh my! Poor Sonja. I hadn't heard that. Did she say anything about it?"

Martin had finished washing the last of the dishes and pulled the sink plug to let the soapy water drain. "No, I never had a chance to talk to her."

"I haven't talked to Nathan since Sonja's return. But I can speak to him tomorrow. We're on duty together. Or you can ask her next time you're helping out."

"Yeah, if I get a chance." Martin dried his hands and headed upstairs to his room.

The next day, as soon as his grandmother returned from observer duty, Martin came downstairs.

"What did Nathan have to say about Sonja's scar?"

"Not much, I'm afraid. Having just met Sonja, he didn't realise that the scar was recent. He didn't ask her about it because he didn't want to make her uncomfortable." Seeing the disappointment on Martin's face, she added, "Now that he knows this happened recently, while in detention, I think he'll ask her about it next time he has an opportunity."

Martin went back to his room, closed the door, and sprawled out on his bed. What could have happened to Sonja in detention that resulted in such a disfiguring scar? If he had gone to the police right away, her face would still be unblemished. But he couldn't have known this would be the outcome. And he did eventually go to the police—ending his only friendship in Weymouth. Anyway, nothing he could do now to change what had happened.

He had been looking forward to working on the farm, because he wanted to see Sonja. Now, it felt uncomfortable to be around her. How could he talk to her when he could barely stand to look at her? Maybe he would quit the farm, but his grandmother probably wouldn't allow it. Nathan really needed the help.

When Martin returned to the farm the next day, Nathan was supervising Sonja and Audrey, who were working with several ewes in the shelters that ran along the side of the main outbuilding. They all looked up at his arrival, but Martin avoided eye contact with Sonja and didn't go over to see what they were working on. Nathan finished his instructions and then came over to tell Martin he would be needing his help with the last of the shearing. Martin was relieved to be working away from Sonja and the discomfort he felt around her.

With the Land Girls working full-time, Nathan invested more time teaching them about animal husbandry. Martin was there for only three half-days per week and was given heavy jobs such as loading feed and cleaning out stalls.

Even though Martin was not old enough to drive on the roads, his grandmother had taught him how to operate his grandfather's motorcar, practicing up and down the long drive to Elm House. Nathan showed him how to operate his old Morris lorry, so that he could help with the transport of supplies around the farm. Martin had been maintaining his grandfather's motorcar ever since moving to Weymouth, and Nathan was happy to have him assume responsibility for maintaining the lorry as well. Martin liked working on engines. He found that he had a knack for finding inventive ways to make do on repairs, given that it was near impossible to obtain replacement parts.

By the end of the second week, work patterns were well established. And by the end of the third week, Martin's body was not complaining quite so loudly as when he first started. Pedalling towards home, he thought that farming might be putting some muscle on his skinny frame, and that brought a small private smile.

He was so involved in his thoughts, that he didn't realise who it was that his bicycle was overtaking along the side of the road until Ellis turned to look over his shoulder. The encounter he had been dreading had come. His heart pounding, he stopped his bicycle in the middle of the road and looked over at his former friend.

"You've been avoiding me," Ellis said as he walked over.

"I've been working on a sheep farm." Martin's voice betrayed his nervousness.

"So I've heard." Ellis did not sound hostile.

"How did you hear about that?"

"Sonja."

Martin was dumfounded. "You've been talking to Sonja?"

"Writing. The judge told me about her detention, so I wrote her a proper apology. She wrote back, and we've had a few letters. She's trying to improve her English."

Martin wasn't thrilled that Ellis was writing to Sonja. "Did she tell you about her scar?"

"Yeah, I heard about her scar."

"Did she say how it happened?" Martin walked his bicycle to the side of the road as a motorcar passed them.

"Maybe you should ask her. Seems I'm not the only one you've been avoiding." Ellis started walking away, towards his house.

Now that Martin knew Ellis wasn't going to be angry at him, he didn't want the conversation to end so quickly. He called after him, "So, when do you head out?"

Ellis turned. "A week from Monday."

"What about your father? What'll he do for an assistant?" Martin took a few steps to close the distance.

"Not a problem, seeing as he lost the military contract. But this way I can send him some of my military pay." He started up the drive to his cottage.

Martin called out after him. "Well, maybe I'll see you before you head out."

Ellis turned again and looked Martin square in the eye. "I don't blame you for running to the bobbies. This mess was my making. See ya around." He turned and continued up the drive.

CHAPTER 14

Weymouth, May – June 1940

THE MORNING WAS BRILLIANTLY sunny, promising to be the sort of day Alice had longed for throughout the cold, rainy expanse of winter into early spring. Yet the warm weather could not diminish the apprehension that constricted her chest and clouded her thoughts.

The newspapers delivered a steady stream of catastrophes, each one deepening her sense of dread. First there was the disaster in Norway. Then, reports that the Nazis had raced through the Netherlands, Luxembourg, and Belgium as if those countries were made of matchsticks. The Meuse River which should have taken four days to cross was bridged in a day. They ploughed through the Ardennes Forest as if it were a cornfield. As a result, the Maginot Line, the great assemblage upon which France had built its defence, was rendered useless in a single stroke. It now seemed inevitable that France would fall, leaving Britain nearly alone in its stand against the German advance.

Throughout Weymouth, the talk was of one thing—when would the invasion come? At school, Martin heard a rumour that two German spies had landed under cover of darkness near Lulworth Cove. But Alice doubted the rumour was true. There was no mention of it in the newspapers.

As Alice waited in line at the butchers, she watched the workmen pulling down street signs. They had been systematically working their way across Weymouth and the surrounding area, removing anything that might help orient the invaders. The sign out front of the merchandise shop across the street came down as well because its signage included the name Weymouth.

The authorities issued detailed instructions on how to avoid aiding the German invasion. Never give directions or assistance to strangers. Leave no bicycles lying about. After each use of Edgar's motorcar, Alice removed the rotor cap, as instructed, and locked the shed where she stored the vehicle. Disrupting potential aids to transport and navigation for Germans parachuters was of critical importance.

Alice turned back to face the queue. Weymouth was a resort town, and they were used to hordes of visitors each summer. So, it seemed particularly out of character for the townsfolk to be peering suspiciously at anyone they didn't recognise. The two ladies standing ahead of her in line were familiar, although she couldn't recall their names. She was so absorbed in thoughts of invasion, that she didn't immediately register what it was they were discussing. Suddenly, it became all too clear.

"...yes, the wife died years ago, but now he has another German working for him. And I heard he petitioned for her specifically," the taller of the two was saying. "And their farm has a view to the bay, so they can track every vessel that enters or leaves."

The second lady was closer to Alice's height, so she had to look up to speak to her companion. She dropped her voice, and Alice listened hard to catch what she was saying. "So, do you think he's spying for the Germans?"

The taller lady shifted her shopping to her other arm. "Well, he certainly seems sympathetic to them. But there's more, he works in the Observer Corps, so he has access to all their sightings as well."

Alice had heard enough. "Forgive me, but I couldn't help overhearing your conversation. You might be interested to know that the German Land Girl working for Mr. Stone is Jewish. She fled the Nazis, so she's hardly likely to spy for them. Also, I work with Mr. Stone in the Observer Corps, and I can assure you that he is not a German sympathiser. His son is currently serving in France."

The two women looked back at Alice. The shorter woman gaped at her while the taller one appraised Alice, her eyes narrowing. With just a hint of a smile, the taller lady placed her hand on her companion's shoulder, and they both turned away, their backs to Alice. The taller woman leaned in close to her friend, whispering something Alice could not overhear. Alice decided she didn't care what they thought of her. She was not going to let these rumours go unchallenged.

The next day, Alice was back on observer duty. The previous night she had debated with herself whether to tell Nathan about the gossip she had heard. Upon further reflection that morning, she decided it was better for him to know what was being said so that he could be prepared, than to try to spare his feelings. When they reached a lull in activity, she relayed to Nathan the conversation she had overheard.

"Can't control what folks say." Nathan set down his binoculars for a minute. "Or what they think, for that matter."

"Well, I thought at the least you should know."

"I appreciate your concern, but this time around, I don't have a wife or any children they can threaten, so I'm not too bothered. Just don't give them cause to wrap you into this."

The distant sound of a single-engine plane provided a convenient distraction, saving Alice from having to respond. It wouldn't surprise her if the rumours surrounding Nathan had already expanded to include her. She put it out of her mind as she picked up the clipboard to record the incoming aircraft. Now that the Germans had gained control of nearby airfields in Belgium and northern France, they were seeing more hostile aircraft and more aerial skirmishes.

The following week, the news from France went from disastrous to catastrophic. An appeal went out calling all sea-worthy craft into service. Alice and Nathan watched from their observer post as boats of all sizes and descriptions left Weymouth heading east. Their purpose became clear when the craft began returning, packed to capacity with evacuees. Most of the vessels refuelled and turned immediately around for another trip. Through her binoculars, Alice picked out the steamer *St. Helier*, on which she and Edgar had booked passage for a holiday on Guernsey in the Channel Islands three summers ago. Now, that time felt like a different age. Over the next two weeks, their observer post recorded eight evacuation crossings from the *St. Helier* alone.

The townsfolks looked on solemnly as long lines of refugees snaked up from the harbour to hastily organised clearing stations. Weymouth had sent its sons, brothers and husbands to France with bravado and pride. In their stead, they received evacuated British, French and Moroccan troops. Their vacant stares and hunched shoulders communicated more clearly than any headline a message of battle trauma, loss, and retreat. In addition to the evacuated soldiers, the town's refugee count swelled with thousands of Dutch and Belgium civilians, most of whom fled the blitzkrieg with only as much as they could carry. The Weymouth Town Clerk appealed for temporary shelter, and Alice found room to house six of the refugees by turning Edgar's former study into an additional bedroom and moving Irene in to share her own bedroom. Martin was delighted and Irene disappointed when the schools closed temporarily so they could be used to billet overflow refugees.

Sightings of enemy aircraft continued to grow. Alice and Nathan watched helplessly while six German bombers flew over Weymouth. Alice could think only of her two grandchildren at home on their own, and it took great effort to carry on with her Observer Corps duties. But the aircraft continued out over Portland and back over the Channel. The six bombs they dropped all landed harmlessly in the sea.

That evening Alice reviewed and practiced the evacuation procedures with Martin, Irene, and Rosa. She also double-checked the emergency supplies in her cellar which served as their air raid shelter. In addition to the food, water, candles, matches, and torch that were already set aside, she added extra batteries, games, books, pillows, and blankets.

Alice suspected that the war still felt like an adventure to her granddaughter, and that the prospects of invasion and combat were too abstract for a sheltered girl just turned nine. Alice worried that her mental state could plunge should actual fighting reach their community.

As for Martin, ever since the theft at Walbridge Manor, he spent most of his time in his room. He rarely left the house except when necessary. Alice knew his change in behaviour had nothing to do with the war. Everything changed when Sonja went into detention. She didn't know what to say or do to help Martin. She had passed along the bit of information she had gathered from Nathan—confirming that Sonja had received the scar while in detention. But Sonja had been reluctant to discuss specifics, and Nathan had not wanted to pry. As far as Alice could tell, Martin had not yet talked to Sonja about her experiences.

As the month of June closed out, Alice let go of any hope that the war would not reach Weymouth. Italy's entry into the war, the Nazis' march through Paris, and the surrender of France were all devastating blows to morale, but the fall of the Channel Islands felt personal. Weymouth was the closest British port to the Islands, and they had been a favourite vacation destination for her and Edgar. As the invasion drew close, she watched thousands of fleeing Islanders walking up from the harbour, many carrying baskets of tomatoes that they were loath to leave behind for the Germans.

No one seemed able to stop the German advance. Scenarios that a year ago would have been laughable, were now not only possible but probable. How would she respond when their tanks came rumbling down the streets of Weymouth and the Gestapo arrived to set up headquarters in the Weymouth Guildhall. With France defeated and Germany bolstered by Italy's entrance into the war, Alice felt the Nazi machine as a physical, everyday presence, with all of its enmity focused on Britain.

In the months following Edgar's passing, Alice had savoured her independence. Now, she found herself thinking of him often, especially when she faced difficult decisions that impacted the safety of her household. Despite the mismatch between her and Edgar, he had provided a sense of authority and confidence. Now, she felt it was up to her to keep her grandchildren both mentally and physically safe.

CHAPTER 15

Weymouth, July 1940

WHEN THE AIR RAID alert sounded, Rosa almost dropped the platter carrying that evening's pie.

"Can't we just have our supper first?" Martin was famished. Besides, there had been a number of alerts, but nothing ever came of them.

His grandmother smiled. "Quickly—Martin, you grab the platter. Rosa and I will grab the plates and forks."

Martin rather liked eating in the cellar by candlelight. He had just finished when the all-clear sounded. After helping carry dishes back to the kitchen, he raced up to the lookout. He couldn't detect any damage but noticed a flurry of activity near Chisel Cove in Portland. The following day at school, he heard that an unexploded bomb had landed near the Cove—the first to fall on land in their vicinity.

The following week, Martin had the entire house to himself. That almost never happened. Whenever his grandmother was out, he invariably would be stuck looking after his little sister. This morning, however, it was Rosa's day off, and his grandmother had taken Irene down to Woolworths to find some new play dresses. She had hit a growing streak, and with the disruption of cloth imports, clothes that fit had become as rare as chocolate.

Martin couldn't get into the book he was reading. He set it aside and wandered downstairs. The house felt empty, but he didn't fancy going out either. He noticed his grandmother's binoculars sitting on her desk and decided to see what was happening out on the water.

He was spending more time in the lookout lately, there being so much activity on view. He had been fascinated and demoralised to watch the hordes returning from Dunkirk. He still didn't know if Ellis had been somewhere in their midst. If the Germans did come to England, where would everyone evacuate to?

He surveyed the length of Weymouth Beach and then the area around the Portland Harbour. He noticed an increase in defensive structures and in the number and size of ships stationed in the two harbours. He had started memorising the names of the larger military ships in case any were mentioned in the *Dorset Echo*.

He completed his usual surveillance. Everything looked pretty much business as usual. He was checking out some activity on the Portland Harbour when the air raid sirens suddenly started. He almost dropped the binoculars. He needed to get down the four flights of stairs to their cellar, and quickly. But something gave him pause. He was curious about what had triggered the alert. No harm in taking a quick look. How often would he find himself already at the lookout when the siren went off? The air raids never seemed to amount to much anyway.

He scanned the horizon but couldn't see anything out of the ordinary. Except—he paused to get a better look—there was something to the east. At first it looked like a dense flock of birds. Martin realised it was moving too quickly and getting bigger. That must be it—a German squadron heading their direction. As the formation drew closer, he could see that there were close to twenty aircraft. Then he heard the drone of their engines, growing louder. His heart started pounding in his chest.

He lingered a moment longer. There was still time to get to the cellar. Besides, they would target the Portland harbour and military installments, not the homes up here on the hill. He knew he was cutting it very close. He should head to the cellar now. But he wanted to watch just a bit longer.

It seemed that the formation covered the remaining distance in no time at all. What was he doing still at the lookout? He realised with a thrill of horror that he was witnessing actual bombs exploding around the Portland Harbour. Seconds later, the sound of the explosions hit him. As the terror of what he was witnessing sunk in, he thought maybe he was going to need to run to the bathroom, but he couldn't take his eyes off what was unfolding in front of him.

A group of aircraft broke away and began an attack on the *HMS Foylebank* which Martin had spotted earlier in the harbour. The Foylebank was returning fire, but it looked outgunned by the Germans. Martin watched in horror and fascination as one of the ship's gun turrets exploded. Then another was hit, and the ship erupted in flames. The squadron made one last circle over Portland harbour, dropping more bombs in the vicinity before heading back out over the Channel.

As quickly as it started, the attack was over. Black smoke billowed from the ship in waves that reminded Martin of boiling water. A gust momentarily pushed the smoke to one side, and he caught a glimpse of the ship already sinking into the harbour. He continued watching as fire hoses were brought out, and medic vehicles arrived. He saw what he thought were dead bodies lying on the ground near some piers.

With a start, Martin remembered his grandmother and sister. But they were in Weymouth, so they were well away from where the bombs had landed. Even so, he needed to get down to the shelter before they returned home and he was caught out. He raced down the four flights to the cellar and sat down before realising he was still holding the binoculars. If his grandmother saw them, would she guess that he had stayed out to watch the raid? As he debated whether to run them back upstairs, the all-clear signal came through. He climbed the stairs and returned the binoculars to his grandmother's desk.

"Martin?" His grandmother and Irene had just returned.

"I'm in here."

"Thank goodness you're alright. You were in the cellar?"

"Yes, of course." Martin was surprised at how easily the lie came.

"We were able to shelter in the basement of one of the shops. But on our way home we noticed a great deal of smoke in the direction of Portland."

"Really? I wonder what was hit?" Martin wanted to tell them all about what he'd witnessed, but he had to keep it to himself. If Ellis were still around, he could have told him. "I'm going to the lookout to check it out."

Later that afternoon, Martin stood looking out his bedroom window. From the upper floor, he could just make out a glimpse of the Island of Portland through the trees. Today, he had witnessed first-hand the destructive force of the Germans, and he couldn't erase the images of dead bodies and the burning ship sinking into the harbour.

He thought of Leo who had turned eighteen last week and was in the process of enlisting. What if Leo ended up dead just like the men he had seen today? What if Ellis were to be killed in battle? Would that be Martin's fault? And in a few years Martin would be expected to enlist—that is, if they still had a country left at that point.

And why were the Germans bombing us in the first place? What had the people of Weymouth done to deserve to be blasted from their homes? For the first time since the war had started, Martin felt ready to fight. You couldn't be attacked like that and not want to fight back.

He was due to help at the farm starting around lunchtime. Despite the bombing raid that morning, Martin couldn't find a reason for not carrying on as usual.

He arrived at the farm with a strong sense of resolution. Only, he wasn't quite clear on what it was he was resolved to do. Then he saw Sonja taking a break, sitting on her own on the wooden bench that was built into the side of the bunkhouse where she and Audrey stayed. The bench offered a sweeping view across the bay. The June sun lit up Sonja's face, and her scarred skin appeared shiny and garish in the bright sunlight. He walked up to her.

"Hi," he said.

"Hello."

"Mind if I sit down?"

Sonja shook her head and gave a small smile. Her smiles would never be the same.

Martin sat a little away from her. "Do you like working here?"

"Yes—much. Farming suits me. And Nathan is good teacher."

"I'm a slow learner when it comes to sheep." Martin looked out over the water. It still felt uncomfortable to look directly at Sonja.

"Once I told you, you have future of farmer in you. You've had not so much time with sheep as Audrey and me."

Martin realised that, even with her once-perfect complexion irreparably marred, Sonja still retained her kindness and that her kindness was also part of what originally attracted him. "Do you mind if I ask? What happened in detention?"

Sonja looked out over the water. Her smile was gone, but she did not close down as she had before when Martin questioned her about her past. "To the British, all Germans are same. Nazis and Jews together—not problem. I was forced to live with Nazis." She looked directly at Martin, pointing to her scar. "This is why I must leave my home. This is why my parents not allowed to leave with me. It is called hatred."

Their eyes met for a moment, until Martin looked back out to sea. A flock of dunlins swept out across the water far below them and then darted back towards the rocks, out of sight. "I'm sorry they did that to you." The words sounded feeble, but it was all he could come up with. "I'd better go see what Nathan has for me today." He rose from the bench and walked up to the farmhouse, feeling self-conscious knowing that Sonja was probably watching him walk away.

He thought about what Sonja had just told him. He knew the Nazis hated Jews. But for that to happen to a young woman here in England? He wondered what really led up to the incident. How did the others even know she was a Jew, unless she told them?

Martin tried to imagine the scenario. He had seen Sonja's independent and, at times, defiant nature. If she had kept her head down and minded her own business, would this have happened to her? She didn't seem to want to talk about details around what took place. Was that because she realised that she had partly brought this on herself?

As he approached the farmhouse, a wiry young man charged out the front door. He looked up at Martin in surprise. "Can I help you?" he asked.

"Um, I'm looking for Mr. Stone."

The man stuck his head inside the open doorway. "Pa," he yelled. He sat on the bench next to the front door and pulled on a pair of well-worn wellingtons.

The man didn't say anything further to Martin. "Are you Mr. Stone's son?" Martin asked.

At that point, Nathan emerged from the house. "Yes, this is Emil." Turning to Emil, "Martin's helping out part-time. He's the late Judge Standfield's grandson." Turning to Martin, he added, "Ready to get started?"

"Yes."

"Great. Emil's home on a few day's leave, and I'm hoping to make a dent in the backlog of carpentry repairs while he's here, especially the fencing. He'll show you what to do."

Without saying anything, Emil headed for the outbuilding, and Martin assumed he was supposed to follow. Martin observed in Emil the confident gait and fluid motions of someone used to physical activity and being outdoors. Emil gathered some tools into a small knapsack, and they headed uphill across the pasture.

From what Martin could tell, the fencing appeared to prevent the sheep from doing three things—wandering into the road, invading their extensive vegetable garden, or dropping off one of the cliffs into the Channel. Being a city boy, Martin did not have much experience with carpentry. Emil demonstrated a repair and then wordlessly handed the tools to Martin so he could have a go. Being used to working under his father's supervision, he kept expecting that Emil would snatch the tools out of his hands and show him the correct way to accomplish the task. Instead, he was given space to work on mastering his technique, with just an occasional adjustment or encouraging comment from Emil.

As the afternoon progressed, Martin became more comfortable working with Emil, and their teamwork became more efficient. Mid-afternoon they took a break, sitting on the grass and taking swigs of water from Emil's canteen. "So, you were stationed in

France?" Martin asked. He was eager to gather as much information as possible about life as a soldier.

Emil nodded his head but continued staring out across the Channel.

"Were you part of the evacuation from Dunkirk?"

"Yep, but not though Weymouth. We landed at Southampton."

"Where'll you go next?"

"Don't know. Lot of our boys are getting shipped to Africa." Emil jumped to his feet, and they continued on to the next section of fencing.

Martin spent two more afternoons working with Emil before his leave expired, after which Nathan judged him as fully capable on minor carpentry projects, and that became part of his responsibilities. At first, he had been put off by Emil's silences, but he had grown to enjoy working with him and trying to extract as much information as he could about his experiences in France. He was sorry to see Emil go, but the farm work was more enjoyable when it included some carpentry.

That Friday, the telephone rang a short while after supper. His grandmother picked up the receiver and after a brief conversation, handed the telephone to Martin. "It's your father."

"Hello," Martin said.

"Martin—wanted to let you know that Leo passed his medical exam. He's reporting for service on Monday."

Martin sank down onto the chair next to the telephone. "Where is he heading?"

"Well, training to start with. We don't know where he'll end up once he's completed that."

"Can I come see him this weekend?"

"I'm afraid that's not an option. We don't have the petrol to run down to Weymouth unless it's an emergency."

"I could take the train."

"The trains are swamped and unreliable too. They need to be kept open for essential travel. But I thought you might like to speak to him. Here he is."

"Martin?"

"Hi."

"How're things in Weymouth?"

"Okay." Martin noticed his grandmother watching him. He was still taking in the news that Leo was heading off to war, and his mind seemed to go blank. "Where is your training?" he finally said.

"Don't know. Somewhere in Surrey."

There was silence. Martin couldn't think of anything else to say. "You want to say hello to Irene?"

After a short conversation with Irene, Martin's grandmother got back on the telephone to talk to his father some more. Martin went up to his room and lay down on his bed. Growing up, he had always been annoyed that his older brother could do things he was not yet old enough to do. And Leo would go out of his way to make sure his younger brother did not tag along. Martin had never considered that he might miss him.

Did he envy Leo? Partly yes. Martin was always second in his family, and there was never the same level of excitement and anticipation the second time around. But when it came to going to war, he wasn't too bothered about being second. As much as he hated the Nazis, the thought of fighting them still terrified him.

CHAPTER 16

Weymouth, Late July 1940

ALICE LEFT HER BICYCLE near the entrance to the Weymouth Guildhall, where, several months ago, she had met with the Chief Inspector to see what could be done for Sonja. This time she climbed the stairs to the upper floor—familiar territory from the days when her husband presided at court. But instead of heading for the courtroom, she entered the Council Chamber and took a seat near the back. The Air Raid Precautions Committee was meeting with the Town Council to review defence preparations. Nathan asked her to attend as the representative from the Observer Corps, and she reluctantly agreed.

She was hoping her role would be limited to that of an observer. The order of business ran through fire and ambulance response, blackout enforcement, steps to mitigate the alarming impact blackouts were having on pedestrian, bicycle, and motorist accidents, emergency housing for bombing victims, and a report from the Home Guard. At the end of the agenda, there was an opportunity for general questions or concerns. Alice noticed Elizabeth Chambers' gloved hand in the air.

"Yes, Mrs. Chambers?" the Chair of the Air Raid Precautions Committee tried to smile but was only partly successful.

Elizabeth stood up. "Mr. Chairman, given Weymouth's strategic location, I was wondering if you could provide an update on efforts to ensure that no one from our community is passing vital information into the wrong hands."

The Chair's attempted smile crumpled. "Are you concerned that we might have a spy in our community?"

"Of course, the citizens of Weymouth are dedicated to supporting the war effort, but there are some known to have German... affinities. Some with extraordinary access to the activity taking place on our waters and in our skies." She looked around the room with a fixed smile.

"Yes, well, if you have concerns about possible spying, you should take it up with the War Office. That is not within our purview."

"Of course, you are correct. I just thought that we should all be made aware and alert to any unusual activities. I think most of you know to whom I am referring."

A murmur rose as hushed side conversations spread across the room. The Chair looked around the chamber and then tapped the podium to regain the audience's attention. "The War Office is the correct venue for that. I'm sure none of us would want to be too hasty in reaching conclusions about our neighbours."

"Yet, we all have a duty to be on our guard. That's all. Thank you." With another smile around the room, Elizabeth sat down.

Alice seethed. She wanted to say something, but Elizabeth was careful not to mention Nathan by name. If Alice had spoken up in his defence, it would have been an acknowledgment that he was the one under the cloud of suspicion.

She remembered the rumour Helen had shared—that Elizabeth's husband was profiting off the black market. Alice considered that the rumour was probably true. Maintaining a show of wealth had always been important in their family. The hypocrisy of that woman, questioning Nathan's patriotism.

When the meeting ended, she was so absorbed in her thoughts that she failed to notice Elizabeth, with her smile of triumph, bearing down on her.

"Alice, I'm sure you've had time by now to sort through Edgar's things. The women's auxiliary will do you a world of good, and I won't take 'no' for an answer."

Alice looked up, startled. "Do you really think I would join your little group after you've just denounced a perfectly innocent man about whom you know nothing?" Nearby conversations fell silent, and Elizabeth's smile vanished.

Alice immediately regretted her outburst. Not waiting for a response, she left the building as quickly as possible. All the way home, Alice wondered how many of her fellow townsfolk had witnessed the exchange and what the fallout would be from her loss of temper.

The twilight had fully converted to night by the time she approached Elm House. She noticed that her kitchen window had not been shuttered. Her house stood out like a beacon, the only source of light in the surrounding neighbourhood. Alice sighed. Observing blackout was Martin's responsibility on nights when she was out, and she had tried to impress upon him just how serious that was. The patrols were not forgiving of lapses.

Alice stored her bicycle and shuttered the kitchen window. She found Martin and Irene reading in the sitting room. They both looked up at her—not used to their grandmother bursting in on them.

"Martin, I've tried to convey to you the importance of observing blackout. I'm not sure what more I can say to convince you take it seriously. You do know that people's lives depend on our adherence?"

"Yeah, sorry." Martin looked defeated as he headed off to his room, and Alice wondered if she had been too hard on him.

Most evenings, after Irene went to bed, Alice looked forward to a bit of reading in her favourite chair. Tonight, she couldn't stop thinking about Elizabeth's comments and the whispers that slithered through the audience. She tried to concentrate on her book, but in the silent house, the grandfather clock seemed unnaturally loud and menacing, like the timed activation mechanism for a bomb. She wandered into Edgar's study, found his decanter of brandy, brought it out to the sofa side table, and poured a generous shot.

As she sipped, she reflected on her interaction with Martin regarding the open shutter. It was the first time she had been truly angry with him, and she realised her temper may have had more to do with what had transpired at the meeting, than what had transpired at home. When she considered all the circumstances, her two grandchildren were adapting remarkably well.

She glanced up at the grandfather clock. The hour was later than she usually stayed up. She rose from the sofa and was heading back to the study to put the brandy away when a harsh jangle shattered the silence. She nearly dropped the decanter. Who was telephoning at this hour?

"Hello."

"Mrs. Standfield?"

"Speaking." Her heart was still thumping from the suddenness of the telephone call.

"Sorry for the lateness. I'm Arthur Miller, and I live next door to your son, Henry."

"Is everything all right?" Alice sank into the chair next to the telephone, the decanter still dangling from her left hand.

"I'm afraid I have bad news for you. Are you alone?"

Alice felt her throat tighten. Her heart seemed to jump in her chest. "The grandchildren are in bed. Please, just tell me what's happened."

"It's Henry and Kathleen. We've had another bombing raid tonight, and I'm afraid they are both casualties."

The decanter fell from Alice's limp wrist. It didn't break but tipped sideways upon hitting the floor, its liquid spreading in front of her like a pool of amber blood.

"Mrs. Standfield? Are you okay?"

"They're dead? Both of them? But how did this happen?"

"Yes, I'm terribly sorry. They were heeding the air raid—in their shelter—but it took a direct hit. I'm sorry. It was just a horrible circumstance. The house is still mostly intact. That's how I found your number. I'm calling from their house. We don't have a telephone."

Alice felt the room sway but tried to pull herself together. "Thanks for letting me know. Thank goodness the children are here. And Leo, he's away at training?"

"That's our understanding, yes." After a pause, "I can stay the night here if you'd like. There've been problems with looting, and the police can't patrol all the bombing sites—too many of them."

The conversation didn't seem real. They couldn't be talking about something so horrible in such a mundane manner. "Are you sure? What about your family?"

"They'll be right next door, so no trouble at all. Is there anything further we can do for you at this point? Is there someone who can be with you?"

"No, I don't think so. Thanks for your help." Alice hung up the telephone, but she didn't get up from the chair or clean up the brandy from the floor. She sat alone and wept. In the depth of the night, Elm House felt large and empty and silent as a tomb—except for the clock, its ticking magnified by the silence.

The next morning, Alice called her grandchildren into the sitting room to sit on either side of her on the sofa. It was easier that way—not having to look directly into their faces as she delivered her news that their mother and father were gone, that they were now orphans, that their stay in Weymouth had become permanent. How was it that just last night she had been upset about a shutter left open? She so regretted her loss of temper.

Irene burst into tears, and Alice put a comforting arm around the young girl as she buried her face in her grandmother's side. She raised her other arm to draw Martin in as well, but he stood up and walked slowly out of the room. Alice suspected he did not want to cry in front of his grandmother. She wanted to go to him, but at this moment, Irene needed her. Perhaps it was best for Martin to have some time alone to comprehend and process all that this would mean for him and how profoundly it would change his life.

As she sat comforting her granddaughter, she thought of the myriad questions that kept her awake the previous night. They had flashed through her mind like the ominous headlines in the newsreels they screened at the cinema these days. How was she to get word to Leo? Would he be granted compassionate leave? She would need to go to London to see about the house and their belongings. Should the children come with her? Should she put their furniture into storage, or try to sell it? Did her son have a solicitor? Did he have a will? Would the children automatically come to her, or would this need to go through the courts? There was no doubt in Alice's mind that she would take the children. She knew Martin was in need of strong guidance. Was she up to the task?

Eventually, she got up to make tea for Irene, breaking into their precious supply of biscuits. She took a tray up to Martin. He thanked her but wanted to be left alone. Returning downstairs, she pulled out *The House at Pooh Corner*, one of Irene's favourites and a story with no references to mothers or fathers.

CHAPTER 17

London, Early August 1940

ARTIN STOOD IN THE empty bedroom that he used to share with Leo. There had been just enough room for the bunk beds, dresser, and small desk. Leo always claimed the desk, making Martin do his homework on the floor or at the dining room table downstairs.

This was the house in which Martin had spent his entire life, up until the war. It felt small and confined compared to Elm House. And it felt cold and empty with so much of the furniture removed, not to mention the removal of his parents. Seeing his home uninhabited made the loss of his parents real. He was used to his father being away at work, but always his mother had been there—busy perhaps, yet still there.

He looked out the second-storey window to their back garden, which was now a crater. No sign of the shelter, and no chance of harvesting any vegetables. He thought back to the previous summer when he, Leo, and his father had laboured over the Anderson shelter that had now double-crossed them. It was supposed to be a refuge, but it turned out to be a death trap.

He wandered into Irene's room, remembering the day when he and Leo were sent to the neighbours, waiting long hours before being allowed back home to find out they had a new sister. That marked the point when his mother no longer had time to read to Martin in the mornings after Leo left for school.

Irene had stayed in Weymouth with Rosa, but Leo met up with them at the house. Together they helped his grandmother sort through the family belongings, deciding which items to take to Weymouth for storage and which items to offer up for sale—the final act in the complete dismantling of his family. His grandmother said that they should put the house on the market, although whether it would sell in the midst of a war, they didn't know.

They spent a last night bunked down in his childhood home, and then it was time to drive away. It was a different Leo who said his goodbyes. He had already become a soldier, the brother who used to smirk at him. He gave Martin a solemn one-armed hug, standing alongside him. Then Martin watched Leo walk away, heading to the tube station that would take him to the train station that would take him back to training camp, that would take him off to war—and Martin couldn't say where war would take him.

Through large stretches of the return trip to Weymouth, the group remained quiet, lost in their private thoughts. The family's furniture and personal belongings were stacked and crammed into the bed of Nathan's lorry and covered with tarps. The lorry laboured under the heavy load, making for a long journey during which they felt every bump.

Wedged between his grandmother and Nathan, Martin's mind remained blank. As they approach the outskirts of Weymouth, Martin's grandmother sat up straighter and looked over at him. "I forgot to tell you that the *Dorset Echo* printed a small article about your friend."

"Who? Ellis?"

"Yes, he received a commendation—mentioned in despatches."

"What's that?"

"It means a superior officer mentioned him by name in his report. The article said that Ellis's section and two other sections were pinned down by Germans during their retreat to Dunkirk. Apparently, he kept his nerve and found a way to get the men free of their predicament."

They reached a point where the Channel came briefly into view, and Martin could see the Island of Portland in the distance. He thought of the bombs he had watched dropping on that island and the dead bodies he had seen strewn about. He wondered how he would respond to Germans firing at him. Would he keep his nerve?

Two days following his return from London, Martin was back helping out at the farm. He had not wanted to come. The thought of staying in his room and not having to see anyone appealed to him. But he knew if he did that his grandmother would come knock on his bedroom door and ask what was going on. He didn't want to talk about it, partly because he didn't understand what he was thinking or feeling.

As he rode his bicycle through town, his thoughts began to focus. In the first days after the news of his parents' deaths, it hadn't felt like they were really gone. While in Weymouth, he had become used to being separated from them. A part of him kept thinking that if he made a trip up to London, they would be there waiting for him. But he had made that trip, and it was now clear that they were not there waiting for him, that they would never again be there.

Martin had never imagined a future for himself without his parents. They would not be there to help him decide what he should study at university. He would never bring a lady friend home to meet them. If he was drafted to fight in the war, they would not be worried about him, and they would not write to

WILLIAM MCCLAIN

him nor receive his replies. There were so many things that were
now not going to happen. It was too much for him to absorb.
He concentrated on the physical work of fence repair, and this
occupied his mind with the task at hand, instead of with his future.

He had just finished a repair and was picking up his tools to
move to the next site when he noticed Sonja walking up the slope
towards him. He stopped to watch her approach.

"Working under sun, I think good to have cold drink." She
offered a glass of tea that she had cooled in the ice box and then
unfolded a napkin with two biscuits.

"Wow—thanks." Martin took the drink and sat down, leaning
against a fence post.

Sonja sat down on a rock opposite him, surrounded by wild
marjoram already gone to seed in the summer heat. "I'm sorry
for your mother and father."

"Thanks." Martin didn't know what to say, so he took a bite of
the biscuit. Sonja hadn't touched hers.

"How does Irene with her loss?"

"She's carrying on okay, I guess. Thanks for asking." The truth
was, Martin hadn't given much notice to how this was affecting
Irene. But when he thought about it, he realised her cheerful
disposition had disappeared right along with his parents, as if
they had taken it with them for a souvenir. Then something else
occurred to him. "Have you heard any news from your parents?"

"There is not news—because of war." Sonja looked out over
the harbour.

Martin thought of what he'd heard about German detention
centres. He hadn't connected that to Sonja's family, but maybe
her parents were in one of those camps. "I guess we have that in
common, being separated from our parents. I hope you will be
reunited with yours when this war is finally over."

"Thank you," Sonja said, but her face looked blank as she stood up and collected the glass and napkin. "I must be return to work." Martin watched her walk back down the hill towards the farmhouse. As he watched, he realised that they had just carried on a conversation during which he had not thought about her scar.

CHAPTER 18

Weymouth, mid-August 1940

ALICE WAS ADAMANT. SHE would not step down from her Observer Corps duties.

Nathan persisted. "This posting is a far-cry more dangerous than I reckoned when I recruited you."

The bombing activity had increased dramatically, both in Weymouth and across Britain. Ominously, the Germans were no longer focused solely on military objectives. Hitler was now targeting morale as much as machine. The list of Weymouth families who had been bombed out of their homes continued to grow. Thankfully, the list of casualties had remained moderate.

"I appreciate this concern, but this is my post, and I'm staying."

"But I keep thinking on Martin and poor little Irene, should something happen to you. My mistake in asking you to place yourself in harm's way."

Alice felt her blood pressure rising. "How was that a mistake? Has my work here fallen short of your expectations?"

"No. You know that's not the case. It's just that I realise now that this is not a safe assignment for a woman. It's nearly as dangerous as being in combat."

She faced Nathan square on. "Is it safer then, for men?"

"You know what I mean." Nathan tried to give a conciliatory smile, but to Alice, it felt condescending.

"I'm afraid I don't know what you mean. We're every one of us in danger, and we all have others depending on us. If I step down, it would only be to place someone else into that danger, whether they are a man or a woman."

With the installation of an RAF base nearby at Warmwell, Nathan and Alice had witnessed up-close some spectacular and frightening aerial battles. Alice found no thrill in watching such things, but she was not to be deterred from her responsibilities at the post.

Their discussion was interrupted by the roar of Spitfires and Hurricanes taking to the air. Being close to the airbase gave them a minute of advance warning. Whenever the planes took off *en masse*, they knew the air raid sirens would soon follow. Nathan and Alice scanned the horizon.

"Holy Christ!" Nathan was the first to spot them. They watched horrified as the formation grew closer. It far exceeded any previous attack they'd witnessed. There appeared to be well over a hundred planes bearing directly down on Weymouth.

As the RAF planes flew out to meet the squadron, the Messerschmitt escorts engaged, leaving the Stuka bombers free to break formation and fan out towards their targets. Alice and Nathan watched in dismay as the Stukas crossed over onto land. The staccato of anti-aircraft guns and the shriek of falling bombs were followed by waves of explosions, erupting in billowing, grey plumes that stretched across the landscape, drifting east in the steady wind. Even at some distance from the drop sites, they felt the delayed barrage of sound through their entire bodies as the carnage spread out in front of them. Through her binoculars, Alice could see a large fire breaking out near the Portland dockyard, but it did not appear that the nearby oil tanks had ignited as yet.

With effort, Alice held her binoculars steady. *Not Irene and Martin, not Irene and Martin* she kept repeating to herself. Surely, they would be sheltering in the cellar. They were well provisioned there. The bombings clustered around the south side of Weymouth Harbour and around the naval base at Portland—east and south of her own neighbourhood. She forced her attention on to the work of trying to track all the air activity taking place in front of them.

The Stukas were circling back out towards the Channel, unloading the last of their payloads over Portland and the harbour. As quickly as the attack had materialised, it had ended. Nathan looked over at Alice. "Okay, I concede. If you're still on your feet after all that, you're made of sturdier stuff."

Turning away from Nathan to cover her small smile, Alice started on the work of documenting the attack. "Thank you," she replied without looking up.

***

The following Saturday, Alice, Martin, and Irene walked down to the annual fête sponsored by their local parish. The morning was sunny but not overly hot, and already there was a sizable crowd. Over the years, the fête had grown into a major event in the community thanks in large part to Elizabeth's relentless drive and iron-strong organisation. This year, rather than benefiting parish programmes, proceeds were going to a fund that helped families who had lost their homes to the air raids.

Alice felt her participation would not only support a most worthy cause but also might help mend fences with Elizabeth. She didn't trust the woman but saw no harm in trying to keep their relationship as positive as was possible. During the week, she had sent Martin with several bicycle loads of clothing and other items of Edgar's to be sold in the bric-a-brac stalls. This year, despite the fact that the stalls had half the usual amount of goods on offer, shortages of almost everything had generated long queues that threatened to block foot traffic.

Missing, of course, were the food stalls with their abundant offerings of lamb, jugged steak, local cheeses, fish stew, and apple cakes. For such an agriculturally blessed region as Dorset, their absence felt like an insult to local pride.

Alice spotted Elizabeth's daughter, Lydia, running the donkey rides for the children. She noticed Irene watching the animals and asked her if she wanted to take a ride, which was a mistake. "Donkey rides are for children," Irene emphatically informed her grandmother.

They moved on to 'guess the weight'. This was traditionally played using an enormous fruit cake. However, this year they had substituted a large and very irregular piece of shrapnel. Alice paid for each of the three of them to enter a guess.

They were wandering over to the ring toss, when raised voices caught Alice's attention. Turning towards the sound, she spotted Sonja standing near the tea tent with her fellow Land Girl, Audrey. Four young men close to Martin's age approached them. One of the young men called out to Sonja. "Bloody Kraut! Why are you here?" He spat on Sonja's shoe. Audrey gasped and stepped back, pulling on Sonja's arm. But Sonja held her ground and stared defiantly at the young man. "Too ugly even for your Nazi soldier friends?" he asked.

The crowd in their vicinity went quiet. Even the donkey ride stopped. Alice noticed Martin tense up, his fist clenched. But at that moment, Ellis emerged from the crowd. He stepped in front of Sonja and faced the young man. In uniform and several inches taller, there was a lean toughness to Ellis, as if he had faced much worse than the likes of this particular troublemaker. "Parker, bit of advice." Ellis spoke calmly but with icy authority. "You don't want to go about bullying Jewish refugees. Might give folks to think you're the bloody Nazi. You're not, are you?"

The young man stared back at Ellis and looked to be considering a response. But he finally turned to his cronies standing behind him. "Let's go. This whole bloody place is a joke."

The crowd's attention dispersed. Sonja and Audrey had faded back into the crowd. Alice stepped forward. "Hello, Ellis. You must be on leave."

Ellis turned, saw Alice, and tipped his cap. "Mrs. Standfield. Martin. Irene. Yes, two days leave before we ship out. Destination unknown."

"I don't know if you heard, but the *Dorset Echo* printed a piece on your award—mentioned in despatches. Congratulations!"

Ellis smiled. "That's right kind of you, but I figure the credit's down to you—helping me avoid His Majesty's hospitality."

"Clearly a good investment. How is your father?"

"Yeah, he gets on. Thanks for asking." Ellis made a quick survey of the crowd. "Great seeing you folks. If you'll excuse me, I might just check up on Sonja." He turned and gave Martin a gentle box on the shoulder and a smile. "Martin."

"Ellis," Martin replied.

As Ellis walked off into the crowd, Alice noticed Elizabeth watching from inside the open-sided tent where she was hosting tea. She could only assume that the entire interaction had been witnessed. She turned to Irene and Martin. "Would either of you like some tea and refreshments?"

"Okay," Irene responded, but Martin shrugged, then shook his head.

Alice took Irene's hand and marched up to Elizabeth. "The fête is a triumph as always. Congratulations!" she said brightly.

"Thank you, Alice. Please have some tea," Elizabeth replied, but her lips were thin and unsmiling as she handed them cups. She immediately turned to talk to the lady standing beside her. *Well, I made an effort*, Alice thought to herself as she and Irene exited the tea tent.

They stood sipping their tea, and Alice looked around for Martin. He had wandered over to the donkey rides and was talking to Lydia. Alice guessed that they knew each other from school. As she watched, Lydia laughed at something Martin told her. She decided that it was probably a good thing Elizabeth was inside the tent and could not see her daughter fraternising with the enemy. Lydia appeared to be all smiles for Martin.

CHAPTER 19

Weymouth, Christmas 1940

MARTIN COULD NOT SLEEP. For the first time in his life, he was not looking forward to Christmas. It would be the first without his mother or father. In fact, he would never again celebrate Christmas with his parents. His last Christmas had not gone well, and at the time, he had thought he would be fine if they had stayed in London. Now, he knew that wasn't true.

He also missed Leo, and that surprised him. And he missed his friend, Ellis. Although he had come to know some of the other students at his school, he didn't consider any of them to be a friend in the way that Ellis had been a friend.

It was just Irene, his grandmother, and Rosa. It might have helped if they could look forward to a normal Christmas tea like they used to have before the war. But Martin knew that wasn't possible. Rosa and his grandmother tried their best, but there was only so much you could do with potatoes.

When he was younger, he would find it hard to sleep on Christmas Eve because of the excitement. Tonight, he found it hard to sleep because he was so very unexcited. He decided to wander downstairs. They had lit a fire earlier in the evening, and there might be some embers left that he could sit next to.

He entered the family room to find he was not the only one who couldn't sleep. His grandmother was sitting in her favourite chair, watching the fire. She must have added more wood, and with all the lights out, the light of the fire softened the room, drawing Martin in towards the intimacy of its glow. The grandfather clock showed that it was past midnight—already Christmas.

Hearing footsteps, his grandmother turned to see who it was. Martin was shocked to see her eyes shining in the firelight. She had been crying.

"Is something wrong?" He sat on the sofa, close to her chair.

She smiled back at him. "No. It's just your silly old grandmother being a bit maudlin."

Martin was used to his grandmother being predictably even tempered. He had never spared much thought as to how all the losses might be affecting her. "You're missing your son?"

"Yes, I do miss him and Kathleen. And your grandfather. I'm quite grateful to have you and Irene around, however."

They stared into the fire for a while. Martin thought about the fact that his father had been his grandmother's only child and how that must make the loss harder to carry. "Had you hoped to have more children?"

Martin's grandmother didn't respond. She continued staring into the fire. After a bit, she looked over at Martin. "Did your father never tell you about his brother and sister?"

"What do you mean? I thought he was an only child."

"No, he had a younger brother, James, and a younger sister, Lilian. They both died of diphtheria. Your father was only six at the time."

"He never told us." Martin was stunned. How was it that he hadn't heard about this? Did Leo know? It struck him that his grandmother had now lost all three of her children. "I'm sorry. You have a lot of people to miss."

"Yes, well that tends to happen as you get older."

Martin stared back into the fire. "Why do you suppose father never talked about this? I should think it had a big impact on him."

"Yes indeed. It changed everything in our family. You carry on, but after something like that—none of us were ever the same. I think your father has had difficulty connecting with you, Leo, and Irene because of what happened when he was a child."

Martin looked up at his grandmother. It had always seemed to him that his father never had time for him, but no one in his family ever talked about that, or even acknowledged that it was true. Apparently, his grandmother had noticed. So maybe there was some truth to it—it wasn't just his feeling sorry for himself.

He turned back to stare into the fire. Something fell into place. He had assumed his father's attitude towards him was due to his own shortcomings—that he hadn't measured up to his father's expectations. If what his grandmother said was true, it might have more to do with his father and what happened to him as a child. Martin found it hard to imagine his father struggling with his own childhood memories. He had always come across as self-assured.

Martin and his grandmother sat for a while in silence. Finally, Martin got to his feet. "I'm going back to bed."

"Me too." Martin's grandmother stood as well. She put an arm across Martin's shoulders and gave him a squeeze. "Merry Christmas."

CHAPTER 20

Weymouth, June 1941

MARTIN HAD SLEPT WELL into the morning when the distant jangle of telephone broke the silence of Elm House. He could hear his grandmother answering downstairs. The slanting morning sun was already illuminating his bedroom with garish light, inconsiderate of his sleepy morning stupor.

It was Martin's first week of summer holiday, and thankfully, today was not one of his farm days. Determined to take full advantage, Martin rolled away from the window and tried to return to blissful unconsciousness. But his grandmother's voice was animated and difficult to filter out. He lay in bed thinking about the summer ahead of him. Last week they celebrated his sixteenth birthday—his first without his parents. He could see that his grandmother had made an effort, but the day felt flat with just his grandmother, Rosa, and Irene.

He slowly got dressed and went downstairs in search of breakfast. His grandmother was still sitting in the chair by the telephone. She looked up, as if surprised to see Martin. "Who telephoned?" he asked her.

"That was an old acquaintance of mine who works despatch at the police station." Ignoring the questioning look from Martin, she remained in her chair for a moment. She then stood and placed a hand on Martin's shoulder, guiding him into the kitchen. "Sit down. I'll make some tea."

Martin sat, wondering what was up.

"There was a fire at the farm last night," she told him as she lit the stove.

Martin's eyes widened. "Is everyone okay?"

"I don't know. She didn't have any details, just that the Fire Brigade was summoned quite early this morning. She knew I shared Observer Corps duty with Nathan and thought I should know."

"Can we call Nathan?" Martin started to get up from his chair.

"No, I just tried. Their line is dead."

"We need to get out there."

"Yes, we do. Can you find yourself something quick to eat? I will let Irene know we're going out." Martin was relieved that his grandmother agreed with him and was treating him as an adult. He cut two slices of bread and a thin slice of cheese. Then he and his grandmother retrieved their bicycles from the shed and started for the farm.

The smell of smoke hit them before the scene came into view. The first thing Martin noticed was that the bunkhouse had disappeared. In its place were scattered charred timbers and smoking embers. The area had been roped off about a yard out from the outline of the foundation. This was the place where Sonja and Audrey slept. Looking around, he spotted Nathan sitting on the bench beside the front door to the farmhouse, staring out at the ruins. His border collie, Moss, was seated next him. Sonja and Audrey were nowhere in sight.

Martin's grandmother called out to him, "Nathan, what's happened?"

Nathan turned. "Hello. The bunkhouse caught fire overnight."

Martin began to panic. "Where are Sonja and Audrey?"

Nathan stood up and started walking towards them. "They're being treated for smoke inhalation, but they should be okay. We're fortunate they escaped in time."

Alice placed a comforting hand on Nathan's shoulder. "Any damage, besides the bunkhouse?"

"Fortunately, we were able to prevent it from spreading to the other structures, and the livestock are all okay."

Martin turned to examine the outbuilding, and it was then he noticed the messages. Someone had crudely spelled out in bright red paint "Hun go home!" and beneath that, "Traitors will pay".

Martin felt a chill run through his body. This was hatred on a new level. He walked up to the police cordon and examined the remains of the bunkhouse. Heat still flowed from the charred timbers, radiating anger. Martin felt his body absorb the anger, fanned by the adrenalin still flowing from his recent moment of panic. "Where are the police? Why aren't they investigating this?"

Nathan stepped in closer to Martin. "The fire brigade and policeman just left. They're sending down an arson expert from Southampton—should be here around midday they said."

Martin still felt on edge. He turned to Nathan. "Where are Sonja and Audrey being treated? We should check on them."

Martin pedalled his bicycle back into town to their small hospital while his grandmother stayed to provide support to Nathan. He thought back to the confrontation at last summer's fête and how Sonja had refused to back down when confronted about being German. Why did she need to provoke these people? She should realise that patriotic feelings were going to run high when we were at war.

He enquired at the front desk and was led back by a stoop-backed nurse who looked older even than his grandmother. He felt impatient with her snail-like pace, but their slow progress forced a pause for Martin—his first chance for reflection all morning. In that moment, he realised that he still cared for Sonja, despite her stubbornness. He would no longer let the scar distract him.

Before opening the door to their room, the nurse stopped and turned to face Martin. "They need to avoid talking too much or exerting themselves, so you'll need to keep your visit short. Most of all, they need rest."

She knocked and then opened the door. "Are you up to having a visitor?"

"Martin," Sonja replied. Her voice was hoarse. He was used to her having a strong voice. Both faces were red and blotchy, with red-lined eyes.

Martin sat down in one of the two guest chairs. "How are you doing?" he asked.

"Could be better," Audrey answered for them.

Martin realised he had not thought to bring them anything. Feeling awkward, he cast about for something to say, remembering that they were not supposed to talk too much. "That's horrible what they wrote."

Sonja's bleary eyes widened. "What is this writing? What do you mean?" she breathed in her raspy voice.

Hadn't they seen the message of hatred left on the outbuilding wall? Perhaps it was still dark when they were taken to the hospital. But it was too late now. He couldn't see a way to backtrack what he'd just said. "Someone painted some words on the outbuilding." He paused but could see from their looks that he was going to have to explain more. "Something about 'Germans go home'." He tried to soften the message.

Audrey gasped, and Sonja's expression hardened. Martin met Sonja's eyes but then had to look away. He felt angry at the people who had given her the scar, angry at whoever had burned down the bunkhouse, and also angry at Sonja, that she didn't know when to keep her head down and look the other way. And once again, he was reminded that, had he acted sooner, her perfect face would have remained unblemished.

He tried to think of something to say that would calm Sonja. "An arson investigator is coming from Southampton. Hopefully they'll catch the idiot who did this."

Sonja did not respond. Her expression was unreadable. Martin looked over to Audrey, but she seemed to be lost in shock. Martin realised that they both had been under the impression that the fire was accidental. Now they knew they had been targeted. Why had he opened his big mouth? Nathan could have covered up the message or removed it before they returned to the farm. Now it was too late. He had wanted to bring support and comfort. Instead, he had upset them both. He felt increasingly uncomfortable. Remembering the nurse's admonition to keep the visit short, he decided he should leave.

"Get some rest, both of you. The nurse didn't want me to stay very long."

"Bye," they both croaked.

CHAPTER 21

Weymouth, December 1941

"**F**ACTORY WORK, FARM LABOUR, Home Guard—I doubt there'll be any jobs left that aren't being done by women," Nathan said as he surveyed the horizon. Alice looked over at Nathan, wondering where the conversation was leading. "It'll be interesting to see what happens once the war is over. Will it all return to the way it was?"

They paused to track a friendly Beechcraft expeditor on what appeared to be a low reconnaissance flight down the coast towards Weymouth. When the plane passed out of sight, Nathan set down his binoculars. "Can we return to the way we were? Pandora's box has been opened. I don't think things will ever be the same once this war's done."

"All those returning service men—you don't think they'll demand their jobs back?"

"Yes, I expect they will. But will women be willing to relinquish them?"

"I doubt they'll have a choice." Alice said the last bit under her breath.

As Alice pedalled home, she thought about the changes war had visited on them. It had ground on for well over two years, and there was no end in sight. She was sick to death of shortages.

These next few weeks, they would need to scrimp even more to save enough from which to make an appearance of Christmas for Martin and Irene. She dreaded yet another Christmas time with the glaring hole left by their missing family members. Both Irene and Martin had become distant since the loss of their parents—especially Irene. Alice couldn't seem to reach across the chasm to help them. And she was so tired.

At least Leo was still alive. They had received a letter today, posted from Egypt. Skimpy on details, but the important part was that he had survived thus far. She couldn't imagine what it would do to her grandkids to lose their brother at this juncture. Best not to think about that.

When she reached home, Alice brought her never-ending pile of mending into the kitchen and sat at the table so she could talk to Rosa while she tried to fashion a pie for their tea with very little meat and no butter. Good thing Martin had an adolescent's appetite. He would eat most anything that was put in front of him. Irene was pickier, and Alice worried over her skinny frame.

Alice thought again about how fortunate she was to have Rosa. Many of her acquaintances from Edgar's social circle were having trouble retaining domestic help. With labour shortages, both men and women could earn more money and achieve greater independence working in the factories. She looked over at Rosa. "I hope you're not leaving to work in one of those war factories."

Rosa scowled. "No. Not for me that factory work. I'm too old to be learning new tricks."

"I'm grateful. Not sure how we'd carry on without you."

At that moment, the telephone rang from the hall. Startled by the sudden noise, Rosa's hand slipped, and her knife cut into her index finger. Alice rushed over to her, but Rosa waved her away. "I'll live. You go on, attend to your telephone call." She rinsed her hand and grabbed a towel to catch the blood, while Alice went out into the hall to answer the telephone.

"Hello?"

"Alice. It's Nathan. Go turn your wireless on."

"Why? What's happening?"

"Just turn on the BBC. We can chat later. Got to go." He had hung up.

That man can be so frustrating! Alice thought to herself. She went back to the kitchen to check on Rosa before heading to the sitting room to turn on the wireless. Irene was on the sofa reading. "What's going on?" she asked.

"Nathan called to say there's a report on BBC we should hear."

The announcer's voice gained strength as the wireless warmed up. Having missed the first part of the report, Alice struggled to make sense of what they were going on about. Then, their meaning sunk in. Japan had attacked the United States. She sat down on the sofa next to Irene, staring into the space in front of her.

Irene looked over at her grandmother. "What is it? What does that mean?"

Alice collected herself. "I'm not sure, but I think it means that the war has suddenly become much bigger."

Irene put her book down. "That's not good."

"No, dear. And it's especially bad for the people who were attacked today, but I think it may be good news for us. I think it means that the United States will join the fight at last."

While they were talking, Martin returned home. December being a slack time at the farm, he was helping just one day a week.

He had kept busy that autumn helping Nathan build a new bunkhouse. They simplified the design to reduce the amount of material needed. Then they collected all the re-useable scrap lumber and nails they could find scattered about the farm. Even after these economies and taking into account their status as a vital industry, their order for building materials had taken several months to arrive.

But the project had been beneficial for Martin. Not only had he improved his carpentry skills, Alice observed a change in character as well. The hesitant, indecisive boy was transitioning into a more self-confident man.

Martin joined them in the sitting room. "What's up?" he asked.

"Japan attacked the US in the Pacific. Looks as if America may be joining the war."

Martin stood for a moment, taking in the news. "That sounds like the US is at war with Japan. Does that necessarily mean they'll fight Germany as well? What if they're too busy with Japan? They may be less likely to help us with Germany."

"I don't know, Martin. That's a good point." Alice had been buoyed by the news, but now she wasn't sure what it meant.

Martin left to catch a bath. A short while later, Helen stopped by.

"You've heard the news about Japan attacking the US?" Alice asked her.

"Yes, I heard that news. I also heard the other news." Helen took a chair as Alice turned off the wireless.

"What news is that?"

"While everyone's all in a flap over Pearl Harbour, Thomas was pointing out Japan's other big move."

"I don't know what you're referring to."

"Japan also launched attacks on the Malay Peninsula, Singapore, and Hong Kong. As if Europe, Africa, and the Middle East weren't enough, now we're fighting in Asia too. I'm worried Sid could be sent out east to God knows where."

Helen's middle child, Sidney, was in the Royal Navy. She and Thomas lived on an emotional rollercoaster—deep dread that his ship might be sunk by a German U-boat, punctuated by periodic reports that he was, so far, okay. Their older daughter was married with a two-year old at home and a husband away fighting in North Africa. Their younger daughter had signed up with the Women's Land Army and was working on a farm near Dorchester.

"Dear me. I hadn't heard that." Alice could understand the angst of having a child posted on the other side of the globe. "Would that at least get him away from German U-boats?"

Helen looked at Alice sympathetically. "The Japanese have submarines too, you know."

"Yes, I suppose you're right." Alice realised how uninformed she was on military matters. She decided she should pay more attention to the news bulletins. "Let's hope the Americans can help bring a swift end to the whole mess."

"Not according to Thomas. He says the Americans are not at all prepared for war, and I don't suppose the bombing of their Pacific fleet has helped matters."

CHAPTER 22

Weymouth, September 1942

MARTIN FELT CONSPICUOUS AS he leaned against the brick wall and watched people queueing up to the ticket booth and filing into the theatre. It had been bad enough to put up with Irene's teasing him for going out on a date. He didn't think he could take the embarrassment if his date was a no-show. He decided that if he were stood up, he would wander Weymouth until the show was over. He didn't want to return home early, and he didn't want to sit in the theatre surrounded by strangers who would think he had no friends and had taken to attending the cinema alone.

He chose the Regent over the Odeon where, in the past, his grandmother had taken him and Irene. The tickets were a bit pricier, but the Regent had more class. Most of the ten shillings he made each week working at the farm went into war bonds, at his grandmother's insistence. His small allocation of pocket money had been accumulating for tonight's splurge. Now all he needed was his date. Where was she? It was almost curtain time.

He looked around once more. With blackout enforced, it was difficult to distinguish faces in the fading twilight. He didn't recognise Sonja until she was only a few yards from him, smiling as she walked swiftly towards him.

"Sorry for lateness. It was busy farm day today." She was wearing a simple red dress that reached just below her knees, and she wore it quite well. Martin had never seen that dress before, and the considerable wear indicated that she likely picked it up second- or third-hand.

Sonja took Martin's arm, as they walked into the cinema. Martin hadn't realised how good that would feel. He scanned the crowd to see if there was anyone he knew who could see him with a beautiful woman on his arm, even if she did carry a prominent scar.

The movie, *The Maltese Falcon*, was proceeded by news reels, and those were already running as the pair took their seats. There were scenes from the Battle of Stalingrad and then a report about the sinking of the *RMS Laconia*, which had been carrying civilians, Allied soldiers, and Italian POWs. The reporting seemed to bother Sonja, but Martin was just eager for the movie to start.

When the movie was over, they lingered nearby to talk. "So, what did you think of the movie?" Martin asked.

Sonja hesitated. "For me, too much of bad people and murders. That we have already, so I don't have need to see more with movie."

Martin had loved the movie, but Sonja had clearly hated it. She seemed to sense Martin's disappointment and quickly added, "But acting very good. Mr. Bogard is very good actor."

Martin thought that Sonja's English language limitations probably made it harder for her to understand the suspense and plot. "Next time I think you should pick out the movie." He depleted his spending money for something that wasn't appreciated.

Picking up on Martin's resentment, Sonja smiled at him apologetically. "It was kind for you to have me to movie. Thank you."

"Shall we get our bicycles?" They had agreed that Martin would accompany Sonja back to the farm, so that she wouldn't be traveling on her own at night.

The night was cool, but they had brought jackets. Martin picked out a route along the waterfront, providing views of a full moon rising over Weymouth Bay. He wished they could stop and sit together, staring at the moon, but the military barrier and coils of barbed wire between the road and the beach didn't seem to set the right tone.

When they reached the farm, they set their bicycles against the outbuilding. Martin stepped in close to Sonja, and she turned to face him. "Thanks for the movie. And thanks for riding back with me."

"Thanks for the evening," Martin replied as he leaned in close to her. Sonja smiled, but turned her head slightly so Martin's kiss landed on her cheek—the cheek without the scar.

This was the first time Martin had kissed a girl, so he didn't know what to expect. He wanted to do more than kiss Sonja's cheek, but he also felt some relief that he didn't end up kissing her on the mouth. He was not sure he knew how to go about it properly. Sonja was always so serious that it made him nervous about making a misstep.

During the long bicycle ride home, Martin replayed the evening in his mind. Here he was seventeen and only now having his first real date. Of course, dating opportunities had been thin due to the war. Still, he had hoped the date would be more than just a girl on his arm and a peck on the cheek.

Even more frustrating was that he had no idea what Sonja was thinking. Did she enjoy the evening, or was she going out with Martin just as a favour to him? She certainly hadn't enjoyed the movie. Was she interested in a more serious relationship?

That night Martin dreamt about having a girl on his arm. They walked at dusk down to a moonlit beach. It must have been summertime because they didn't have jackets but there was only a slight chill in the evening air—just enough to drive them tightly together for warmth. The beach showed no signs of war, only the distant crashing of waves below them and the lonely call of a plover in the fields behind them. They settled into the dunes, and Martin kissed the girl—properly—on the mouth.

Martin woke feeling snug and content in his warm bed. Then he realised the girl that he had dreamt about had not been Sonja. It had been Lydia.

That afternoon, Martin was due to work on the farm. He felt uncomfortable about seeing Sonja again, partly due to the fact that their evening the night before had ended a little awkwardly and partly because he thought somehow Sonja would be able to tell that he had dreamt about Lydia. To Martin's relief, he was busy on fences all afternoon, and their paths did not cross.

He did, however, cross paths with Lydia as he passed through town on his way home. She was wearing a long skirt with a white bib apron and white sleeves and a funny sort of hat. He stopped his bicycle on the street corner to chat with her.

"What are you wearing? It looks like a nurse uniform."

Lydia smiled at him. "Perhaps that's because it is a nurse uniform, Sherlock. Nurse Assistant actually. I'm volunteering at the hospital."

"Doing your part, I see. What's it like working there?"

"Well, it's not Harrods but more interesting than being stuck at home. What about you? Done with your sheep for the day?"

"Yes. And starving. What I don't understand is, with all those sheep on hand, why we can't just eat one or two of them. I am so tired of potatoes."

Lydia laughed at that. "See you at school."

As Martin pedalled uphill towards Elm House, it struck him how much easier it was to talk to Lydia than to Sonja.

CHAPTER 23

Weymouth, November 1942

MARTIN TOLD HIMSELF THAT he had no reason to feel guilty. Even so, he looked up and down the Weymouth side street before parking his bicycle and entering the small café. A quick glance around the nearly empty dining room told him that Lydia had not yet arrived, so he picked out a table and sat down to wait. The taped-over windows, the pastry cabinet empty except for a few exhausted dinner rolls, the worn-out chairs and tables all added to the generally dismal atmosphere.

Lydia had initiated their meeting. Although she told Martin she needed help with maths, he suspected that wasn't really what she wanted.

Martin still felt that Sonja was the gal for him. But he had to admit that he was growing tired of her being so serious so much of the time. Lydia was just easier to be around. She always had something to talk about, and it was never anything too heavy.

Sonja was still upset over the article that had appeared in the Daily Telegraph last summer. Nathan had come across it and shared it with her. Martin wished he hadn't. He had learned that being at war meant having to deal with rumour and hysteria. Clearly that was the case with this news article. It claimed that 700,000 Jews had been executed in camps in Poland. Even the Nazis weren't that inhumane. Martin was good with numbers, and he understood what most people didn't really grasp—just how large a number that was. Most people in Weymouth would never be in the company of more than a few thousand people at one time. So, seven thousand or seven hundred thousand, it was all the same to them. It just meant lots of people. Martin knew that to execute seven thousand would be astonishing but still in the realm of believability. Seven hundred thousand was clearly a number someone had made up.

He had tried to reason with Sonja. None of the other newspapers carried the story, so it had to be a false report planted as anti-Nazi propaganda. But that upset her all the more. She refused to look at things rationally.

Martin looked around the café, his eyes momentarily meeting those of the lone waitress who appeared bored and perhaps a little resentful. Martin figured she must be tired of customers ordering just tea. But most people couldn't afford to waste precious ration coupons on restaurant food. It was a joke, really, to go "out" these days.

He wished the waitress had something to keep her busy. He felt uncomfortable sitting there being watched and having nothing to do. His mistake in arriving fifteen minutes early.

As he waited, he grew morose. He was tired of always being hungry, and he was especially tired of potatoes. He used to like potatoes, but he would challenge anyone to try having them as the main course every meal for months on end. And forget about ever owning anything new. Earlier in the year the government expanded the long list of rations to include electricity and coal and had lowered the rations on clothing. Nothing was ever thrown away, and everyone wore clothes that had been patched, altered, or repaired in some way.

The bell hanging from the front door jingled, and Martin looked up. Lydia's entrance brightened the entire room. "You came!" she beamed.

"Yes, I said I would." Martin stood up and pulled out one of the well-worn wooden chairs for Lydia.

Lydia sat opposite Martin at the small table, set the menu aside and peered over at him. "My mum thinks I'm working a shift at the hospital." She gave a conspiratorial smile.

"My grandmother only cares that I'm home by tea-time." Martin felt slightly self-conscious at the intense gaze from Lydia.

"It's not fair that boys are given so much more freedom." She laughed and picked up the menu. "What will it be? Tea? Or did you rather have your heart set on tea?"

At that point, all eyes turned as a pair of young men entered the café. They were dressed in uniforms unfamiliar to Martin and talking loudly in accents that Martin recognised only from the cinema. Lydia stared intently at the newcomers, with her mouth slightly ajar. She leaned in close to Martin, speaking into his ear. "Crikey! I think those are Americans."

Martin had never seen an American before, and he studied them as best he could while trying not to stare. One was tall and the other medium height. They both appeared well fed. In their crisp new uniforms, Martin was forced to admit that they were an impressive presence against the backdrop of the dingy café. From their casual self-assurance, you would never guess they were thousands of miles from home.

Martin turned back to face Lydia, but she was still watching the Americans, who were ordering meat pies. He wished they would leave. They were latecomers to this war that the British had been enduring for three long years. Now they were over here eating our food. He tried to think of things to say to Lydia but she kept glancing over at the Americans who had lit up cigarettes while waiting for their order. One of them pulled a small tin of peaches from his overcoat pocket. Martin had not seen canned fruit in over two years, and he stared in envy as the American used a small knife to pierce the top of the tin. The American tipped the can into his mouth, drained all the syrup, and then set the tin down. Martin watched the can sitting on the table. The American seemed to have forgotten it. Wasn't he going to eat the peaches? The inexcusable waste felt like an insult to the sacrifices they had all been making.

Trying to regain Lydia's attention, Martin considered suggesting they work on their maths, seeing as that had been their pretext for meeting. But noticing the expression on her face as she watched the two newcomers, he thought better of that idea.

The Americans didn't linger over their meal. They settled their bill and left without completely finishing their meat pies. Shaking her head, the waitress swooped in to salvage the tin of peaches along with the half-smoked cigarettes left behind in the ashtray.

With the Americans gone, Lydia once more focused her attention on Martin. "You really are lucky that your grandmother lets you roam wherever you want. My mum keeps tabs on me every waking minute. Little does she know all the ways I've learned to evade her." Once again, the conspiratorial smile.

"Yeah, my mum was almost as bad, but my grandmother trusts me." Martin wondered if he should confide in Lydia all the things he and Ellis had gotten up to, but he wasn't sure what Lydia would think of Ellis. Her family was well-to-do. "On velvet," was how Ellis would have described them.

"Is it just you and your sister left, with your parents gone? I hope you don't mind my asking about your family." Lydia's face had transformed into a picture of concern.

Martin wasn't used to so much close attention. He leaned in, as if what he had to say was just between the two of them. "No, that's okay. I have an older brother. He's stationed in Africa. Just got a letter from him, so I know he's okay—at least so far."

Lydia's eyes went wide in a way that made Martin feel proud of being close to someone stationed so far afield. "I can't imagine having a brother so far away. You must miss him."

Martin had found that he did miss Leo, although he was usually loath to admit it. With Lydia, however, the concept of missing a family member took on a different meaning. "Yeah, it's not the same with just me and Irene. But we all do our part." Suddenly he was proud of Leo, off fighting the Nazis and not loitering around Weymouth having a good time like the Americans.

Martin started to form a picture of Leo pursuing German infantry with dogged determination, but he was distracted when Lydia looked up abruptly, staring over Martin's shoulder while her face went slack, and her mouth dropped open. Martin turned to find Mrs. Chambers striding towards them, her mouth clenched in the thinnest line of rage. "Extra hospital shift indeed!" was all she said as grabbed Lydia's shoulder in a vice grip, her contemptuous gaze sweeping over Martin before turning to march Lydia from the premises.

With Lydia gone, Martin paid for their teas—the waitress barely able to hide her smile at having witnessed such a gossip-worthy spectacle—and bicycled towards home. He also had to smile to himself as he thought about Mrs. Chambers frog-marching Lydia from the café. Being with Lydia was definitely a hoot. Yet, there was something that made Martin hesitate—something about her that lacked depth. She could shine a spotlight on you when you had her attention, but that attention was easily distracted, as Martin had seen when the Americans came on the scene.

Martin tried to tell himself that none of that mattered. He was just a seventeen-year-old looking for some fun and laughs at a time when those were a bit thin on the ground. Especially with the shadow of enlistment drawing closer. In less than a year, he would be following in Leo's footsteps and that put a different light on many things, including who he might fancy as the person waiting for him back in Weymouth.

CHAPTER 24

Weymouth, Early June 1943

"WILL YOU WRITE TO me?" Martin looked over at Sonja. They were on break, watching a raptor circling at eye level, just past the cliff, taking advantage of the updraft rising off the beach. Martin's grandmother would know what species of bird it was. But his inability to identify it did not lessen the beauty of its effortless flight.

Sonja hesitated. "Yes, of course." Her scar, although still jarringly obvious, had faded somewhat, the shade of red no longer as angry. Martin still found it difficult to look at.

Three years of helping part-time on the farm had wrought a transformation in Martin. The heavy work had added muscle to his lean frame, and his walk and movements conveyed his newfound confidence in his physical body. But he continued to struggle with transferring this confidence to his words. He wanted to say more to Sonja but was not comfortable translating feelings into sentences. He always felt that Sonja saw straight through him. Surely, she must know what he was feeling.

They were interrupted by Emil, slowly working his way around the corner of the outbuilding on his crutches. In the mountains of Tunisia, a bullet had callously selected his left ankle for destruction. Two entire days of intense pain had transpired before he was able to reach a field hospital. In the end, he was grateful that it was only his foot that was left behind to be buried in North Africa. He was now wait-listed for a prosthetic and meanwhile had taken to tying his trouser leg closed with string to prevent it from flapping about.

"Nathan was looking for you," he said to Sonja.

Sonja sprung from the bench. "Thanks," she replied. Turning back to Martin, "See you around."

Emil continued over to Martin. The man who had once been so agile, lowered himself heavily onto the bench and breathed a sigh. "God, I wish this bloody foot would quit itching." He looked over at Martin. "When do you report?"

"In three days." Martin tried to avoid looking at the leg that ended in puckered fabric instead of a foot. But his eyes were drawn to it as if it were a weird form of pornography. He looked up at Emil. "Do you still plan to carry on farming despite your...?" Martin wasn't sure what label to attach to the injury. He didn't know why he felt a sense of shame about it. Emil seemed unbothered. He was watching the same raptor Martin and Sonja had been watching. It had been joined by another, and they were circling each other in the updraft.

"Don't know. I think my foot is trying to tell me it's time to move on."

That made no sense to Martin. He looked out again as the two birds set off down the coast.

"Farming was all I knew until this bloody war came along and kicked me in the arse."

"What about your father? How much longer do you think he can handle the place?"

Emil pulled a cigarette from the pack in his shirt pocket and lit up. "Pa will sort that. Once the war is done, there'll be plenty of help looking for work." He took a long draw from his cigarette. "You know who really has a nose for tending sheep? That Sonja."

Martin turned to look over at Emil again. He knew Sonja liked working there, but he had always assumed that, once the men had returned, she would move on. Emil continued, "She's a strong one, that gal. Lucky chap who catches her fancy."

Martin's eyes widened slightly as he studied Emil, trying to decide what he should read into his last remark. Surely, he wasn't thinking that Sonja might fancy him. Emil must be around fifteen years her senior.

Emil rose from the bench, managing to work the crutches with the cigarette still dangling between his fingers. "Reckon I better start back for the house. At my pace, be doing well to make it by tea." He paused at the corner of the outbuilding, twisting on his crutches to look back at Martin. "You'll do okay, kid."

Martin sat watching the clouds drift over the Channel. A destroyer made steady progress across the bay towards Portland Harbour. After nearly four years of watching men in various uniforms, he was, at last, about to join them.

Martin collected his bicycle and started for home. Shortly after crossing the Town Bridge, he spotted Lydia walking up the hill carrying a bag of shopping. He braked to a stop so he could say hello. She smiled brightly at him. "Where are you off to, Martin Standfield?"

"Home now, but in three days, off to training camp."

Lydia's smile transitioned to concern as her soft brown eyes grew large. "It's so sad. All the boys from our year are heading out. Are you joining the army?"

"That's right."

"I hope you'll take care. Don't want anything happening to you." She paused, but when Martin didn't respond, she continued, "Would it help to have folks writing to you?"

"That would be most kind of you." Martin felt a bit uncomfortable, as he had just asked Sonja to write to him. But he told himself that he was not making any commitments to Lydia and that it would be unkind to say no.

Lydia was smiling again. Hers was a sweet smile, refined and gracious. "Well, I think you are very brave. I'll look forward to hearing about training camp."

Martin arrived home to find Irene reclined on the sitting room sofa with Oscar asleep on her lap. As usual, her nose was buried in a book, and she did not look up when he entered. Over the past three years, she had become more withdrawn and since Martin's call-up papers had come through, had hardly spoken to him.

Her grandmother tried to interest her in sewing, knitting, sketching, painting, chess, babysitting, cooking, and gardening. Irene would do as asked but only half-heartedly. When left to herself, she always returned to her reading. Her grandmother finally gave up and focused instead on providing her with a varied selection of appropriate books.

Martin went up to his room and stretched out on his bed. He liked the idea of Lydia writing to him, even though it was Sonja who loomed large in his mind. If only she hadn't been sent into detention. He still blamed himself for that, and he was reminded of his failure whenever he looked into her scarred face.

His thoughts drifted, and he started to worry again about training camp. The stories he heard from Leo sounded horrible—working from dawn to dusk, terrible food, no privacy. But when they were growing up, Leo had always made things sound worse than they really were just to spook his younger brother.

Martin didn't mind that he was leaving Weymouth. For him, home had continued to be London, but that place was gone now. They had managed to sell the house despite the war, thanks to a bombing-induced housing shortage. He would miss his grand-mother, but she would write to him. He would miss Rosa's cooking! Even with shortages of everything, she managed to feed them reasonably well.

He was less worried about being in combat, now that he was in good shape physically. Plus, he had heard from lots of people who had been in the armed services – Leo, Emil, and folks he had come to know in Weymouth. He felt that he now had some idea of what to expect.

Martin didn't realise he had drifted into sleep until he heard his grandmother calling him down for tea. He had been having a very strange dream. His drill sergeant was screaming at him to unlock a large wooden chest that stood directly in front of him. He desperately wanted to do that but had no idea how. Leo was watching but wouldn't say anything. He seemed slightly amused by the whole scene. Emil was watching as well. All he said was, "you'll know when you know." Then he walked away on his crutches. He made it about thirty yards when his crutch triggered a land mine, and he disappeared in a huge explosion. Martin lay on his bed trying to recall the details of his dream, but he couldn't remember what it was locked away in the wooden chest.

"Martin! Tea is ready." The sound seemed to come from far away. Martin dragged himself from his bed and slowly made his way downstairs to supper.

CHAPTER 25

English Countryside, Late June / July 1943

MARTIN AND THE OTHER enlistees were corralled into a former warehouse and told to strip. Their clothes were taken away to be mailed home. Martin was pleased to find that the new shirt he was issued was a bit tight across his chest. He was less pleased to be handed boots that looked like leftovers from the Boer War. Next, they were subjected to brutal haircuts and even more brutal dental exams. Thankfully, he had not toppled over during inoculations as two others had done.

The army apparently found no value in allowing new soldiers the opportunity to get acquainted or settled into their new surroundings. They were immediately assembled into sections and platoons, handed wooden poles to use as pretend rifles, and sent on a march—a very long march and at a pace that could not be described as leisurely. By evening, everyone was learning about first aid for blisters.

Leo had not been lying about how atrocious the food was. But that was among the least of Martin's worries. Sergeant Mallory had singled him out, almost from the moment he first opened his mouth in response to the orders being barked in his ear. Martin's kit and bunk could be the cleanest, most orderly in his barracks, but that would not deter his sergeant from finding miniscule faults which would become near-capital offences, resulting in the extra guard duty, the additional parade marches, and the foulest cleaning jobs.

Martin couldn't work out why Mallory took against him. He decided it must be something to do with his background. It was clear that Mallory favoured those who shared his hard-scrabble working-class roots. Those few whose manners and language marked them as coming from privileged backgrounds were treated by Mallory with distain tempered by restraint. But Martin fit neither category—clearly not one of the boys but also not from a family with sufficient status to threaten repercussions.

Martin took on the challenge. The more he was singled out, the more determined he became to provide nothing, not a scrap, that could be used as fodder in justifying his mistreatment. It would have helped to know that some of his fellow enlistees were on his side, but it seemed to be each man for himself. The man who lined up for inspection on his left just smirked at Martin, reminding him of Leo, while the enlistee to his right, a slightly older chap named Jack Green, gave nothing away. His gaze remained fixed straight ahead and his expression blank, as if he saw nothing, although Martin suspected that he saw more than most.

One enlistee in their group came under even worse treatment than Martin. Howard Walker was short, skinny, cautious, and soft-spoken. A pair of small, metal-rimmed glasses perched incongruously on his long angular face. When he moved about, he seemed to be all elbows, knees, and long skinny fingers. Martin could not imagine a less likely soldier. Everything about him seemed to be a magnet for bullies, and Mallory would have been unable to resist—not that he ever tried. Martin couldn't help feeling sorry for Howard. At the same time, he hated to think that he had anything in common with the poor fellow, as their similar treatment might imply.

In the third week, boxing was added to their regimen. Martin had never boxed and was eager to pick up everything he could about the sport. He overheard talk that Mallory had trained at Repton Boxing Club, and he certainly looked the part. After a couple of days of instruction and drills, they were paired up and provided opportunities to spar. When Howard's turn arrived, it was quickly apparent that he was every bit as hopeless at boxing as one might expect. His sparring partner took it easy on him, not wanting to overwhelm the poor bloke.

Mallory goaded them on with a steady stream of insults. Finally, he threw down his clipboard, and donned his boxing gloves. Stepping into the ring, he leered at Howard, his fists hanging at his side. "My guard's down. Pretend for a moment I'm a Jerry. Give me best you've got."

Howard's eyes widened in alarm. He hesitated a moment before delivering a wild, straight-armed punch at his sergeant, which Mallory easily blocked.

"You've got to be kidding me. Did your little sister teach you to box? Do you always stay close to your mum for protection?" Mallory then went to work on Howard, who withdrew behind his boxing gloves, not knowing how to parry the attack. Minutes later, Howard lay sprawled on the ground, blood on his cheek and oozing from his nose. When he didn't move, Mallory ordered a pair of enlistees to carry him out.

"Anyone else keen to find out how it's done?" Mallory looked around the room triumphantly. The room was quiet. Martin looked down, hoping to avoid Mallory's eye. He felt someone brush past him. Jack Green entered the ring with his shoulders hunched and his gaze down, his face devoid of emotion. He was about two inches shorter than Mallory. Where Mallory had a broad physique, Jack could best be described as scrappy.

Mallory's face slowly broke into a greedy smile. The two men raised their gloves and began to circle each other. Mallory threw the first punch, which Jack seemed to take as a signal. His punches came in rapid fire and from all directions. It soon became clear that Mallory's strength was no match for Jack's speed and agility. As the sergeant's anger rose, his technique suffered. But Jack kept after him with unrelenting, clinical determination. After just one round the red-faced Mallory called for an abrupt halt to their boxing session and ordered the men out on an extra march. With great effort, no one in their group broke a smile.

So it was that quiet Jack Green joined Martin and Howard on Mallory's shit list, while at the same time he became a bit of a legend among the boys.

The next day, Martin noticed Howard struggling to clear a wall in full gear. With a quick glance to make sure Mallory was not watching, Jack grabbed Howard's boot and gave him the extra push that got him over the obstacle.

Two days later, they were on a brutally long march. Howard was at the back of the pack and in danger of falling further behind. Jack waited for Mallory to be distracted.

"Hold still a sec, Howard." Jack quickly fished through Howard's backpack and pulled out two of the heavier items. One, he handed to Martin. "Be a mate and find a spot for this." The other he stashed in his own backpack. Martin was happy to oblige—it was a way to fight back.

They started looking for other ways to help Howard. It was tricky making sure their assistance went undetected by their sergeant. And Howard came in handy when training on new equipment. He was consistently the first to finish in cleaning and reassembling anything put in front of him.

A few days later Martin was standing guard duty when he overheard a pair of enlistees walking past.

"The look on Mallory's face. You'd think he'd swallowed a hornet's nest."

"Apparently, he didn't know about Jack Green."

"Know what about him?"

"North Counties welterweight champion, that's all!"

"Ha. That explains things."

Martin had not known Jack had such an accolade in his background. But there was no swagger to the man. He reminded Martin of his friend, Ellis—comfortable in his own skin and the same strong sense of fairness.

When word came down about the formation of a new battalion, the three of them decided to volunteer in the hope that they could remain together.

As they approached the end of their six weeks, Martin sensed a small shift in Mallory's behaviour. Slowly, begrudgingly, the sergeant had begun to respect their determination. Nonetheless, it was Martin's sincerest ambition that they would never again cross paths with him.

CHAPTER 26

Weymouth, July 1943

NATHAN TOLD HER THAT it was the four-year anniversary of the day they first met. That was the first thing to catch Alice off guard. Then he went on to propose to her. "You're a special lady. I could spot that at the start. I would be honoured if you could agree to spend our remaining time together. And you've Irene to raise, a household to manage. That's too much for one person."

Alice didn't know how to respond. She was sixty-two and a grandmother. Marriage had not been in the picture for her. It must have shown.

"I can see that I've presumed upon you," Nathan said. Then added, "I'd be grateful if you'd consider it. If it isn't right, I just hope this doesn't end our friendship."

Later, as she sat at her writing desk and looked out on her beloved elm, its leaves quivering in the afternoon sun, she realised she had been naïve. Nathan had in many ways taken on the burdens of a husband. Over the past several years, out at their observer post in all types of weather they had helped each other through the challenges of family and the hardships of war. But the exchange had not been even. He stepped in when she lost Henry and Kathleen. She was grateful for his help and counsel, especially his insights on helping Martin navigate the loss. She struggled with raising Martin on her own and with how to help Irene.

Her worry for Irene persisted, a wound that refused to heal. Her granddaughter's sullen presence constantly reminded Alice of the cheerful young girl they had lost to the war. This essence of worry and loss shadowed her daily life, seeping into every room of the large, empty house.

Outside at her observer post, Alice could find perspective on her grandchildren. And Nathan had been both patient and insightful. Was it fair to take all that support from him expecting there would be nothing in return? Did she love him? She did as a friend. She wasn't sure if she loved him as a husband. What did that even mean at this stage in her life? She had no plans to remarry—in fact, she had been looking forward to her independence.

And did Nathan really love her, or did he simply want to take care of her? He had a caring nature. Alice thought that was what led him to become a veterinarian. His proposal had been caring, but where was the romance? Maybe that's what romance is once you've started your seventh decade—caring for each other.

Alice realised that she felt beholden to Nathan for the care and support he provided. Was she going to marry him out of obligation? No, she made that mistake once before. But her sense of obligation clouded her vision. What were her feelings for Nathan?

She tried to focus on the letter she was drafting to Martin. But her house was too silent. With Martin away at training, Irene had become part of the furniture, glued to the sofa with the shades drawn and her nose in a book. She had not made friends at school.

The silence was complete except for the incessant ticking of the grandfather clock, the clock that had never belonged to her. Just like Elm House, it was part of Edgar's family. But Edgar's family were all dead, and Elm House felt like their mausoleum.

She had been given four glorious months between Edgar's passing and the start of war. She looked up, imploringly at the clock. *Is that all the time you've allotted me?* The clock remained resolute.

Alice put down her pen and turned to Irene, who was on the far side of the room, sprawled on the sofa with Oscar in her lap.

"Come walk with me," she said.

Irene's eyes appeared over the top of her book. Her forehead creased, and Alice guessed there was a frown hidden behind her book. "It's too hot for walking."

"I've been watching our elm tree, and there's a steady breeze off the Channel. I want you to come with me. Please." Irene sighed and dropped her book, and they headed out the door. Alice grabbed her binoculars on the way out.

They walked up the street, away from town, and then set out across an open meadow, waist-high with summer grass. A cooling breeze bent the tall stalks in waves, as a pair of orange and black checkered fritillaries meandered across the meadow and continued up towards a line of trees. In contrast to their silent house, the meadows were alive with the sounds of insects and birds, and of the wind tossing branches full with leaves. They reached a gentle stream and followed it to its source—a pond bordered by bending trees and shrubs.

It was Irene who spotted the kingfisher, motionless on a bleached snag that stretched out over the pond. Alice handed her the binoculars. She knew the bright orange and iridescent blue-green plumage would not fail to impress. Irene gasped when, without warning, the kingfisher darted into the water with a gentle splash. It reemerged onto a log holding a fish that looked entirely too big for such a small bird. Not to be deterred, it set about banging the fish against the log. "That poor fish," Irene said as she continued to watch through the binoculars.

"Yes, not a good day for that particular fish. But, if it wasn't for the kingfishers, there would be too many fish in that pond and they would all run out of food."

That seemed to satisfy Irene, and they set off again, climbing gently uphill. Alice noticed with satisfaction that Irene did not return the binoculars. When they reached the top of the rise, Alice stopped to wipe the sweat from her brow. Irene flattened some of the tall grass creating a place to sit. The view stretched towards Chesil Beach over gently sloping grass meadows and low trees. In the distance, they could barely discern the Island of Portland through the summer haze.

As Irene studied the scene through her binoculars, Alice's thoughts turned again to Nathan's proposal. At a loss, she was tempted to ask her granddaughter for her thoughts but quickly dismissed the idea. That would be an unfair position in which to place the young lady.

But she needed to talk to somebody. It occurred to her that, although she knew many of the people in Weymouth, there were few with whom she had developed a close friendship. Really, just her neighbour Helen. The assumption from Edgar had been that her world should revolve around him and his social circle. There had not been the freedom to develop a life outside their home. Besides that, there were no women she knew of who shared her unconventional interests.

With a start, she realised that her granddaughter had asked her a question. "Sorry, dear?"

"Are you ready to hike back?" Irene appeared slightly amused by her grandmother's lapse.

"Yes, let's." Stiff from sitting on the ground, Alice struggled to regain her feet.

While Irene raced ahead, Alice descended the hill at a slower pass to help cushion her aging knees. At age twelve, Irene remained an innocent—for now. Alice worried about the change and disruption that lay ahead for her. She thought of her own awakening to the world of men and the expectations placed on young women. Even as a teenager, Alice found it difficult to make close friends, difficult to become interested in the things that dominated the attention of others her age. And her mother kept her on a short leash. Perhaps if she had joined in the whispering and giggles, perhaps then she would not have been quite so naïve about men. But she had never felt comfortable in the society of teenage girls.

At age eighteen, she took the path of least resistance. She had been flattered by the attention from someone who was tall, handsome, cultured, and well established. As for her mother, it had been a foregone conclusion that her daughter would say "yes" to such a promising suitor. But Alice had sensed something more from her mother—an implied threat. To turn down an excellent prospect would send the wrong signal. She would be tainted as not being serious about marriage, and others would be wary of pursuing her. She had been made to feel that this might be her only chance at happiness. Now, after all these years, she was in danger of making the same mistake—taking the path of least resistance.

Irene was waiting for her by the pond, excited that her friend, the kingfisher, was back at his post at the farthest tip of the dead snag, watching for his next meal. As Alice walked home in companiable silence with her granddaughter, she decided to see what her neighbour Helen was up to. She needed someone who would listen and provide perspective free from judgement.

Helen and Alice had become closer since Edgar's passing. Thomas often helped Alice with tasks that Edgar would have taken care of and that Alice found difficult to do on her own. In exchange, Alice shared apples and firewood from her garden, which was considerably larger than the Bascome's small plot of land. On days when Alice was not on observer duty, Alice and Helen often shared morning coffee, or rather what the shops tried to pass off as coffee.

Once Alice and Irene arrived home, Alice stopped just long enough to change out of her walking shoes before heading over to her neighbour's. Helen was in the back garden harvesting runner beans. They had converted both their front and back gardens into victory gardens. Their treeless property received more sun than did Alice's.

Helen looked up from her harvesting as Alice approached. "Just got a letter from Sidney."

"Marvelous!" Alice sat down on their back step in the afternoon shade. "What does he have to say?"

"Well, you know Sid. Man of few words." Helen continued her picking. "Besides, he can't talk about what he's up to. But he's safe for now. That's what matters."

Helen finished the row of beans and sat on the step next to Alice. "So, how are you?"

Alice decided she should just put it out there. "Nathan proposed."

Helen turned to face Alice. "Wonderful! That's a development," then, seeing the expression on Alice's face, "or is it?"

"I'm flattered, of course. But this was not expected, which was probably naïve on my part."

"From all that you've told me, he seems very respectable."

"Yes, and I love him dearly but as a friend. Marriage was not in my plans."

Helen put her hand on Alice's. "So, you're going to turn him down?"

"I think so. But I feel horrible doing that. He's provided so much support, with the war, the grandchildren, and everything."

Helen looked directly into Alice's eyes. "Yes, and you're grateful for all that. Doesn't mean you have to marry the bloke."

Alice smiled nervously. "You're right, of course. I have a hard time not doing what's expected of me. I thought that might end with Edgar gone, but it hasn't."

"The way I see it, there's only one person who can change that, and I'm looking at her."

Helen always seemed able to cut straight to the heart of a matter. Of course, offering advice was easy. Helen didn't have to face turning Nathan down.

CHAPTER 27

Southern England, August 1943

THE HEAT, THE LACK of air circulation, the lurching movement of the train, the smell of close-packed sweating
bodies—it all threatened to make Martin physically sick.
Standing in the aisle, he occasionally caught glimpses past the
seated passengers to the sunbaked fields passing by much too
slowly.

While he was excited about finishing basic training, the
uncertainty of what lay ahead kept him on edge. He thought of
Ellis—mentioned in despatches. Martin felt sure he would not
be earning the same accolades. He was just not a quick thinker
on his feet—his brain froze in stressful situations. And he didn't
consider himself especially brave. He just hoped not to embar-
rass himself.

Howard Walker leaned over towards Martin. "Been looking
forward to this trip. Thought we'd be putting our boots up at
last. Now, I can't wait for it to be done."

"Yeah, shame the window's stuck. Could use some cross
breeze—not that we're moving fast enough to create any."

Howard had received the same assignment as Martin, along
with Jack Green, who was leaning against the far wall. Jack
took the suffocating closeness and the uncertainty of their new

deployment with his usual equanimity. There were six others from their basic training camp who were assigned to the same deployment.

To Martin, it made a world of difference having his two friends to share his new assignment. Would Howard prove to be an asset or liability? Either way, they would be looking out for each other.

He had hoped to catch up on his correspondence, but writing was impossible on the packed, swaying train. Any seats that became available, the men left for the women and children sharing their journey. Hopefully, folks back in Weymouth would understand how difficult it was to find scraps of spare time and that when those rare respites occurred, how completely knackered they all were. Many times over the past six weeks, Martin's greatest ambition had been a few minutes left alone to stare at the ceiling above his bunk and to not move.

His own lack of letter writing had not deterred Lydia, whose letters arrived faithfully week after week. Her sweet, mostly banal chit-chat was a welcome spot of colour in his drab existence. She wrote about the creative ways they were adapting to shortages and shared bits of gossip about townsfolk and sometimes the sad news of a war casualty from among their former classmates.

Irene had posted several letters as well. These were unimaginative reports on daily life in Weymouth. Yet, Martin had been surprised at how much he welcomed hearing about the familiar and mundane. His grandmother's letters were more informative— war news picked up from newspapers and the wireless, updates on Leo, updates on Nathan's farm, and bits on how Weymouth was adapting to war, disruption, and ever-increasing shortages. Martin was not thrilled to hear that spotting Americans was no longer the novelty it had been just a year ago. His grandmother was not allowed to share anything related to her Observer Corps duties but seemed determined to report on every bloody bird that crossed her path.

In contrast, Sonja had only written once, explaining that the extra farm work left little time for letter writing. The Ministry of Agriculture had inspected the farm last February and had mandated that, in addition to raising sheep, they needed to start cultivating flax which was a critical war supply.

Martin struggled to interpret the tone of Sonja's solitary letter, with its grammatical irregularities and uncustomary word choices. He understood that the farm kept her busy and that composing letters was time-consuming when writing in a non-native language. Even so, he had begun to resent mail call and the repeated disappointment of receiving nothing from her.

The train screeched to a halt, rousing Martin from his thoughts of home. He and his comrades pressed to one side of the compartment to make room for the disembarking passengers who collided and scrambled with nearly as many boarding passengers. When the train began moving again, Martin glanced up and down the compartment, confirming that all seats remained occupied. But the aisle was now less crowded, allowing clearer views of the passing landscape. The brown fields and hedges gave way to roads, bridges, the backside of buildings, and to spaces where buildings once stood—sometimes entire city blocks turned to rubble. Martin decided this must be London. The train moved even slower, swaying and bumping while Martin's mind turned inward to thoughts of Lydia and Sonja. He watched the city without seeing it, until a familiar scene caught his eye.

"Hey, my old primary school." He leaned over and pointed it out to Howard. "And our fish and chip shop. There, next to the greengrocer. My father used to take us there Saturday nights in the summer."

"You're lucky, growing up in London. Not much excitement in our town, unless you count cows getting loose and roaming the streets."

Martin didn't consider himself lucky. But in the stuffiness of their cramped train car, he lacked the energy to explain to Howard how he was never allowed to do anything or go anywhere in the big city.

It surprised Martin how little time it took to pass through the neighbourhood that had comprised his entire world for most of his life. Strange to think that his home no longer welcomed him, being occupied now by strangers. He felt detached, like one of his grandmother's birds blown out to sea by a passing storm. His focus was on surviving the storm. Once the war ended, he would figure out where to land. Elm House had only and always been temporary.

The scenery transitioned back to fields punctuated occasionally by towns passing too swiftly, as if the lives spent there were of no matter. When at last they reached their stop, the sun had dipped below the low hills.

The nine men waited for transport, seated on the ground, leaning against their gear. Breakfast seemed long ago, and Martin's stomach rumbled uncomfortably. Mercifully, it had cooled, although the air was still. Mosquitos materialised out of the darkness, in search of dinner. Nearby fields hummed with crickets. The moon had not yet risen, and with blackout in place, the dark was absolute except for the stars.

Two of the men shared off-colour jokes, substituting Mallory into the most unflattering of roles. Jack sat quietly, his arms wrapped around his knees, staring into the blackness.

Howard leaned over to Martin, speaking so the others would not hear. "I know you might think me daft, but I've something to ask of you."

"What's up?" Martin always felt cautious about getting pulled into the quagmires that seemed to follow Howard everywhere.

"If something should happen to me, will you visit me mum and dad? There're no brothers or sisters at home—I'm all they've got."

"Of course, Howard. But yeah, you are being daft. Nothing's going to happen to you, me, or Jack. We're going to look out for each other. You can be sure of that."

Dimmed headlights appeared in the distance. Their transport truck had arrived.

Their new base camp was shut down for the night. A lance corporal emerged from one of the buildings. "Sorry gents—the kitchen's locked up. You'll have to wait till morning."

This was met with a chorus of complaints and groans, until Jack Green raised his hand, motioning silence. He took the lance corporal aside. Martin couldn't hear Jack, but he could hear the lance corporal responding, "I'll see what I can do."

He returned a short while later with a disgruntled-looking, hastily dressed private who unlocked the mess hall. The men dined on cold leftover stew—the fat congealed in a thick top layer—and break-your-teeth biscuits, and for that they were grateful. After the hasty meal, they were led to barracks filled with snoring men and assigned to the few remaining empty bunks.

Martin was relieved to be assigned to the same newly formed section as Jack and Howard. He suspected Jack had a hand in keeping the three of them together. It turned out there was a group of lads from Jack's home town of Sunderland, and they all seemed to know him.

He was also relieved to escape the heel of Sergeant Mallory. In contrast to Mallory's attempts to degrade those under his command, their new leaders worked to identify and reinforce the contributions each man had to offer. Martin, with his experience driving and maintaining Nathan's lorry, was taught to operate and make repairs on any means of transport, from motorcycles to tanks. They quickly spotted Howard's mechanical aptitude and trained him on maintaining and repairing technical equipment. Jack, who was respected by all, seemed destined to leadership.

Being out of basic training allowed more time for writing, and Martin sent letters back to Lydia, Sonja, and one addressed to both his grandmother and Irene. He also posted a letter to Leo, even though Leo had not written to him since his enlistment. He imagined swapping stories with his brother, once they returned from the war. They would be on a more equal footing by then.

Lydia, his grandmother, and Irene continued writing on a regular basis. He even received a second letter from Sonja. Unfortunately, the short, factual letter didn't relieve his anxiety over her feelings towards him. He was brought up to speed on flax and sheep but remained clueless about Sonja.

Martin's company was sent on a nighttime training exercise. They were dropped near the water and sent jogging the length of the beach, Howard falling further and further behind in the soft shingle. At the far end, they were to climb a rocky escarpment to the summit of a headland. Jack and Martin waited for Howard. He would need help scrambling over boulders and scaling the steep banks. At the top, the rest of the company sat in a grass field, waiting for the three stragglers. No one spoke to them as they joined the group.

"Who's the skinny bloke what needs his mates to climb a bleeding hill?" Martin heard the hushed voice in the darkness behind him.

"Howard Walker. Sure as hell hope he doesn't stay in our company. If this were the real thing, he'd have us all killed."

Martin felt an urge to slink off so he could sit somewhere away from Howard. He was an embarrassment. What was this friendship costing him in terms of respect and friendship from the rest of his new company?

CHAPTER 28

Weymouth, October 1943

THE AMERICANS WERE EVERYWHERE, infiltrating cafés and pubs, clogging roads, and turning farms into military compounds. They even infiltrated the neighbourhood around Elm House. American officers replaced the British officers billeting at Walbridge Manor. The victory garden in the front grounds transitioned overnight into a camp for American servicemen. Alice's bicycle ride to her Observation Corps post became an obstacle course, requiring all her cycling skills in dodging military vehicles and avoiding potholes and ruts torn up by the tanks and heavy trucks.

Alice heard plenty of complaints about loud music and loose morals. She didn't feel quite so negative about the Americans. It did seem that Weymouth no longer belonged to the English, but being overrun by Americans was infinitely better than being overrun by Nazis.

One demographic was definitely not sorry to have Americans around. It seemed that every female in Weymouth between sixteen and twenty-five was taken by them. Alice could understand the attraction of these easy-going, easy-talking young men in their new uniforms and their ready access to both cigarettes and chocolate. Everywhere they went they brought music and dancing unlike anything Weymouth had ever seen.

It was strange to see Walbridge Manor a hive of activity. Alice was used to the property being quiet, almost derelict. As she watched guards on duty and soldiers scurrying back and forth between camp and manor, she felt fortunate that Irene had not quite reached the age where the visitors were of great interest.

Alice continued past the property, then left the road, following a path through a meadow towards a gentle hill. The Home Guard took exception to civilians roaming the coastal foot paths with binoculars in hand, so she had to content herself with exploring nature inland. She had explored this walk numerous times with Irene after discovering her granddaughter shared her interest in the natural world. Today, Irene was too engrossed in her current read. She had discovered Agatha Christie.

Alice paused for a small flock of blue tits hanging upside down in a stand of oaks, feeding on an abundance of insects. Though common, their canary-yellow breasts and black and white masked heads were always a cheery sight. She continued, then paused again when a merlin, her first of the season, glided low over the meadow. *Any field mice best beware*, she thought as she watched through binoculars until the bird flew out of sight.

When she turned to continue uphill, a man was coming down the trail towards her. The path, never heavily used, had become quite solitary since war had broken out. The man wore an American uniform but looked older than the typical GI— late forties or early fifties she guessed, his dark hair edged with a bit of grey. His skin looked sun-tanned, even though that was not possible in Weymouth in October. As he drew closer, she spotted binoculars.

"Good afternoon," he called out as he approached. "Are you out birdwatching?"

Alice was unaware of any restrictions on citizens wandering about carrying binoculars in this area but had learned that the rules change frequently in wartime.

"Yes. Is that a problem? My home is just down the road from here."

The man smiled. "No problem as far as I'm concerned. I was out doing the same. I'm a bird watcher back home. But this is a real treat—a chance to observe your British birds. Only wish I had more time to get outdoors."

"Then, did you see the merlin just now? He was flying just there." Alice pointed off to her left.

"Is that what that was? I thought perhaps a kestrel, but I wasn't close enough for a good view. Merlins are not common back home."

"Where is home for you?"

"Athens, in the state of Ohio. I doubt you've heard of the place. It's a small town."

"No, you're right. I haven't. Are you stationed at Walbridge Manor?"

The man smiled again. "Yes—you've noticed us?"

Alice picked up on the sarcasm. "It would be hard not to. I live immediately next door, to the west."

"A lovely home you have. And I'm guessing not as drafty as the grand old manor."

"Perhaps not." Alice couldn't think of anything to add to the conversation. "Pleasure talking to you. I hope you have more opportunities to view our wildlife during your time here." Alice turned and continued a few steps up the path but then stopped and turned back to face the man. "I hope you don't think I'm being forward, but I was just thinking, if you would like a guide sometime, I'd be happy to show you some of the better locations in the area for observing birds."

"That's very kind of you. I'd like that very much. My schedule can be unpredictable. Can I send word should an opportunity present itself?"

"That would be fine. Most mornings I'm on observer duty, but I'm often free in the afternoons."

"Great. I'll check my schedule for a free afternoon. Thanks so much."

The man was about to set off down the path but then turned around. "I almost forgot—I'm Major Peter Gurin. I don't believe I caught your name."

"Alice Standfield."

As Alice continued her hike, she thought about having adult company on her birding excursions. She realised that was something she had missed since Nathan had become too busy between his farm work and his Observer Corps duties. She also thought she might enjoy comparing experiences with someone from another continent. She had no acquaintances outside of England. In fact, her life experience was confined to Dorset and the Isle of Wight where she spent her childhood. She had only ventured beyond their boundaries for brief holidays to the Channel Islands or the Lake District, or for occasional trips up to London.

By the time Alice returned home, Irene had finished *The Mystery of the Blue Train*. Alice suggested that, if she enjoyed that book, she might want to read *Mystery on the Orient Express* next. Then she reminded her that she had a town council meeting that evening. She had been attending regularly as the representative from the Observer Corps. Nathan liked to stay informed on what the council and the Air Raid Precautions Committee were up to, but it was easier for Alice to attend as she lived closer into town.

Unfortunately, it started raining just as she set out on her bicycle. She noticed a young woman walking briskly down a side street, also heading towards the town centre. Her head was covered against the rain by a red scarf. She looked up, startled by the sudden approach of Alice's bicycle, then quickly turned away. Even in the semi-darkness of dusk, Alice recognised the young woman. She was surprised to see Lydia Chambers out on her own at night and was sure her mother would not approve. Nor would Elizabeth approve of Lydia's skirt, which was barely touching her knees.

It was obvious what was going on. Both of Lydia's parents would be attending the council meeting. This was Lydia's chance to sneak out of the house, likely headed for one of the pubs taken over by the jazz-playing GIs. Alice had heard her fill of handwringing over the loud music and provocative dance moves. She was inclined to be more tolerant. But perhaps she would feel differently if Irene was of age.

Alice quickly dismissed the idea of saying something to Elizabeth. This was their mother-daughter squabble, and she wanted no part in it. She did, however, experience a measure of smug satisfaction in knowing that Elizabeth's family was not quite the tightly run ship that one might expect.

Once more, Alice sat near the back of the room, hoping to remain an observer. The threat of invasion had receded, and these meetings no longer held the sense of urgency that gripped them at the beginning of the war. Alice's mind wandered—she considered which bird species her new American friend might appreciate, should the opportunity materialise.

Elizabeth's gloved hand rose into the air a few rows in front of Alice. Before she could catch herself, Alice gave an involuntary small groan and was embarrassed that the scowling lady sitting next to her appeared to have noticed.

"Yes, Mrs. Chambers?" The council chair did not attempt a smile this time.

"I was just wondering if you might share with us the council's views on the segregation of American negroes when using Weymouth facilities. As I'm sure you know, that is the custom in the United States, and it is my understanding that the inconsistency during their stay here has resulted in confusion and in incidences of violence."

"Thank you, Mrs. Chambers. But I think it perhaps best to leave it to the Americans to deal with incidents involving their own personnel as they see fit. While segregation may be the norm in the United States, it is not the norm in England." He looked around the chamber. "Any other items before we adjourn?"

Alice recognised the grim smile on Elizabeth's face and knew that she contained her frustration with effort. But she did apparently, have the sense to realise that the council had no appetite to take on her issue, and her gloved hands remained neatly folded in her lap.

Pedalling up the hill towards home, Alice considered the issue raised by Elizabeth. She had never seen a negro before the arrival of the Americans and hadn't given much thought to segregation. She knew what Hitler would have to say on the matter. There were people who reacted negatively to those whose looks, customs, or beliefs were different from their own. That was not how she felt. Perhaps because she often felt herself to be the outsider.

As she walked her bicycle up her drive, she decided she should make acquaintances with people from outside her small corner of the world. Her life was confined by geography and society. She hoped the American major would take up her offer of a birding expedition.

CHAPTER 29

Weymouth, December 1943

ALICE SET DOWN THE letter from Leo—the first in several months. They had reached the Garigliano River in their march up the boot of Italy. That was all he could disclose about their situation. She studied the map of Italy pinned to the wall in Edgar's study until she found the Garigliano River. She wrote next to it the date from Leo's letter. Based on news releases and any information from Leo that survived the censors, she followed the Allied advance as best she could. The important thing was that her oldest grandchild was still alive.

She received a letter from Martin with the same post. Thankfully, his unit was awaiting deployment and using the time to further their training. He had three days of leave the week before Christmas, which would be their first opportunity to see him since he had set out for basic training. They would adapt by holding their family Christmas celebration a week early.

Alice was still planning a special tea for Christmas Day, and thought she would invite Nathan, Emil, Sonja, and the new Land Girl, Betty, whom Nathan had hired when Audrey moved back home. She also wanted to invite Peter Gurin, the American who had become her birding companion. She hoped that wouldn't be awkward for Nathan.

He responded as a gentleman when Alice turned down his proposal of marriage. They remained friends, but their friendship was not the same. A degree of discomfort tainted their relationship, like a batch of soup with the wrong spice added. The soup was still proper food, but the taste was off.

She hoped Nathan would not view Peter as competition. They were both bird enthusiasts, so they had that in common. She needed to decide today, because she and Peter were to go on another birding walk that afternoon, which would likely be her last opportunity to extend an invitation.

On one of their recent walks, Peter shared some of his experiences teaching civil engineering at Ohio University. She was interested in finding out more about this mysterious American who seemed so different from the GIs that were everywhere in Weymouth.

"Irene, I'm heading out," she called up the stairs. Irene was spending more time in her bedroom and less time in the sitting room. Alice took that as a sign she was entering adolescence. She made hikes with Irene a priority—the one activity she seemed to enjoy sharing with her grandmother.

Alice retrieved both her own bicycle as well as Henry's old bicycle that had been so well used by Martin before his enlistment. Peter stood waiting for her at the end of the drive. With the coast off limits, they decided on Radipole Lake, just upstream from Weymouth Harbour and surrounded by marshlands.

Upon reaching the trailhead, they hopped off their bicycles and walked them down towards the lake.

"What was the path that led you to becoming an army major?"

"I joined the army straight out of school. Seven years later we shipped out to Germany. It was serving in the Great War that offered the opportunities for advancement." Peter stopped to unsnag a blackberry vine that had caught his jacket.

"And what led you to choose engineering as your field?"

"Working bridge crew during the war—that sparked my interest in civil engineering. After the war, I attended college and continued serving in the army reserves. Then when Pearl Harbour happened, I knew I'd be called up. Bridges are very strategic."

They reached the lake and stopped to survey the steel grey surface and surrounding reeds. There were gadwalls, teals, shovelers, and widgeons, but Peter's attention was drawn by the kingfisher. The bird flew past and landed on a snag, all the time scolding them in his harsh, screechy voice. Peter gave a hearty laugh.

"We have kingfishers, but they're not such flashy dressers as yours."

"Yes, they are quite colourful." Alice studied Peter as Peter studied their surroundings. His joy in nature was intense, childlike. It made their expeditions fun. She felt relaxed.

Nathan also appreciated nature, but it involved notes on behaviours and ranges, lists of birds seen, when and where. With his training as a veterinarian and his occupation as a farmer, he encountered animals as either patients or commodities.

"Do you have family back home?" Alice asked after the kingfisher moved on.

Peter paused before responding. "No. Between soldiering and academics, not much time for romance."

Alice turned to look out over the lake. Had she intruded into personal territory? But she wanted to know more. Peter seemed aware of others, sensitive to what they were thinking and feeling. He didn't fit her conception of career soldiers. Was she falling for this American? She reminded herself that marriage was not in her plans. Plus, based on what he told her about his life, he was around ten years her junior.

The marsh went quiet, and the songbirds disappeared. Both Alice and Peter knew what this signalled. They scanned the horizon.

Alice spotted the raptor, soaring above the marsh at eye level. Then Peter spotted it as well. They both stood motionless as he flew towards them. He passed within a few yards then veered, crashing through reeds and branches. The chase was quickly over, and the raptor landed on a high branch, a bundle clutched in its talons.

Peter looked over to Alice. "Your local harrier, I presume."

"Yes—a marsh harrier. I have fond memories of them as a child. They had disappeared by the time I was twenty. Poaching and the draining of our swamplands, I suspect. But in the past few years they've made a small comeback."

They followed the pathway around the side of the lake. "So, you were interested in birds as a child?" Peter asked.

"I grew up on the Isle of Wight—not far from here. My father built his wealth in shipbuilding there. As a young girl, I was allowed to roam the beaches and the seaside meadows. It was an idyllic childhood. Being outdoors allows me to connect to that time." They paused to negotiate a particularly soggy section of the trail. "What about you?"

"I grew up on an Island as well. Although I think the similarity probably ends there. My childhood was spent on Baranof Island, in the town of Sitka, Alaska."

"That sounds very different. What was it like?"

"Cooler and much rainier—similar to Northwestern Scotland, I hear. And isolated. The only way to get around is by boat."

"But surrounded by nature, I would imagine."

Peter smiled. "Yes, there's no shortage of nature. Everything in Sitka revolves around fishing. But there's also a lot of hunting. I was never that interested in either. But living in Ohio, I find I miss the wilderness."

They reached the next viewing point and stopped to survey their surroundings. "Why did you leave Sitka?"

"My father's family was Russian. My mother came from the Tlingit tribe. I didn't feel I belonged in either group. Joining the army was a way to escape the island. But then, I'm not sure how well I fit in the army either. They tolerate me because of my engineering skills. I ended up in Ohio, because I wanted to teach, and that's where I found a post."

The daylight was waning so they decided to retrieve their bicycles. Amidst all the disclosure, Alice felt embolden to ask, "You mentioned that you have no family in Ohio. Did you ever marry?"

"No, never married."

Alice waited for some elaboration, and when it didn't come, she persisted, "Was there ever someone special in your life?"

Peter hesitated. "Yes, there was someone very special, but that person is no longer living."

"Forgive me, I should not have intruded."

"That's okay. It happened ten years ago. I don't mind sharing that with you, but I would appreciate it if you could keep that to yourself. I try to keep my personal life separate from my army life."

"Of course."

Silence fell upon them. Alice felt that her insensitivity had spoiled what would otherwise have been a special day. Little conversation passed between them on the return ride. When they reached Alice's drive, she turned back to Peter.

"I've invited a few friends for Christmas tea, and it would be lovely if you could join us."

Peter smiled again. "That's very kind of you. I'll look forward to it."

CHAPTER 30

Weymouth, Christmas 1943

LICE, IRENE, AND ROSA spent the past several days in the kitchen attempting feats of magic, with mixed success. Shortages were so integral to their way of life that they had become quite adept at improvisation. But to pull together something that resembled a proper Christmas tea for guests was beyond the limits of their creativity. Two things had saved them. One was Peter's generosity. He stockpiled his chocolate rations and sent them over as his contribution to the meal. The other was down to Sonja's enterprise. She had snared three rabbits, and they were to feature in their main course.

Over the past several years, Alice's household gathered and cut up the branches that fell in the small woods at the back of Elm House. This provided the comfort of a wood fire for special occasions or on their coldest winter nights. The evening satisfied both criteria. It had been an exceptionally cold and clear Christmas day, and the temperature was already plummeting with the onset of darkness which comes so early that time of year.

Peter arrived shortly after Nathan and his crew. Alice made introductions. She noted that Nathan and Peter seemed to be getting on—sharing notes on bird activity they'd observed recently. She seated Nathan next to her, with Irene on her other side, and

Peter near the other end of the table along with the two Land Girls, Emil, and Rosa. She sought to avoid any sign that Nathan might wrongly interpret.

After dinner, they retired to the sitting room. Sonja sat near Irene and asked about the books she was currently reading and what she liked and disliked at school. The group gravitated towards the fire, drawn by its warmth. Alice found the faint hint of woodsmoke more relaxing even than Edgar's whisky or Nathan's mulled cider. As was her Christmas tradition, she set up the gramophone and selected a Mozart concerto. For once, Elm House felt like it was her own and not the home that used to belong to the Standfield family.

Nathan, Emil, Sonja, and Betty decided it was time to head home. After they left, Irene retreated to her room to read, and Rosa headed for bed. Alice was left with Peter, who stared into the fire, seemingly lost in his thoughts. He set down his whisky tumbler and looked over at Alice.

"There's something I need to tell you. Something I feel I can trust you to keep confidential."

"Yes, of course Peter." Alice was suddenly alert. This sounded serious.

Peter turned back to stare into the fire, as he continued. "You asked me if there had been someone special in my life, and I told you that there was. What I didn't tell you was that this special person was a man."

Peter paused to allow his last words to sink in. Alice had not expected this. "I see," she responded, trying to sound neutral. She had, of course, heard of homosexuals but had never known any and had never given it much thought. She knew the church considered it sinful, but Alice was not deeply religious, and she liked to draw her own conclusions about these types of things.

Peter looked back over at Alice, trying to interpret her reaction. "I would not have burdened you with this information, except that I value our little expeditions, and even more I value our friendship. I want to be sure that I don't create expectations beyond that of a close friendship."

It was true—Peter had occupied her thoughts recently, although the notion of them together seemed silly, given their differences in age and nationality. Alice decided right then and there that she didn't care what the church or the law had to say about Peter. He was one of the most genuine persons she had met. She had been thinking their relationship might be heading beyond friendship, but now she knew that was not to be. It suddenly made their friendship simpler and in some way that she could not explain, richer.

She looked over at him with a new sense of love and respect. "Thanks for your confidence in me. You're right in that my feelings were starting down that path. Now, I very much hope we continue as friends."

"Good! I do as well."

"I imagine that if word got out, it would create problems for you with your superiors."

"It would be the end of my military career and probably also my position as a professor."

Alice set down her mulled cider. "That *is* serious. I'll guard this confidence carefully." She remained thoughtful while they listened to the reassuring sounds of the fire. "This very special relationship of yours, I presume it had to stay hidden."

"Yes." Peter continued staring into the fire.

"The isolation is a disease," he finally said, "every much as deadly as typhoid. It became too much for him, the isolation and constantly being on guard, constantly in fear of being found out. He took his own life."

Alice rose from her favourite chair and sat on the sofa next to Peter, taking his hand. "I'm so sorry for what you have been through." They sat for a time, watching the fire burn low, then Peter took his leave. Alice remained by the fire. She wondered how it was that the two men currently in her life had each suffered the same loss.

The next day, before heading out for observer duty, Alice posted the note she had written the previous night, shortly after Peter had left, thanking him for joining their Christmas tea and expressing her hope that they would enjoy many more birding expeditions in the new year.

***

The cold weather continued into Boxing Day. The bicycle ride out to the observer post was even more challenging when wrapped in multiple layers against the cold. And it was hard to gain any feeling of warmth sharing the post with Nathan.

"Thanks for the lovely evening," he told her. But his tone was clipped and formal. She suspected that her rejection of his proposal of marriage had wounded his pride and that her friendship with Peter added to that injury. There was nothing she could do to reassure him. She was committed to keeping Peter's confidence safe. She decided the best path was to ignore his coolness and act as if their relationship remained unchanged.

She returned home exhausted. This was partly due to enduring such frigid weather in the strained company of Nathan and partly due to the post-Christmas let-down. They were back to their everyday existence which at times felt quite bleak.

She heard a knock at the door. The young man standing on her front porch looked entirely out of place. "Mrs. Standfield?"

"Yes." Alice felt her throat constrict. Her pulse began to race, making her light headed.

"Telegram for you. I'm very sorry, ma'am."

She leaned against the door frame as she ripped open the telegram, not trusting her legs.

The War Office regrets to announce that your grandson LAC Leo Standfield has been reported missing in action in Italy. His exact whereabouts and condition unknown. Letter to follow.

"Thank you. No reply." Alice managed to say, her throat suddenly dry.

"Sorry," the lad mumbled, uncomfortable.

Alice closed the door. She needed a chair. She sat and focused on her breathing. *He's not dead. There's still hope,* she told herself. She managed to stand and walk to the telephone.

"Nathan. It's Alice. Leo has been reported missing in action."

"I'll be right over."

Alice felt the pressure across her chest lessen. "I was so hoping you would say that."

CHAPTER 31

Weymouth, January 1944

LYDIA ONLY HALF-LISTENED TO Lois's detailed account of the alterations to her satin-blue dress—quite a lucky find at the secondhand store. Her attention kept turning to the soldier in the corner of the café. Lydia had seen only a few negroes in her life, all in the past year and at a distance. This was her first close encounter. She detected wariness in her friend's face when the man entered the café. But Lydia was not wary. She was curious.

Lydia and Lois were only having tea, of course. They couldn't spare the extra ration coupons for a meal out. The man in the corner ordered a sandwich. Lydia kept stealing glances as he lit up a cigarette, took a worn paperback from his coat pocket and began to read while he waited for his order. He was a tall man, with legs that barely fit under the table. He seemed comfortable with his surroundings and absorbed in his book.

Lois looked up at the wall clock. "Well, got to dash. Heaven forbid I overstay lunch. Mr. Bernard'll be nasty all afternoon." Lois had found work as a typist and secretary for a local solicitor.

Lydia's shift at the hospital didn't start for another hour, so she lingered at her table, happy to be out of the cold and rain. She was still curious about the man in the corner and continued watching him while pretending to read the copy of the *Dorset Echo* left behind by another diner.

The waitress brought over the man's lunch order, and he wasted no time digging in. At that moment, three American soldiers sauntered into the café. One of them was relaying a story, apparently about someone in their regiment. They broke into laughter as they took up a table in the centre. The storyteller looked over at Lydia. "Hey, beautiful. There's an extra chair. Why don't you come join us? Lunch is on us."

Lydia smiled. "Thanks gentlemen, but my shift is about to start." She stood up and gathered her belongings. When she turned to leave, she saw that the man in the corner had gone, his sandwich left almost entirely untouched on its plate. Lydia stepped outside, looking left and right. She spied the man on the next block. He had just settled onto a bench and was pulling out his book.

She walked over and smiled. "Pardon me, but couldn't help noticing you didn't finish your lunch. Was the food not to your liking?"

He looked up, surprised. "No mam. The food was fine. Thanks for asking."

Lydia was mystified. She decided to press on. "Are you feeling poorly? Excuse my asking. It's just that we're not used to food going to waste around here."

"No, back home my mama wouldn't stand for that neither." He didn't offer any further explanation, but he smiled up at Lydia, so she didn't think her questions were being interpreted as hostile.

"So, where is home for you?"

"Chicago."

Lydia had heard of Chicago. It was the setting for a gangster movie she'd seen a few years ago. "Do you like it here in Weymouth?"

"I do, except the rain. You sure do get a lot of rain around here."

Lydia nodded. She didn't like unsolved mysteries, so she persisted. "I still don't understand why you didn't finish your lunch."

The man rolled his eyes and sighed. Then he looked straight at Lydia. "Let's just say my presence was no longer welcome."

It took a moment for the meaning to sink in. "You mean the other soldiers?" Lydia was incensed. "But you were there first. That isn't right. You had to leave just because they happened along?"

"No, it ain't right. But that's how things are." He smiled again.

For once, Lydia didn't have a response. She'd heard about segregation in the States, but this was Weymouth. They should be following British customs, not bringing their own bigotry over here. She decided to let the matter drop. "My name is Lydia, by the way."

"Anthony. Pleased to meet you."

"My shift at the hospital is about to start. Would you like to walk over with me? They have a small canteen, and you could pick up a bite. I can show you where it is."

"That sounds right kind of you."

When Anthony stood up, he towered over Lydia, who was a bit shorter than average compared to other girls in her year. She liked walking next to him. He had a gentle and thoughtful manner of speaking, and it made her feel safe. "So, what were you doing in Chicago before the war?"

"I was in school—Chicago Teacher's College."

"You were studying to be a teacher?" Lydia didn't know why that surprised her.

"Yep. Studying to be an English teacher. I've always liked stories."

"Reading stories or writing stories?"

"Both. My mama read to me when I was little, and that got me started. Writing was what kept me in school."

Lydia had not been expecting that a negro would be an avid reader. But now that she thought about it, why not? "I admire that. I've never been able to generate a lot of enthusiasm for reading."

Anthony smiled again. "Maybe you haven't been reading the right books."

They had reached the hospital, and they paused just outside the entrance. "Well now, that's an interesting thought. Do you have any suggestions?"

"Wow—where to start?"

"We could start at the library. Do you think you could pick out some titles for me to try?"

Lydia and Anthony agreed on a time that they could meet during Anthony's next day of leave. Lydia went with him to check out the few options at the hospital canteen. Once Anthony settled on something, she left to start her shift.

Lydia thought about Anthony all through her shift. She had become acquainted with a number of Americans during those evenings she had snuck out of the house. She loved jazz, and had fun learning the latest dance moves. The soldiers she met were a hoot, but she knew what they were after. She realised that people thought she was not very bright—that she was the type who could be easily manipulated. She let them think that. But she knew what was important to her. Anthony was the first serviceman for whom she thought she might feel differently. He didn't make her feel that he was just after her skirt.

It bothered Lydia that her mother didn't trust her. Lydia needed to do things, get out and see people, have some fun. But she knew enough to stay out of trouble. She wasn't going to do anything that she would later regret.

Her mother expected her to follow in her footsteps, say all the correct things, always be in the right sort of company, always do what was expected. From what Lydia could see, that path had not brought happiness to her mother, and she was certain it wouldn't serve for her either. She entertained no hopes of discussing this reasonably with her mother, so Lydia opted for passive resistance. Say "yes" but do otherwise. What her mother didn't know wouldn't hurt her.

CHAPTER 32

Southern England, April 1944

MARTIN COULD SEE SOMETHING big was in the works. Intensive training on beach landings—it didn't take a genius to figure out what that meant. They all knew Churchill would invade the Continent at some point. The only questions were when and where.

Strange to think that he had nearly a year of service under his belt. It seemed longer. The army had become a part of him. He knew how to drive and repair pretty much anything the army had on wheels and was eager to put his knowledge to work. He was ready for something to happen.

Assigned as a driver for their brigadier, he'd made trips to briefings in London and last week, in Southampton. He viewed firsthand the mobilisation of troops and machinery, all migrating south.

Driver duty entailed extended periods of waiting while meetings took place behind a strict wall of security. His thoughts strayed to Leo, wondering if he was dead or alive and if alive, what he was enduring as a prisoner of war. The rumours filtering back from escaped POWs spoke of conditions that could feature in nightmares. He also wondered where Ellis had been deployed and what he was up to. He knew that local casualties were posted in the *Dorset Echo*, and that his grandmother would inform him if anything were to happen to someone he knew.

Mostly, he thought about Sonja and his visit to the farm during his December leave. She had inquired about his life as a soldier but didn't, as far as Martin could tell, provide any clues as to whether her interest extended beyond that of simple friendship.

With only three days leave, there wasn't time to see Lydia. He wondered if that explained why her letters had become scarce. Only two from her since the first of the year, and they were shorter, less personal. Maybe she had simply tired of writing, especially given Martin's much-less-frequent return letters.

Of the two, he laughed more with Lydia. But with Sonja there was something he couldn't quite place his finger on—a depth that drew him in. Martin shared a bit about his conflicted feelings with Jack, who just smiled and made some comment about women having the ability to make a perfectly sane man not know up from down.

***

"Time to get up, mate." Howard shook Martin's shoulder.

"Okay, okay. I'm getting."

Martin pulled himself from his bunk. As his brain cleared, he remembered that he wasn't needed on driver duty that day. That meant he was stuck with his battalion on yet another simulated beach landing. He used to believe that there was no such thing as being overprepared. Now he was starting to question that.

Martin and Jack would stay close to Howard who, of course, didn't know how to swim. Martin felt sorry for Howard, but secretly felt there was only so much you could do for someone like that. He might have dropped Howard as a friend if it had been just him. But Jack was adamant about sticking together and watching out for each other. Martin supposed Jack was right. But that didn't stop him from resenting the fact that they were the last group in every exercise.

They started the day executing a transfer from a large transport ship to smaller landing crafts. This involved climbing down scramble nets carrying full gear and a rifle slung about the neck. Adding to the difficulty, the two differently sized boats refused to synchronise their rising and falling in the swells.

It was their turn down the net when the landing craft suddenly dropped into a trough. Martin heard Howard cry out as he lost his balance, grasping wildly for the nearest thing. Unfortunately, the nearest thing was Martin's arm. Before he could react, he was following Howard into shockingly cold water and sinking quickly due to his heavy backpack. An involuntary gasp brought sea water instead of air. Martin kicked and paddled with all the muscle of his years of being a farmhand while trying to wrestle free from the backpack. Just as he broke the surface, two arms locked themselves around his legs. Howard was hanging on for dear life. Suddenly unable to kick, Martin felt himself sinking once more.

He tried to kick his legs free, but Howard, in his panic, would not let go. Lights started to pop in his head. Martin felt a wall of rage. Because he had befriended this loser, he was going to die. His young life was ending, and he wouldn't even be a war hero. People would shake their heads reading in the *Dorset Echo* that he had died in a stupid training exercise.

Then he felt an arm grabbing him under his armpit, then another arm, and he was being hauled over the side of a small patrol boat. "Fucking idiots," he heard someone say overhead as he lay in the bottom of the boat coughing and gasping.

In the mess tent that evening, Martin endured the pointing and the humour at his and Howard's expense. Howard apologised as they were readying for bed. Up till then, Martin had been holding in his anger. Howard's feeble apology pushed him over the edge.

"What the hell, Howard! If you can't swim, did it ever occur in that pea brain of yours to keep to the inside? I'm done watching out for you. If you want to die like a sodding idiot, rule me out."

Howard mumbled another "sorry". He climbed onto his bunk, which was just below Martin's, and was silent. Martin felt bad about exploding at Howard, but that day a line had been crossed.

The next day Jack pulled Martin aside. "Shame about the swim yesterday. I know Howard's a pain at times, but the kid's got a good heart. And you just never know when you might be the one to need a friend."

That's all Jack said, but it was enough for Martin to regret his outburst. It took a couple of days, but they were back to being a threesome; watching out for each other. Nonetheless, Martin remained cautious. He was willing to help Howard, but he was never again going to risk dying for him.

CHAPTER 33

Weymouth, May 1944

NYWHERE THEY WENT, THEY attracted attention. They met twice at the library, but that was pushing their luck. They tried cafés, different ones each time, but people would stare, and waitresses would act strangely. Some were cold and disapproving. Worse were the ones who smiled knowingly, regarding them with what? Lydia wasn't quite sure. Pity? Ridicule? It was just a matter of time before the gossip reached her parents.

As the weather improved, they started meeting up in the countryside, taking long walks along lonely treks and talking about anything and everything. They found common ground in the boundaries they pushed against. For Anthony, it was racism. Racism packed onto ships and carried across the Atlantic by his fellow servicemen. For Lydia, it was a mother who wanted control over every action, and worse, every thought.

Anthony dreamed of showing young people from similar backgrounds the path to understanding a greater world, the path of reading. Lydia's dreams were less defined. She wanted more from her life than the role dictated by her mother. But what was that alternate path? She had no specifics. That's part of what excited her—an open door to the world full of possibilities.

Today they climbed a hillside with a view out towards the bay. The sun kept disappearing and reappearing from behind puffy clouds that reminded Lydia of the cotton gauze used by the hospital nurses. Warmed by the climb, they sat in the sweet-smelling spring grass, enjoying the cool breeze off the Channel and watching the ships in the distance. Lydia had brought a few slices of their wartime wheatmeal bread, grey and crumbly, and a jar of tea to wash it down. Anthony had brought his chocolate ration to share.

"What will you do, after the war?" Lydia asked, still staring out across the bay.

Anthony glanced over at Lydia. "Don't know. Maybe see if I can't return here. I could get used to this place."

Lydia realised he was asking a question. "I would like that. Do you think that's possible?"

"Don't rightly know, but don't see why not."

Anthony leaned over, and Lydia turned her face up to him. But they didn't kiss. At that moment, Lydia noticed the approaching hikers. A man and a woman. With a start, Lydia recognised the woman. It was Martin Standfield's grandmother. She was with an American serviceman.

"Oh no—she knows my mother." Lydia looked around, trying to find a way to avoid this encounter, but she realised they had already been seen. It would appear worse if they scampered off, as if what they were doing was wrong. And Lydia was adamant that there was nothing wrong with going on a hike with an American GI who happened to be a negro.

Anthony jumped to his feet and saluted the major, while Lydia composed her face into one of her cheery smiles. "Mrs. Standfield, nice to see you."

"And you Lydia." Turning to Peter, "Peter, this is Lydia Chambers. Lydia, Major Peter Gurin." Turning back to Lydia, "and your friend?"

Anthony stepped forward, "Private Anthony Lewis, ma'am, sir."

Peter reached out to shake Anthony's hand. "Pleased to meet you, Lewis. Don't let us disturb you."

Lydia looked over to Mrs. Standfield. "I'm so sorry to hear that Leo is missing. Do you have any word on him?"

"Thanks for asking. No, we haven't received any further news."

Lydia studied Mrs. Standfield, trying to make up her mind. "Mrs. Standfield, may I have a word?"

"Of course." If Mrs. Standfield was puzzled, she didn't show it.

Lydia led her a short distance down the trail and then turned to face her. "Mrs. Standfield, I want you to understand that Anthony is one of the kindest souls I've ever met and that he would never be one to take advantage of me. I'm not sure my mother would be ready to accept him, though. Would you be so kind as to not mention this encounter to her? I would like to introduce Anthony in the right timing."

Mrs. Standfield didn't hesitate. "Of course, dear." She smiled and placed a reassuring hand on Lydia's shoulder. They hiked back to join the two men, who were discussing their respective home towns.

Later, as Lydia and Anthony hiked back, Anthony explained that he would likely not be able to see her for a while. "Rumour is that there'll be a communication blackout soon."

Lydia felt her chest tighten. "Why? What's happening?"

Anthony took her hand. "Don't know. And I couldn't say anything, if I did. Just want you to know that I will always be thinking of you, even if I can't tell you that for a while."

For Anthony's sake, Lydia tried to remain cheerful during the remainder of their walk. Everyone knew that at some point the Allies would invade the Continent. Why else would they have accumulated all this military down here? That would likely mean that Anthony would be sent over the Channel, and that she might not ever see him again. He was unlike anyone she had met in Weymouth—a gentle, thoughtful giant. Never had she hated this war more. But if there hadn't been a war, they would never have met.

Lydia went straight from her walk to her shift at the hospital. By the time she returned home later that evening, she was dead tired. Her mother and father were both in the sitting room, perched on the edge of the sofa. They looked as if they had been waiting for Lydia to arrive. "Hi Mum, Pa. What did you have for tea? I'm famished."

Her parents remained seated. "Lydia, come sit down," her father said.

Lydia sat. Something serious was going on, and she thought she knew what it was. She tried to conjure an innocent expression as she looked across to her parents.

"What were you doing this morning? Before your shift?"

As her heart rate quickened, Lydia worked to maintain her innocent expression. "I stopped by to see Lois. Remember?"

Her mother appeared to barely contain her anger. "No dear. I talked to Lois's mother. Lois helped her with the mending all morning."

Lydia's mind raced. She needed an alternate explanation. "Oh, that's right. They needed me to come in early to cover for someone. It's been such a long day, I'd forgotten."

Her father stood up. "Lydia, don't make this worse by lying to us. It's true, isn't it? You've been seeing an American. A negro! Apparently, the whole town is talking about it behind our backs."

"And so, what if I have?"

Her mother also stood. The two of them looked down on Lydia. "Do you ever consider anyone besides yourself? How am I to show my face in town? And your father is a councillor. Did you think about how this affects his standing?"

Lydia was no longer worried or scared. She was angry. She had never felt this angry. "Yes, that's what really counts for you—your social standing. Forever worrying about what people will say or think. I refuse to live that way. There is nothing illegal or immoral about making friends with someone. Even if that person is a negro."

Her mother's face was flushed. "From what I hear, you're more than friends."

"Nothing untoward has happened. We see each other. We talk. That's it. Who's been talking to you? Did Mrs. Standfield run home and telephone you?

Elizabeth looked perplexed. "Mrs. Standfield. What has she to do with this?"

Someone else then, Lydia thought to herself. She ignored her mother's question.

Elizabeth paced the room, then stopped in front of Lydia. "The point is, their people are different from our people. Different culture, different standards, different morals."

The hypocrisy of her mother's statement hit Lydia hard. "No, you may be right. I think perhaps they don't hold to our moral standards—they hold to a higher moral standard. Anthony is the most kind and respectful person I've met. But all you see is his skin."

Lydia's father spoke next. "Lydia, we forbid you from seeing him. Clearly, he has sweet-talked his way around you. Probably has lots of experience with charming young girls back in America."

Lydia rose from her chair, eye level with her parents. "You may not have noticed, but I'm no longer a girl. I'm an adult, and I'll make my own decisions about who I will or won't see."

"Not while you live under our roof, you won't! We're not having it!"

Lydia didn't say another word. She stormed upstairs, yanked their largest suitcase from the upstairs closet and went into her bedroom to pack her clothes and essentials. When she returned downstairs, she stepped into the kitchen and pulled her ration coupons from the stack on the counter. Passing back through the sitting room, she ignored her parents questioning stares and stepped out into the complete darkness of blackout. Clutching her suitcase, she walked with no destination in mind. She wanted distance between herself and her parents.

Eventually she stopped, set down her suitcase and sat on top of it. For once, she was thankful for the blackout. She didn't want to be seen sitting alone on the side of the road late at night. The complete darkness also meant that she couldn't see anyone who might be lurking in the shadows. She tried not to think about that. She had more important things to worry about.

She had finally stood up to her parents. It was a step that could not be backtracked. She struggled to hold back tears. She needed to think.

The truth was, she had nowhere to go. Lois's home was not an option. Lois's mum was in league with her own mother. In fact, everyone she thought of was connected to her mother or her father. Maybe she could take up an empty bed at the hospital. As she thought about that, she realised the nurses wouldn't allow it. Did she know of any boarding houses? But she had no money to pay her board.

Not knowing what else to do, Lydia remained by the side of the road, perched on her suitcase. The longer she sat, the more she calmed down. Despite all that had transpired, the night outside was pleasant—comfortable with just her cardigan. The Channel winds had finally blown away the clouds, and the air was exceptionally clear. With the town in blackout, the vast landscape of stars was positively dazzling.

But she couldn't sit by the side of the road all evening. The Home Guard would pass through at some point, and they would insist that she return home. She had no plan and no idea where she could spend the night. In the end, she started walking towards the Standfield's, simply because she could think of no alternative. Apparently, Mrs. Standfield had kept her word about not telling her mother. Plus, she seemed genuinely supportive when they met on the trail. Hard to believe their encounter had occurred earlier that day. It seemed ages ago that she and Anthony had parted, not knowing when or if they would see each other again.

Lydia hesitated on the street in front of the Standfield home. She didn't know Mrs. Standfield very well – mostly what she had heard about her from Martin. What if she refused to take her in? She might insist that Lydia return home and work things out with her parents. But Lydia knew things had advanced beyond the point where they could be resolved. She and her parents held very different ideas about how she should live her life. They were too divergent to be reconciled.

Worse than turning Lydia down, she worried that Mrs. Standfield might say "yes" out of pity and that her presence would be an intrusion. This could only be a temporary solution. She would still need to find a permanent place to live.

Reminding herself that there were no other options, she braced herself and walked up the front path.

Lydia was prevented from peeking through any of the windows by the heavy blackout curtains. She knocked on the door and waited. The house remained completely silent. Lydia didn't think Mrs. Standfield could be out of town, as she had seen her earlier that day. She knocked harder this time. More silence and then distant footsteps, drawing closer. The door opened partway, and Mrs. Standfield appeared in nightgown and robe. "Lydia. Is everything alright?"

"Yes. Sorry to intrude at such a late hour. May I come in?"

Mrs. Standfield opened the door wider. Irene was standing behind her grandmother, peering at Lydia with great curiosity.

"Why don't you come sit down." Mrs. Standfield led the way into her sitting room. She turned to her granddaughter. "Irene, I'm going to ask you to go back to bed. We'll talk in the morning."

Irene looked like she was about to protest, but she turned instead and pounded up the stairs. Lydia wondered if Irene would stay upstairs, or sneak back down to listen in from the other room. That's what she would have done in similar circumstances.

Once they were seated, Mrs. Standfield leaned forward. "How can I help you?"

Lydia wasn't sure where to start. "Earlier today you met Anthony. What I told you on the trail is the truth. He's been a perfect gentleman to me, and I have grown fond of him. I've known from the start that my parents would never approve of my seeing a negro. Today when I came home from my hospital shift, they were waiting for me. Someone told them about Anthony and me."

"Oh dear. She didn't hear that from me."

"Yes, I know it wasn't you. Regardless, they confronted me tonight. They forbade me from seeing Anthony again. That's not something I can agree to." Lydia looked up at Mrs. Standfield, who was listening intently. She gave no indication of what she thought of Lydia's story, but she was eyeing Lydia's suitcase.

"Did she ask you to move out?"

"No, not quite. She told me that as long as I stayed under their roof, I would need to abide by their rules."

A board creaked in the hallway. Alice didn't turn to look but raised her voice. "Irene, back to bed." They heard retreating footsteps.

Lydia looked back over at Mrs. Standfield. "Would it be possible for me to stay here for a few days—just until I sort things out? I didn't know where else to go."

Mrs. Standfield didn't answer right away. When she spoke, it was with a calm firmness, but Lydia did not detect disapproval.

"Yes, you can. But one thing needs to happen first. I need to speak with your mother."

Lydia was taken aback. Mrs. Standfield must have noticed, because she quickly clarified. "I won't share anything you have shared in confidence, but your parents need to know where you are and that you are safe. And given what's transpired this evening, I think it might be better if they heard that from me. I encourage you to try to resolve things with your parents, but I don't think that will happen this evening."

Lydia nodded. Mrs. Standfield got up and walked out into the hall. Her voice carried into the sitting room where Lydia sat waiting. "Hello. Elizabeth? This is Alice Standfield. I'm sorry to be calling so late, but I thought you should know that Lydia has turned up at my house. Yes, she's fine. She has asked to stay for a few days while she works some things out. I've told her that she can do that, but I wanted to make sure you knew where she was." There was a period of silence. "No, I..." More silence. "Elizabeth, I've done nothing of the kind..." Yet more silence. "I'm sorry you feel that way." Another pause. "I can ask her." Mrs. Standfield poked her head into the sitting room. "Would you like to speak to your mother?" Lydia shook her head emphatically. Alice returned to the telephone. "I'm afraid she doesn't feel ready to talk at this point. I'm sorry."

Alice returned to sitting room. "Well, that went about as well as I thought it would. But at least they know where you are and won't waste police time trying to track you down. Now, let's get you settled. Would you like something to eat before you head to bed?"

Lydia realised she was famished. "That would be much appreciated. I don't know how I can repay you, Mrs. Standfield."

"Not to worry. But please, call me Alice." Then she called up the stairs, "Okay Irene. I know you're listening. You can come down now."

CHAPTER 34

Weymouth, June 1944

ALICE WOKE TO A deep rumbling that seemed to reverberate from inside her skull. She sat up in bed and listened. Grabbing her robe, she went downstairs, stepped out the front door and walked down her drive. Nothing looked amiss, but there was a definite smell of diesel and the now-familiar sound of heavy vehicles.

"Must be the real thing." The voice came from behind her.

Alice turned to see her neighbour Helen coming down her drive. "It would certainly seem so," Alice replied.

"With all the comings and goings, makes you wonder how the Jerrys could possibly be surprised."

"Let's just hope they are." Alice was careful not to inadvertently disclose information gleaned from her Observer Corps post. But she agreed with Helen. It was clear to most in Weymouth that something was afoot. "I need to get ready for my observer shift. Talk this afternoon?" She walked back up her drive, filled with anxiety.

"I think it best if you stayed indoors for the day," she told Irene over breakfast. But then, she did that most days anyway.

As she set out on her bicycle, the rumbling and the smell of diesel exhaust grew stronger. A roadblock came into view at a major intersection. Ahead of her, an unbroken procession of tanks headed south towards Portland. She stepped off her bicycle and watched. Was this truly the start of the invasion, or just an exceptionally large training exercise?

A soldier walked up to her. "You can't come through here ma'am. I need you to return home."

Alice dug into the knapsack perched on the front basket of her bicycle. She pulled out her Observer Corps card and also the helmet she wore on duty. After consulting with his superior, the soldier directed her forward. The procession came to a halt, just long enough for her to pass.

A short while later, she encountered yet another roadblock. This time, an endless column of transport trucks, each overflowing with American soldiers. They appeared to be heading towards Weymouth Harbour. Once again, Alice convinced the sentries that she required passage. The soldiers hanging out the back of the trucks called out and tipped their helmets to her. "Care for a lift?" one of them asked.

Alice decided this must be the real thing. The invasion had begun. When she thought about all that was hinging on the success of this operation, the worry almost made her nauseous. She wondered whether Weymouth was a special departure point, or if this was playing out all along the south coast?

She was late for observer duty, but no need to explain. From the post, Nathan had been observing the mobilisation taking place throughout the countryside. Alice set down her knapsack and grabbed her binoculars. Hundreds of vessels of all descriptions and sizes clogged the bay between Weymouth and Portland.

Constant air traffic made for a noisy and busy session, leaving no time for discussion. When possible, they tried to include the largest of the ships in their recordings for the day. Their shift passed quickly. Returning down the path together, they at last had time to talk.

"I reckon that Martin's part of this mobilisation somewhere?"

"Yes, I presume so. We haven't heard from him recently. There's probably a communication blackout in place."

They continued their descent. Since the only information they had related to the mobilisation was what they had both just observed, there was little more on that topic to discuss.

"How is Lydia fitting into your household?"

"Surprisingly well. She's a pleasure to have around and always ready to pitch in."

"She seems the friendly sort."

They reached the spot where Alice had left her bicycle. "Yes. What I hadn't anticipated was the positive effect on Irene. I think Lydia is becoming the big sister she never had."

"Is that a fact?" Nathan leaned against a fencepost, facing Alice.

"It's like a cloud has lifted. Irene isn't spending all day in her room—wants to be involved in whatever Lydia's doing."

"You're not concerned about the influence Lydia might have on her?"

"No, I'm not. I think Lydia's a positive influence, actually. It's a shame Elizabeth can't see what a delightful daughter she has."

Alice started walking her bicycle down the footpath towards the farm, and they continued their conversation. "I imagine there's no word from her friend?"

"From Anthony? No. And now, I guess we know why. I think that's why she keeps herself so busy."

"Yes, doesn't do to sit at home and fret."

"What's the latest with Emil?"

"Even with his prosthetic, working the farm is a challenge. He's applied to an accounting programme. Lots of openings with all the young men off to war."

"So, he's not going to wait for the war to end?"

"No. He figures when it does, there'll be a flood of applicants, and he hopes to get a jump on everyone else."

"That makes sense." They arrived at the farm and paused outside the main outbuilding. "Do you think he will want to move to a big city once he has an accounting degree?"

"He reckons there are enough opportunities in Weymouth. He wants to help with managing the farm. Thinks there's potential to expand our operations with the amount of land we have."

"Sounds like he's thought this through. I have no idea what Martin will do after the war. He hasn't shown an inclination towards any particular vocation. And, I'm sorry to say, I don't think he'll end up in farming."

Nathan laughed. "No. He was good help, but his heart's not in it."

***

Alice had an easier time getting to observer duty the next day. The skies and seas were less busy, but the weather had turned stormy.

All day the transport ships remained in the Weymouth and Portland Harbours. Alice and Nathan wondered whether the invasion would actually take place. Perhaps this was just a massive drill?

The following day, they had their answer. By the time Alice arrived, the armada had already begun its exodus from the two harbours. Air activity remained extremely heavy throughout their shift, again leaving no time for conversation. They gave up on recording ship traffic and concentrated on tracking as many of the aircraft as possible.

The sound of air traffic grew throughout the evening and into the night. Alice found it hard to sleep. She kept thinking about

Martin, wondering where he was at that moment and whether she would see him ever again.

Alice awoke to planes. This was beyond anything they had experienced so far. The sound seemed to shake the stone walls of Elm House down to its foundations. She rolled over to look at her bedside alarm clock. It was half past two. People might think she was crazy, but she needed to see what was happening. In her nightgown and robe, she climbed the stairs to their rooftop lookout and opened the door to a wall of sound. Lydia and Irene were already there with her binoculars. A steady stream of aircraft passed overhead, while thousands of winking lights lay spread out across the horizon, working their way east and south.

Irene looked over to her grandmother. "Lydia says they're all headed to France to support the invasion."

"Yes, I believe she's correct." Alice couldn't take her eyes away from the spectacle. She placed her hand on Irene's shoulder as the three watched the sky.

Alice thought again of Martin and Peter. She looked over at Lydia, who had bent over to answer a question from Irene. Of course, Lydia's thoughts would be on Anthony. An operation of this size against an enemy that's spent the past few years fortifying their position—you didn't need a military background to know there would be many casualties.

Alice also thought of Leo. If he was still alive, he was likely in a prison camp. She had read stories about the conditions in those camps. She knew his survival depended on getting him out of the camp as soon as possible. And that meant bringing the war to a swift close. But if this operation failed—Alice couldn't bear to think about it. She squeezed Irene's shoulder. She tried to concentrate on those around her.

CHAPTER 35

France, June 1944

MARTIN'S COMPANY WOVE THEIR way up the beach past blackened tangles barely recognizable as tanks and landing craft. Everywhere they stepped over boots, helmets, discarded cartons, and items of clothing, each telling its own story to anyone who took notice. Above them, the now-silent gun emplacements hung menacingly over the beach. Martin realised just how fortunate they were—assigned to day three of the assault. There had been no debrief on the cost of securing this beach, but they had heard the rumours which their eyes now confirmed. The bodies were cleared, but the men could not escape filling in the blanks, each building their own understanding of the grim toll suffered by those in the first wave.

Clusters of German POWs waited to board the just-vacated transports. He thought he saw relief in their faces. The war was probably over for them. They had survived.

No one spoke as they marched across the sand. The beach had become both terrifying and sacred. When they reached the top of the bluff, Martin soon wished they could return to the beach. The stench was almost unbearable. There had not yet been time to clear away the livestock caught in the crossfire of the intense battle. Howard stepped out of line and heaved his long-ago breakfast into the grass.

The warships just off shore continued sending salvos over their heads as they marched inland under a hot afternoon sun. They passed through an orchard, but the apples were for cider and too bitter to eat. A farmhouse was smoldering at the far end of the orchard. As they drew closer, Martin noticed an older couple, about the age of his grandmother, sitting on a stone bench. They did not turn or acknowledge the soldiers filing past them but continued staring out towards their orchard. Behind them were only piles of brick and charred timbers. They were holding hands. Martin wanted to do something to help them, but his job was to keep marching.

Towards evening the company joined up with the rest of their battalion at a village—only two of the homes left intact. Here, at last, they could catch a meal and some time to write letters home. Martin was eager to reassure the folks back in Weymouth that he was okay. Jack came over to join Martin and Howard. Jack never lacked for friends, but for reasons Martin could not understand, he continued to prefer their company.

They had seen so much that day. For all three of them, this was their first time off the island of Britain. And now they really were in the thick of war. There seemed no hope of sleep, even though their day had started well before daylight. They lay side-by-side, using their packs for pillows, and gazed at the river of stars covering the moonless sky. Explosions continued in the distance. "What do you chaps plan to do, once this bloody business is done?" Jack asked.

Martin had no idea, but Howard responded immediately. Apparently, this was something to which he had devoted some thought.

"Electronics is the future. I've got some ideas I want to see to. The challenge will be which one to focus on first. Just need some space and a bit of equipment." He went on to describe how he taught himself the workings of radios by tinkering with an old broken set. Before the war, he earned money from neighbours and friends by repairing radios, clocks, and anything else mechanical.

"What about you? Returning to your boats?" Martin asked. Like his father and grandfather, Jack had been a shipbuilder before the war. Employment in a vital industry provided a deferment from enlisting. That is, until he reached the point where he could no longer stand remaining on the sidelines.

Jack placed his hands behind his head before responding. "Ship-building's a respectable trade, no question about that. But I might fancy something different. The owners will always have good representation. Someone needs to represent the people who actually build the boats—and the trains and houses and keep everything running."

Martin was dumbfounded. He got up on one elbow to look over at Jack. "You want to be a politician?"

"Don't care much for the word 'politician' but yeah. It's the way things get changed in our country."

Martin wouldn't have guessed that about Jack, but there was no denying that he would likely succeed in getting himself elected. The three men fell silent. Martin tried to think about his future. He had no idea what he wanted from it.

The next morning saw them up before dawn and continuing their march inland. A small village came into view, but German infantry held all the strategic positions and were determined to slow or stop their advance. The village had to be cleared. The ear-shattering shells that flew over their heads all the previous day were supposed to prepare the way for them. But the Germans had simply waited it out in village cellars and reemerged once the shelling stopped.

Martin had pinned his hopes on the success of the D-Day invasion—that it would cause great demoralisation among the Germans. Those hopes were quickly banished. It was Martin's first taste of the ferocity and cunning of battle-hardened soldiers. The fighting progressed slowly from house to house until the few remaining Germans surrendered late that afternoon. The price of the village was three lives, but none of the casualties were people Martin knew. The assault had been led by those with more experience, while those fresh out of training provided cover and backup.

They continued their march eastward. Around dusk, they reached a stream and camped along its banks. Meals only happened when there was a break in the action, and no opportunity went wasted.

That evening, Martin lay awake thinking about his first day of actual fighting. He had seen men killed in battle before, from the lookout at the top of Elm House back in Weymouth. It was different being up close, knowing that you could be next. He wasn't sure he could ever grow accustomed to being so closely acquainted with death. But he found some reassurance in that he had faced his first battle, and now that hurdle was behind him.

Despite all that was circling in his head, his dog-tired body eventually won out. The next thing he knew, someone was shaking his shoulder. It was time to face another day.

They continued their march inland until mid-morning. The battalion paused while Martin's company was sent ahead to deal with a German machine gun post at the top of a hill overlooking the route forward. They had to be dislodged before the battalion could proceed up the road that followed the stream heading east.

The company split into its three platoons. Martin's platoon and one other platoon flanked the post on either side. Their job was to draw attention away from the third platoon, which circled the hill to mount an attack from the rear.

Martin's platoon worked up the left flank through tall grass, pausing when they reached an old stone storage shed. From there they made a dash to a small gulley and then further uphill to the shelter of an outcropping. At that point there was no clear path forward, so they hunkered down to wait for the rear attack to materialise.

Something landed a few feet in front of Martin. For a fraction of a second he marvelled at the luck or skill of the precise throw of the grenade from such a distance. Someone pushed him roughly aside, hurling past him and falling on the grenade just as it detonated, taking the full force of the explosion. There was only one person who had such lightning quick reactions. "Jack!" Martin yelled. He tried to turn over what remained of the body. A hand on his shoulder, pulled him back.

Martin turned. It was Jack's hand on his shoulder. His face was white. Martin turned back to the body. "But, who?"

"Howard," Jack replied. "He jumped before I could stop him." Turning to the rest of the men, "We need to move, now! They've got our number."

Jack grabbed both of Martin's shoulders and turned him away from their friend. The group fell back to their previous position. Eddie took a hit, and dropped to the ground. But he quickly regained his footing, and joined the others.

The group huddled together in the shelter of the gulley. Two of their party attended to Eddie, ripping away his shirt. His shoulder was bleeding profusely, but the wound was quickly wrapped. He looked to be okay.

Martin watched all this as if a long distance away. None of it mattered. He was trying to understand what had just taken place further up the hill. It could not have been Howard who jumped on the grenade. Jack must be mistaken. Howard couldn't react that quickly if his life depended on it. Howard must be somewhere with their group. He looked around at his comrades crouching in the gulley. Everyone was present, except Howard. The realisation hit like a bale of hay dropped from the high rafters of Nathan's outbuilding. For once in his short life, Howard had reacted quickly—when someone else's life depended on it. He had saved Martin's life.

They heard gunshots above them. The ambush had started. His platoon got to their feet. It was time to work their way back up the hill and join the assault.

Martin didn't move. They killed Howard. They meant to kill Martin. Instead, they killed Howard. They took him away just as they had taken away his parents. Germans were not normal people. They thought they were superior to everyone else, but they were common murderers—that's all.

Someone nudged Martin's shoulder. "We need to move out." Martin looked up and stared at him. Suddenly, he jumped to his feet and took off, running past the other members of the platoon, charging recklessly up the hill.

"Martin!" Jack called after him. But Martin ignored him, sprinting past. The Germans would pay. He didn't pause when he reached the top, vaulting over the low wall of the gun emplacement.

The machine guns were all turned, fending off the rear attack. Over the noise of the battle, no one heard Martin land in their midst. Remembering Sargent Mallory's boxing training, he slammed his fist into the back of the head of the closest machine gunner, knocking him onto the far wall. The soldier never knew what hit him. Martin grabbed his gun, an MG42, and pivoted it sideways, mowing down the remaining gunners just as they began to realise what was happening.

It took a minute for the third platoon to realise that the machine guns were silent. Their objective had been secured. Suddenly everything was quiet, except for Martin's panting breath. He didn't wait for the others to reach him. He jumped the wall and trudged back down the hill, past the remaining members of his platoon. Jack jumped up and fell in alongside Martin. Neither spoke while they walked back to where the battalion was waiting for the signal to move forward.

All afternoon they marched east. This allowed plenty of time for events to sink in. Howard was gone. Their threesome had been blown apart. All the times Martin wished they were not saddled with Howard, and now there was a gaping hole that only Howard could fill. He thought Howard was going to get him killed, but it turned out Howard saved his life. He couldn't think about it any longer. Had to get his mind on something else.

Then it hit him that he had killed another human being. In fact, he had killed seven people. Now that they were dead, they suddenly seemed more human. They had mothers and fathers, sisters and brothers. They had probably grown up in circumstances not terribly different from Martin's. Probably some of them—maybe most of them—didn't want to be fighting this war. And now, their short lives were over. He had ended them.

This was too much. Martin tried to focus on the marching. One, two—one, two. Deaden your brain. Stare at the back of the head of the soldier marching in front of you.

That evening Jack and Martin bivouacked on the ground together. The dynamics were entirely different without Howard. Things felt tense and constrained. Jack could often be inscrutable and Martin withdrawn. Although Martin had not realised it, Howard had been their catalyst. His honesty and openness disarmed them both, and the relationship had flowed.

They stared up at the stars, each in their private thoughts. Jack broke the silence. "Storming the gun post like you did today—no denying that was brave, and I understand why you did it. But I hope you don't get into the habit of that sort of thing." Martin remained silent. After a minute, Jack continued. "There's plenty enough of risk already, so no use in adding second helpings. You're no help for us once you're dead. And I've had my fill of saying goodbye to folks I'm fond of."

Martin kept staring into the night sky. After a bit he replied, "Yeah, okay." He rolled over on his side away from Jack.

CHAPTER 36

Weymouth, June 1944

L YDIA RUSHED MADLY ABOUT the house. This was not unusual. She just was not an early riser, and never had been. Irene waited by the door, tapping her foot impatiently. Lydia slipped on her shoes while balancing her breakfast in one hand—a piece of that awful wartime wheatmeal bread. Even toasting it didn't help much.

Lydia was working full-time at the hospital. She had wanted to make that change ever since she left school, but her mother had forbidden it. While she was delighted to be making her own decisions, always in the background she felt the pain from the rift between herself and her parents.

"Finally." Irene's impatience was an act. Tagging alongside Lydia as a volunteer twice a week was the highlight of what was otherwise a rather dull existence. She would do whatever might be needed—fetching supplies, getting glasses of water for patients, even cleaning out bedpans—because she so badly wanted to be considered an adult. She had seen enough of being the youngest in the family.

As they walked to the hospital, Lydia was only half listening to Irene's chatter. Her thoughts were on Anthony. It had been over a week since the big invasion they now referred to as D-Day, and she had yet to hear from him.

The night before D-Day, Lydia, Alice, and Irene stood and watched the planes pass over by their thousands. It made the immensity of the operation apparent in a way that mere numbers could not. They finally returned to bed at half past four. But Lydia hadn't slept. When daylight came, she returned to the lookout. On the eastern horizon the sky glowed red with the battle already underway. The scene set her mind spinning. Did this mark the beginning of the end, or would it backfire, extending the war far into the future? And what was happening to Anthony at that precise moment? It was no wonder she hadn't slept that night.

She had heard the following day that the invasion was a success. What she still didn't know was how much longer she would be made to wait for news from Anthony. She wrote to him immediately after moving into the Standfield home so that he would have her new address. But she wasn't sure if he had received her letter. What if he wrote to her old address? Would her mother open and read her post? Lydia wasn't sure whether she would stoop that low.

Between Irene's endless chatter and her own thoughts of Anthony, Lydia wasn't paying proper attention to what was taking place around her. The lady up ahead stopped to dig something out of her handbag. She didn't register in Lydia's conscious mind. But her subconscious mind recognised the pretense of delicate mannerisms, the respectable knit sweater and skirt, the outdated ivory gloves with their miniature buttons and fine embroidery. Just at that moment, her mother looked up, and they locked eyes. Her mother's eyes narrowed, and her jaw clenched. She crossed to the other side of the street and continued on her way without a further glance at her daughter.

The incident ended so quickly, that Lydia didn't have time to attempt a greeting or acknowledgement. Just as well, she thought to herself. She didn't want make a scene in front of Irene, who seemed unaware of what just transpired. Lydia quickened her pace, determined to put her mother out of her thoughts so she could give her full attention to the demands that waited for her that day.

Quick to follow the invasion had been a flood of casualties making the reverse trip back to England, including both Allied soldiers and some German prisoners. Most of these went to military hospitals, but some of the overflow came to Weymouth's hospital as well.

Lydia found it hard to face the broken bodies, knowing that the same or worse could befall Anthony—may have already, as far as she knew. And it wasn't just Anthony. She also worried about Martin and the many other boys she knew from Weymouth who were fighting overseas. But she was determined to maintain a positive outlook. The wounded were just coming to terms with damage that, in many cases, would be with them for the rest of their lives. They needed her to be strong, and she owed them that, for the sacrifice they had made.

When Lydia and Irene returned home that evening, a letter addressed to Lydia sat in the basket in the front hall. She dropped her things where she stood and ripped it open. Anthony was in France, but that's all he could say about his location. He had not seen any actual fighting, just transport of supplies, disposal of casualties, and road work. Since his regiment was comprised of negroes, they weren't to be trusted with combat roles. While Lydia couldn't understand why negroes weren't considered capable for combat, she couldn't feel the same indignation that she sensed from Anthony. She was relieved that he was safe, and in comparison, none of the rest seemed important.

As Lydia came into the kitchen, Alice looked up from the counter where she was preparing yet another potato pie. It was Rosa's day off. "What's the news from Anthony?"

"He's okay. He's in France, but he isn't able to say where in France."

"Well, thank goodness he's all right. We also received a letter from Martin today, and he's made it safely to France as well."

"What a relief." Lydia started laying the dining table for tea. When she finished, she asked if there was anything else she could help with.

Alice placed the pie in the oven. "No, we just need to wait for that to finish." She set a fresh pot of tea on the kitchen table and sat down.

Lydia sat across from her. "I want to talk to you about my stay here."

"Alright." Alice poured them each a cup of tea.

"I've already stayed longer than I initially thought I would."

"From my standpoint, it's working well to have you with us."

"I'm glad to hear you say that. Would you consider my living here longer term? I'd pay board, of course. I can afford that now with my working full-time." Lydia was studying Alice's reaction.

"Lydia, I'm delighted to have you with us. And, in case you haven't noticed, so is Irene. You've been easy to have around, and there's certainly enough room in this old house."

Lydia broke into a full smile. "Thank you. That's a load off my mind. I feel at home here, and I don't think I'll ever feel that way living with my mother and father. I'm not sure I can ever forgive them for the way they treated Anthony and me."

Alice took a thoughtful sip of her tea before responding. "Your parents no doubt love you. I think your mother struggles with understanding what's important in your relationship. Under all the to-do over what is or isn't proper, I sense a deep insecurity."

Lydia looked doubtful. "I'm sorry, but I have trouble imagining her as insecure."

"Society doesn't make it easy for us women. It places many expectations on us, yet it doesn't relinquish much power over our own lives. It's understandable that your mother tries to exert control in the only way she knows how to."

Lydia was staring into her teacup. "That's certainly a different way to view things. But it's no excuse for the way she treated Anthony, or for making me no longer welcome in my own home. They continue to treat me as a child."

"No, I suspect you're right. There is no excuse for her behaviour." Alice took another sip of tea. "You're of age. You have a right to be treated as an adult. But you can't force your parents to do that. The only part you can control is your response to them."

"So, you're saying it's all down to me to fix this?"

"No. I'm not even sure the relationship can be fixed—not completely anyway. That's why it's important for you to look forward rather than backward. I see promise in your future."

CHAPTER 37

Belgium, December 1944

MARTIN PROMISED HIMSELF THAT if he did survive this war, he would move to the tropics. He couldn't remember the last time he felt warm. He tried to get their jeep winterised. For reasons beyond Martin's comprehension, Colonel Wootten considered that an unnecessary extravagance. His philosophy seemed to be that a first-rate soldier not only endured hardship—he actively sought it out. So here they were driving about in the coldest weather Martin had ever experienced with no heater. Somehow, this seemed to energise the colonel.

Martin had been recommended as a driver, not just due to his mechanical skills. As it turned out, he was a natural at navigation—able to translate maps into visual images of the terrain and vice versa. Wootten requested him as his driver last July, and he had learned to adapt to the colonel's eccentricities.

To pass the time driving through dreary farmland, he often fantasised about the end of the war. His homecoming became even more of a celebration when Leo suddenly appeared, freed from his POW camp and just returned to England. He and Ellis renewed their friendship as they swapped war stories down at the local pub and without shortages. After Sonja's parents made the trip to visit her in Weymouth, she saw that Martin had been right—they had survived living in the detention centre. She was not so serious all the time. They could laugh together. They could relax. It would feel natural to kiss her.

Martin could sustain these fantasies only for short periods. Like trying to balance a stick on the end of your finger. Inevitably, it would topple over. In reality, there was no news on Leo, so in all likelihood, he was dead. He didn't know if he and Ellis would ever be friends again. And letters from Sonja were few and far between and not in any way intimate. He still didn't know how to interpret her impersonal letters. Was it her writing style and lack of familiarity with the language, or something deeper? He suspected something deeper.

Letters from Lydia were also sparse, despite the fact that she was now living with his grandmother. That news certainly caught him by surprise. Neither Lydia nor his grandmother had shared the circumstances that brought about this living arrangement. Irene, however, wrote something about a disagreement between Lydia and her mother. That didn't surprise Martin. He still chuckled when he remembered Lydia's mother marching her out of the café after Lydia told her she was on shift at the hospital.

The road passed over a bridge, and Martin concentrated on negotiating the icy surface. As the steel-grey darkness deepened, the temperature dropped. He fell into his habit of shaking his left leg to stay warm—that is, whenever it wasn't needed to engage the clutch. At least they were heading back to base camp. That meant sleeping inside an actual building and warm meals. They had been on the road for several days, and their jeep was in need of maintenance and reprovisioning, including restocking spare torch batteries and replacing their smashed compass.

They reached camp just in time for supper, and immediately following, Martin fell into bed. The cold air of their bunkhouse kept trying to invade his bed, slipping under the edges of his blanket. He wrapped the blanket tightly around his body. He felt he had only just gone to sleep when someone shook his shoulder.

"Hey, mate. Wootten's asking for you. We're mobilising."

Martin groaned. His body rebelled at the thought of stepping out in the frigid air to dress.

"What's up?" Martin was trying to stall. A light had been flipped on, and he could see his breath. Others were already up.

"The colonel's been called to some high-level meeting. You know what he's like. You best get a move on."

Martin stepped out of bed, dressed, and threw together his belongings.

"Bloody Krauts. Pick the shittiest weather for an offensive," he heard someone complain.

"Heard said they've pushed through our lines at Ardennes," another responded.

Martin recalled Wootten complaining about the Ardennes. Said that it was their weak link, and that it would come back to bite them. Apparently, he had been right. So much for Martin's hope of spending Christmas in the relative comfort of base camp. Outside, he walked briskly to the officer's quarters through a steady wind. A scattering of pellet-like snowflakes hit his face like miniature needles.

As usual, Martin was told where but not why, nor how long. He picked up spare torch batteries, but there was not time to replace their smashed compass. He consulted his maps by light of the torch they kept in the jeep and then waited for the colonel.

By the time they set out, the sky was displaying the first hints of daylight along the horizon. Martin knew from his geography class that, as it was close to winter solstice, the sunrise was in the southeast. They were heading into unfamiliar territory, so Martin memorised the hills, streams, and intersections on their route.

Wootten was less energised than the previous day. At first, Martin put that down to his usual moodiness. He figured the colonel had also been looking forward to a relatively quiet Christmas. Then he heard him muttering about the counteroffensive and the damned Allied overconfidence. Perhaps the situation was more serious than Martin had at first realised. Having ample experience with the colonel's moods, Martin deemed it best to keep quiet.

Around lunchtime, they approached an intersection, and Martin turned right. The colonel erupted. "Where in God's name are you taking us?"

"To the town of Dinant, sir. Did I misunderstand your orders?"

"Dinant is to the west. Why are you heading east?"

Under thick cloud cover, there were no celestial navigation aids, and they had no compass. "With respect, sir, we are heading west."

"And I'm telling you we're heading in the wrong direction. I've been through this country before. Now turn this contraption around."

Martin hesitated. Wootten glared at him. Reluctantly, he did a u-turn. They preceded in the opposite direction for about a half hour, before Martin dared to speak up again. "Sir, can we consult the map? This town should not be on our itinerary."

"Standfield, how many times have you been to Belgium?"

"This is my first time, sir."

"So, you were not here at the beginning of the war? You're seeing this territory for the first time?"

"Yes, sir."

"Yet, you feel sufficiently confident to contradict your superior officer."

"Yes, sir." The words came out before Martin realised what he was saying.

Wootten's face turned Christmas red. "You will keep driving as I say, and I will hear nothing more on the subject!"

Martin was certain they were off course but thought it inadvisable to say anything further. They continued in silence. A short distance further they heard the all-too-familiar sound of shells. One exploded fifty yards to their right. "What the hell! We're being shelled by our own men!"

"Sir, I don't think those are our guns."

"What? No, we're nowhere near German lines."

Another explosion. This time on their left.

"Permission to turn around, sir."

"Yes, and quickly. When I get my hands on the imbecile who ordered these men to fire at us."

Martin did the fastest three-point turn he could and raced off in the opposite direction. The next shell landed just behind them. Martin thought about varying his speed to throw off the sighters, but Wootten told him to floor it, and Martin was happy to oblige.

As they came over a short rise, a cow blocked the road ahead of them. Martin slammed the brakes, sending himself and Wootten onto the dashboard. Martin laid on the horn, but the cow simply looked up to stare at them. And then, the cow was gone.

It took Martin a moment to realise what had just happened. Wooten didn't say anything. He stared straight ahead, his hand on the dashboard as if needing support. Martin realised that, had the cow not obstructed their route, they, instead of the cow, would have met the shell's trajectory. He drove the jeep up onto the verge, around the crater, and they sped on their way.

Wootten remained silent the rest of the trip. He never acknowledged that it was his mistake and his obstinance that almost got them both killed. When they arrived at the town of Dinant, they were more than three hours late.

Two weeks later, Martin was transferred to a new unit. He assumed that Wootten was to blame for his reassignment. He had been in the army long enough to know that, with people like Wootten, to make a mistake was frowned upon, but to prove your superior to be mistaken, that was unforgivable.

CHAPTER 38

Weymouth, March 1945

ALL ACROSS WEYMOUTH, DAFFODILS and blue scilla infused the landscape with colour so vivid it felt like ages had passed since their last appearance. The approach of spring brought an optimism not seen through six long years of war. Everyone was desperately eager for victory, but at least that victory now seemed inevitable.

Alice remained deeply anxious about her grandchildren, Peter Gurin, and others still fighting. And although Helen seldom discussed it during her frequent visits, her anxiety for Sidney was ever present just below the surface. To lose any of them so close to the end would seem especially cruel.

Alice also thought often about Lydia. She was a spark in their household. Why was her mother unable to appreciate the daughter she had? She decided that, unlike her other worries, she could do something to try to help Lydia. Whenever possible, she adjusted her schedule so that her in-town errands occurred in the early morning, knowing that Elizabeth likewise favoured early-mornings.

Eventually, her plan succeeded, and their paths crossed. Alice spotted her emerging from the greengrocer, and made a beeline to intercept her. Elizabeth looked up, saw Alice and started to turn the other way.

"Elizabeth! Please, could I have a short word?" Alice tried to make her face and voice friendly. She was not looking for a confrontation.

Elizabeth looked ready to bolt but hesitated just long enough. "What do you want?"

"I simply would like to talk to you, mother-to-mother. Please. I would consider it a great favour if you could spare a few minutes. Can we sit for a bit?" Alice gestured to the tea shop adjacent to the grocer.

With a frown, Elizabeth followed Alice into the shop where they found a table in a secluded corner. Elizabeth placed her shopping on an empty chair and sat down, staring across at Alice, still frowning.

After they placed their order, Alice looked over and tried to smile without coming across as condescending.

"Mostly, I want to thank you."

This caught Elizabeth off guard. Alice could see her trying to discern what trap Alice had set for her.

Alice continued, "You've clearly done an exemplary job in raising Lydia. We have so much enjoyed her visit with us." She purposely tried to portray Lydia's stay as temporary. "She's a positive influence on Irene. I've been so worried about her ever since her parents were killed. Lydia has brought her out of her shell, something I've been unable to do."

Elizabeth still said nothing, but she looked even less sure of herself. Alice's praise for Lydia and her depiction of her struggles with Irene were both genuine. She thought that openness and honesty might create the best chance to disarm and connect with her, while avoiding loss of face on Elizabeth's part.

Keeping her voice light, she continued. "Also, I was wondering what you've found out, so far, about Anthony?"

"Anthony? Is that his name?"

"Yes. I did have the opportunity to meet him—quite by accident. I thought you might be interested to know a bit more about him?"

Elizabeth looked conflicted. "Did he talk his way past you as well?"

Alice ignored that. "I found him to be articulate. He has an interest in literature. That's what he was studying before the war."

"He was at university?" Elizabeth struggled to maintain her show of disinterest.

"Yes, studying to be a secondary school teacher in literature. He wants to continue his university studies once the war is over."

Elizabeth was silent. Alice could see that the new information contradicted the picture she had formed. Alice continued, "I think that you have raised an astute daughter. She's a good judge of character."

Alice decided that this was sufficient progress for an initial discussion. Elizabeth would need time to consider the new information, and Alice didn't want to push too hard or too fast. Better to leave her wanting more. She took another sip of tea. "Well, that was all. I just wanted you to know we're grateful to have Lydia with us for a time. She's a credit to you." She reached a hand across to Elizabeth. "Your daughter loves you."

She had gone too far. Elizabeth pulled her hand away from Alice.

"What do you know about Lydia? Lying to us. Sneaking behind our backs. Disobeying us." She paused. "I do understand what it is to be smitten by someone, but an American negro? They are from different worlds. Do you really think that could end well for her?" She paused again, studying Alice. "You want to talk about family? I know a few things about yours. You think you kept Edgar satisfied?" She stared at Alice, watching her reaction.

Alice sat back in her chair. It took a minute for Elizabeth's statement to register. "Whatever are you talking about?"

Elizabeth didn't answer. She smiled triumphantly and then rose from the table, leaving Alice to pay for the tea.

Alice couldn't move. What did she mean by, "You think you kept Edgar satisfied"? That Edgar had been unfaithful? Alice had never considered the possibility. Edgar was too formal, too proper. She couldn't picture it. Certainly not with Elizabeth. The thought was ludicrous. But then with whom? He was a judge. There would be too much risk, especially in a small town.

She felt dizzy, almost nauseous. She noticed the waitress watching her and tried to calm herself. That Edgar might have had an affair—it was a ridiculous notion. She tried to force the idea from her mind, but it didn't seem disposed to leave.

When Alice arrived home, she found two letters waiting for her—one addressed to Lydia from Anthony and one addressed to her from Peter. The letter from Peter she tore open immediately.

> *Dear Alice,*
>
> *I hope this finds you doing as well as is possible in these times. I have some news to share. In the military, you become accustomed to the sudden change in plans. Just last week I was across the border into Germany inspecting damage to a strategic bridge, and a few days later I find myself in a field hospital in Belgium. I'm in no danger, but a sniper bullet to my thigh has put an end to my active service. The plan is to ship me stateside for surgery on my femur. I had hopes of stopping by your lovely town upon demobilisation, but that's not to be.*
>
> *Thanks again for your hospitality and friendship in showing me around Weymouth, which has truly been the one*

highlight in this entire ghastly business. I hope that we will have an opportunity for more bird expeditions at some point in the future, but when and on which continent, I couldn't say.

I hope for a speedy conclusion to this awful war and that Martin and Leo will both soon be home, safe and sound. Please keep me informed. I've included my home address below.

Yours,

Peter Gurin

Alice mostly felt relief from reading the letter. She, of course, felt awful about Peter's injury. But now she knew that at least one person from her worry list had survived the war. Leo was another matter. The absence of news was so very worrying. Each day she reminded herself that dwelling on things over which she had no control served no purpose.

She sat down at Edgar's old desk and stared out at the leaves just budding forth on her elm tree. Unbidden, Elizabeth's comment returned. "You think you kept Edgar satisfied?" After almost forty years, had she really known Edgar? Had he ever let down the wall of formality? Ever said anything that was truly from his heart?

CHAPTER 39

Germany, April 1945

EACH NEW VILLAGE LOOKED the same as the last one. Mothers and children, gaunt, empty, and pale, came out to stare. All the able-bodied males had been swallowed by war. Everyone knew the end was near. Their weariness prepared them for defeat—anything to end their misery.

Some of Martin's comrades seemed to soak up the weariness, both from the villages they passed and from the sheer monotony of years at war. You could only spend so long in a state of high alert before that too turned into weariness.

Others in his unit became reckless in a way Martin found disturbing. They took unnecessary risks, broke curfew, ignored orders with no thought for the consequences. There were explosions of violence towards the enemy that went beyond the norms of war.

Martin felt lost, as if alone at sea and trying to swim to a shoreline that was a distant line of grey. He also felt a heightened wariness. He could no longer approach personal danger with the grim fatalism that soldiers, of necessity, adapt. Becoming a casualty no longer felt inevitable. Instead, the prospect of being killed had transformed into an ironic tragedy. To be within sight of safety and then to have your life snatched away. The uncertainty wore on everyone's nerves.

Driver duty provided a reprieve. Motoring an officer around the countryside entailed less risk than clearing the last fanatical holdouts from the ruins of a village. Today they were to take charge of a camp under terms negotiated with the retreating Germans. The camp was experiencing a typhus outbreak, and the Germans were concerned that a disorderly transition could result in disease being spread among the general population.

All camouflage had to be removed from their vehicles. Under a flag of truce, they proceeded through no-man's-land and then crossed over German lines. Their detachment consisted of less than forty men, and Martin felt unnerved to be so outnumbered. The enemy knew they were fighting a lost cause, and Martin understood that such demoralising conditions could produce erratic behaviour. German soldiers lined the road with their hostile stares. None of them talked or moved. The only sound was that of their detachment's vehicles.

They reached the camp without incident. It looked completely unremarkable and mostly empty, with a large parade ground, some barracks, and a few administrative buildings. Behind the barracks stood a pine forest. The silence felt unnatural.

Despite the gathering darkness, they pushed on into the forest, eerily illuminated by their torches. Martin started noticing bodies here and there. He had become used to seeing bodies. He assumed that, with the typhus outbreak, the Germans had been overwhelmed and not able to keep up with burying all those who had succumbed.

The further they went, the more bodies they found, some stacked in small heaps. The air was foul. As they approached the shelters, Martin realised something was horribly wrong. There were bodies everywhere, piles and piles of them. Some prisoners were walking about, but they resembled skeletons more than people. The smell became overpowering. He was thankful his last meal had been long ago. Otherwise, he was sure that he would be seeing it again.

It was a scene worthy of one's most horrifying nightmare, and Martin found it hard to believe the images in front of him were real. He looked over to Andrew, one of his comrades, and he shook his head, saying nothing.

At first, the prisoners shrank from them, those who could move. Then a few realised that their uniforms were British. Word began to spread. There was jubilation as the starving hordes began pressing in on them, begging for food. A man knelt and started kissing Martin's boots. He tried pulling the man to his feet, but he seemed unable to regain his footing. Martin wished he could do something. They had not brought supplies with them.

The prisoners greatly outnumbered the camp guards. Some of the prisoners began to realise that, with the British in charge, the guards were no longer allowed to shoot indiscriminately. Martin and Andrew were pushed back by the swelling crowd. The prisoners became bolder. They demanded food.

"We need to find the others," Martin called over to Andrew. They retreated to joined the rest of their group who were using hand signals to communicate with the prisoners but with limited success. Their group leader was busy identifying those prisoners who could help with translation. The camp had been filled from all corners of Europe, and in the chaos, it was hard to tell who spoke which language. Eventually, they identified a group of interpreters, and they spread the message that they did not have food supplies with them but that help would be arriving soon.

Reinforcements did arrive the following morning. But the daylight illuminated the monstrous conditions with brutal clarity. Martin and Andrew watched as prisoners walked aimlessly, unaware of where they were going. When they bumped into other prisoners, they simply walked off in a new direction. Those were the ones who were well off—still able to walk. Many were too weak to move. Some that they initially thought were dead, turned out to be alive. It was hard to tell the living from the dead. Some from their group shared their rations with the prisoners, and the results were disastrous. The rich food turned deadly for those who had been starved for so long.

Andrew looked over at Martin. "I know the Jerrys had food shortages, but these people are emaciated."

"How long do you suppose the camp's been without food?" Martin promised himself he would never again complain about food rationing back home.

As more help arrived, Martin's detachment returned to the main camp, passing through the pine forest that had felt dark and foreboding the previous night. In daylight, Martin stared at the trees, at the blue sky overhead. How could such tranquility exist alongside what was the closest thing to hell that Martin could imagine? He concentrated on the structure of the branches, the soft spray of needles, the texture of bark. Trying desperately to cleanse his mind of other images that he was just realising would haunt him to the end of his days.

Upon reaching the main camp, they began a survey of the administrative buildings. They found an infirmary, but it was empty. People were dying by the thousands, and no one had been receiving treatment. Another building turned out to be a supply warehouse. Martin stepped inside, and Andrew followed. They stood and stared, not believing what they were seeing. Huge crates of food stocks were stacked into long rows.

"There was no food shortage." Andrew spat the words. "Those bloody bastards have been deliberately starving these people!"

Martin stared in disbelief, incapable of words. He would not have thought humans capable of this level of cruelty. He and Andrew turned to rejoin the others.

Among the German soldiers, they found SS men and women. These were arrested on the spot. Their safe passage was not part of the negotiations with the Germans, and they were put to work burying their own victims. Many of them needed convincing to undertake the work, and Martin and his comrades were only too happy to oblige. They marked off an area the size of a football pitch and began digging a pit large enough to accommodate the thousands and thousands of dead.

The following day, more help arrived, and Martin's detachment returned to their battalion. The rest of the war was a blur for Martin. At night when he closed his eyes and tried to sleep, he saw piles of corpses, while those who were nearly corpses walked about like zombies. His clothing had picked up the smell of the camp, and he'd not had an opportunity to wash or exchange his uniform. He feared the smell would never leave him.

The day finally came when Martin's battalion met Russian forces advancing from the east. For these two armies, the fighting had at last finished. There was no unclaimed territory left over which to advance. Martin should have felt relief, but he could not feel anything. He remained haunted by Bergen-Belsen, the camp they had liberated, haunted by cruelty that far surpassed anything he witnessed in combat.

That night, the British and the Russians came together to celebrate the end of the campaign. Martin had his first taste of vodka and found it quite useful for obliterating the haunting memories. Through interpreters, the Russians told them of other camps further east, camps worse even than Bergen-Belsen. Those camps were built with the sole purpose of efficiently killing Jews and others considered undesirable by the Nazis. The master race had engineered human extermination by the hundreds of thousands. Martin recalled the news article that appeared nearly three years ago reporting executions on such a scale that Martin dismissed the report as totally implausible.

The next morning Martin suffered the worst headache ever. They were given the day to rest, and he tried to do that. But his mind would not rest. He now knew that Sonja had been right about everything. She had been right to be serious. She told him that hatred had given her the scar, and now, at last, he understood.

He had resented Sonja for being noncommittal regarding her feelings for him. He realised that it was he who had been noncommittal. He had been unable to look unflinchingly into her scarred face, unsure about being close to someone who was publicly marked out. He had doubted her account of her own experiences. Now he was a witness to the depth and force of hatred set loose in the world. He wanted to protect her, to always be there for her.

His mind was set on one thing. He wanted to return to Weymouth, to tell Sonja that he was ready to stand with her. The war could not end soon enough.

CHAPTER 40

Weymouth, May 1945

ALICE HAD NEVER SEEN this many people gathered in Weymouth. Hitler was dead, and Germany had surrendered three days ago. Alice, Irene, and Lydia made their way to the esplanade for the VE Day thanksgiving service. The area was already packed with people, so they contented themselves with listening from the edge of the crowd.

Union flags hung from every pole and building. Alice heard a dance band in the distance, and soon the music was coming through loudspeakers set up along the esplanade. Irene wanted to join the dancing. "Fine, as long as you stick close to Lydia," Alice told her. She smiled as she watched the two excited young women disappear into the crowd.

The man standing in front and slightly to the left of Alice happened to look over his shoulder. Their eyes met. Alice recognised him. It was the mystery man who had shown up at Edgar's graveside service six years ago—the man she had chanced upon in town several years ago. Her first thought was that she must be mistaken. She was caught up in the celebrations, and her mind was inventing things. But when the man immediately turned and tried to disappear into the crowd, she knew it must be him. He made little progress through the densely packed throng, bent on celebration. Alice went after him, reaching out to place a hand on his shoulder. "Please, can you stop for a minute. I just want to talk to you."

Reluctantly, the man turned around. Again, he seemed alarmed at the prospect of speaking with Alice. Although he was six years older than when she first spotted him at Edgar's burial, he still brought to mind a younger version of Henry. She was afraid he might bolt at any moment, so she spoke quickly. "I know you were at Edgar's service. Are you his son?"

The shock on the man's face echoed her own shock over the words that came unbidden. The realisation that Edgar had an illegitimate child had been growing in her subconscious, but she hadn't wanted to face it. Gazing directly into this man's face, she knew from his reaction that it was true.

"Please, don't run off again. I simply want to know the truth."

He hesitated. Alice wondered why he was so conflicted about talking to her. Finally, he assented. "Is there somewhere quiet where we can talk?"

Alice doubted that there was anywhere in all of England that was quiet on that particular day, but she suggested a nearby café where they were fortunate to find a small table in a back corner. They ordered tea, and the man began his story.

"You're right. Edgar was my father. I didn't know this until I started university. My mother didn't want to tell me, but I persisted. She finally relented under the condition that I would never share the information, or try to approach your family."

"You've kept your promise. I was the one who approached you."

"No. I shouldn't have come to Edgar's service! I thought I could remain anonymous. I just wanted to know who my father was." The man looked down at his teacup, uncomfortable with what he had shared.

"Of course, you wanted to know. Anyone in your position would have felt the same." Alice thought she would be devastated by the confirmation that Edgar had been unfaithful. But ever since Elizabeth made her veiled accusation, she had been coming to terms with the truth. It fit the pattern of their marriage. Now, she found herself wanting to help this young man who seemed rather lost. And she felt some commonality in that they were both seeking the truth. "Do you mind telling me your name?"

He looked up at her. "James Edgar Moore. Yes, I was named after your husband—my middle name anyway. I have my mother's last name."

Alice stared into James's eyes. She was fighting back tears. "James, do you know who else you were named after?" He shook his head. "You have a half-brother named James. Diphtheria took him when he was only four. We also lost his infant sister at the same time."

James's eyes widened. "Mrs. Standfield, forgive me. It was a mistake to intrude on your family. I had no intention to raise painful memories."

"There's nothing to forgive. I'm glad you've turned up. You've provided missing pieces for me as well. Have you always lived in Weymouth?"

"No. My mother moved to Southampton to live with her sister just before I was born. I moved back here after finishing university. I don't know if you know this, but your husband paid for my schooling. That was partly why I felt I needed to know who he was. My mother always worked outside the home, but Mr. Standfield helped support us. She had originally worked as a clerk in the district courthouse, and that's how she and Edgar met."

Alice leaned back in her chair, cupping her hands around her teacup as if that might provide stability. This was almost too much to take in. She didn't begrudge the money. They always had enough of that. And this young man seemed a grateful and worthy cause. It was the fact that so much had gone on for so many years without her knowledge. Yet it did explain Edgar. He had always been pompous and aloof. But after they lost their two youngest, it was as if she'd lost him as well. There had been no life left in that home.

She tried to refocus on the man sitting in front of her. He met her eyes with a look of concern that she had never received from Edgar. Not wanting to break down in front of him, she grasped for something to keep the conversation moving. "Does your mother still live in Southampton?"

"No. She passed on while I was at university. That was why I felt I could risk coming to Weymouth. She was adamant about not disrupting your lives. But with her passing, I thought there would be nothing left to connect me with your family. That's why I thought it would be safe to attend the service. I hadn't counted on someone so astutely observing."

"You do resemble my son, Henry." Alice started recovering her composure. "There's no doubt that you're a Standfield. Do you live in Weymouth now?"

They were interrupted by cheering and clapping all around the café. Someone had propped open the door to bring in the dance music from the loudspeakers out on the street. Tables were pushed to the side, and several couples started dancing in the centre of the café.

James smiled at all the excitement and then turned back to face Alice. "I've just been demobilised. I was serving in the Royal Navy in the Mediterranean. I'm not sure where I go from here."

"Well, I hope you decide to stay in Weymouth." Did Alice really mean that? Did she want the entire town talking about Edgar and his infidelity?

Alice gave James her telephone number, and he wrote down his temporary address for her. Alice realised she needed to find Irene and Lydia. They would be wondering where she'd gone.

The following morning, she dropped in on Helen. She needed to tell someone about what she'd learned, and her neighbour seemed the safest choice.

Helen was over the moon. She'd just received a telegram from her son Sidney. He was in Naples but would be on a ship home next week. Helen pulled a bottle of sherry from the top shelf of her jam cupboard. "I think this calls for a little celebration, don't you?"

"Splendid idea."

Celebration was a common theme. Personally, Alice couldn't fully celebrate. She kept thinking of Leo, wondering if he was still alive. She would celebrate once she had Martin back safe and at least, knew what had happened to Leo. But she might never know Leo's fate. She had known that sort of thing to happen in the Great War. She wouldn't share any of this with Helen. At least not on this day when she had so much to celebrate.

Over sips of sherry, Helen updated her on her granddaughter, who would soon turn six but was an infant when she last saw her father. "He'll be a complete stranger to her and maybe to the rest of us. Folks are changed by war. We saw that with the last one."

"Sid always was a sensible one. I have great confidence they will be back to being a normal family in no time."

Once they had talked out Sid's return, Alice brought up her own recent revelation. She started from the beginning, the stranger at Edgar's service, the chance encounter in town, the words from Elizabeth Chambers when she was trying to extract revenge on Alice, and finally all that had transpired the previous day.

"He seemed the nicest young man, and he was truly upset that he had betrayed his mother's confidence." Alice stared out

Helen's side window. Yesterday had been sunny—perfect weather for celebrating their victory over Nazism. Today it was raining lightly and windy.

"Do you plan to maintain contact with him?"

Alice turned her attention back to Helen. "I'm not sure that would be wise."

"Why is that?"

"This is just the fodder Elizabeth needs to spread stories all over Weymouth. What will that do to Edgar's reputation? How will Irene and Martin feel about their grandfather when they find out? I'm angry at Edgar. But he's dead. Tarnishing his name won't benefit anyone."

"What about you? What do you want?"

Alice knew the answer to that, but she couldn't respond right away. She found herself instinctively drawn to James. He could never replace her little James, nor Lilian, but he felt like family. And he had no other family left. Alice thought that was what he was really seeking. "I want to adopt him!" she finally said.

"Well, in my view, none of the rest matters. If this damages Edgar's reputation, that's his own doing. As for Elizabeth—the sort of person who gains her approval is not sort I want for a friend. And that person is not the Alice Standfield I've been neighbour to all these years. Time to quit fishing in that pond, from my way of thinking."

Alice laughed at that. "I suppose you're right. Why has her opinion mattered all these years?"

Helen poured Alice a little more sherry. "She's a busybody and a curtain twitcher. My mum used to say, 'Folks who watch and judge their neighbours are the ones most fearful of being judged.'"

"She certainly carries a lot of anxiety about her daughter. That's what drove them apart." Alice took a sip before continuing. "The thing is, Martin and Irene have always looked up to their grandfather. Is it wise to subject them to this? Irene especially is so impressionable."

"Another thing my mum used to say, 'No point telling a child brambles don't have thorns. They find out one way or another.' Don't you think they deserve the truth? And maybe they'd like having another uncle."

"Perhaps they would." Alice was lost for a moment in thought. "Anyway, I'd best be back home. Promised Irene we'd try to find her a new dress today. She's hit another growth spurt." Alice got up from the table. "Helen, you always make things sound simple. I'm not sure this one is."

"Well, you're the one who needs to decide. Just my thoughts, for what they're worth."

As Alice headed home, she smiled to herself, thinking about Helen's advice. She wished things could be as straightforward as Helen made them out. But there were other considerations. For example, she had already taken three people under her wing. Did she have the resilience to become involved with another? Irene was just coming of age. Alice had never raised a daughter, and her own coming of age had been a disaster. She felt daunted by the prospect of guiding Irene through that period. And the poor girl had already experienced the loss of her parents. Then there was Leo. If he does return, what shape will he be in? What help will he need, mentally and physically? And she couldn't forget Martin, the one who always *was* forgotten between his older brother and younger sister. What has he been through, and how has it changed him?

She would turn sixty-four this year. Where was she to find the stamina for all this? She already felt a diminished energy. War had taken its toll on her as well. She'd given up on ever finishing her book on the natural history of Dorset. That was probably never going to happen. A small sacrifice in the context of all that was taking place around her. It was better not to dwell on it.

***

The day after VE Day, Lydia was back working at the hospital. The previous day had been a hoot, celebrating with Irene. The girl was still an innocent. Innocence seemed scarce these days. She thought Irene would come through okay.

She wasn't as sure about herself. It had been a month since she'd heard from Anthony. She prayed that he had survived the war and was doing alright. No telling how long before he would be demobilised. She'd heard from another returning serviceman that the negro regiments were last in line for transport home.

For the past year, all she thought about was whether Anthony would survive. Now, with the end in sight, she had to face the reality of what her future might look like. Contrary to what a lot of people thought of her, she was one to always deal in facts. She allowed others to assume that her thoughts skimmed across the surface. The truth was, she considered her actions carefully.

Was she really prepared to marry Anthony? Yes, she was very much in love with him. But she was not one to believe that love magically fixed everything. First, where would they live? America scared her. She had seen photographs of negroes being lynched. And Anthony would be a target if he was married to a white woman. No use trying to pretend otherwise. She would not live in a place where her life would forever be shadowed by fear.

They could try to live in England, but they would likely be rejected there as well. Were they willing to put up with that rejection? If they had children, how would they be treated? And was Anthony really willing to move here? He said he was, but she knew that saying and doing were two different things. What about his mother living alone back in Chicago? Would he be willing to leave her behind? Would they try to move her to England to live with them? She might not want to leave her friends and move to a new country where it would be unlikely that she would feel welcomed or at home.

And how would they support themselves? There would be no help from her parents. She was sure of that. She didn't think Anthony's mother was in a position to help them financially either. They would be on their own. What were his prospects for finding work? There would be many returning servicemen, and as a foreigner and a negro, she knew Anthony would be last in line.

She loved Anthony, and she wanted it to work. But they needed a plan. She didn't think Anthony was the planning type. He liked to dream. Probably a result of reading all those books of his.

"Lydia, for heaven's sake! Where is your head today?"

It was the charge nurse. Lydia realised to her horror that she had left the patient's used bedpan on the bedside table, as if it were his food tray. She quickly snatched it away. She would have to put away thoughts of her future. Time to concentrate on the day in front of her.

CHAPTER 41

Germany, June 1945

A MONTH HAD PASSED SINCE they liberated Bergen-Belsen. Still the nightmares continued. Emaciated corpses clawing and pulling, begging for help. Sometimes it was Sonja being pulled into the vast pit where they had buried the thousands of victims, sometimes it was Leo, and sometimes it was Martin himself. He was ashamed of all the times he awoke in the night, screaming, jumping out of bed. The others in his unit told him they understood. But those who had not been there, had not seen with their own eyes, they would never really understand.

Their work now consisted primarily of sorting refugees. There seemed to be no end to them and from all corners of Europe speaking all manner of languages. Everyone was in search of lost family members. In fact, most were on their own and desperate for word on what had happened to their loved ones. Their job was to help them register and provide some food. Then they were sent on their way, as desperate as when they arrived.

Martin heard it said that their battalion was staying mostly to prevent the Russian advance from swallowing all of Germany. Already the powers-that-be were calibrating for the next conflict.

The news that kept Martin going came via a letter from his grandmother. She had heard from Leo. After being taken prisoner in Italy, the Germans shipped him to a prisoner of war camp in Poland. The camp was liberated by the Russians, after which it had taken weeks for him to be turned over to the British. But he was on his way home, which is more than Martin could boast. His grandmother had no news on Leo's condition, physically or mentally. What they did know was that a year and a half in a German prisoner of war camp could not be good.

Martin's camp was near a forest. Whenever Martin had free time, that's where he went. He wandered with no destination in mind, finding tranquil settings where he would sit and observe. He became familiar with the red squirrels and red foxes. The different types of birds became recognizable by sight and sound, although he didn't know their names. He came to realise that their world existed entirely separate from Martin's. They did not care that a war was now over, nor who had won. They only appreciated that quiet had a last come to their forest, that they could now go about their lives with less disturbance.

Bergen-Belsen lurked in his head as a deep foreboding, a siren of alarm running night and day, disrupting his ability to concentrate. The forest seemed to be the only thing that muffled his sense of alarm. Sitting among the trees, the siren sounded distant and unimportant.

Martin thought constantly of his return to Weymouth and seeing Sonja. He thought that once he made things right with her, perhaps the sense of alarm would fade. All his focus and energy went into anticipation of his return. He hoped never to set foot in Germany again.

A small village sat near their camp, and Martin walked past it on his way to the forest. He despised the villagers. He knew it wasn't rational, that they personally had not created Bergen-Belsen nor the other German concentration camps. But he still held them responsible, along with every other German. He ignored the villagers as he walked past, and they returned the favour.

He had passed the village, heading towards the forest, when he noticed a cart off the side of the road. He could hear a woman speaking German. She was in the roadside ditch, hidden from view behind the cart which tilted halfway, as if deciding whether to join her. If his German were better, he would be more certain, but he thought he heard language that his mother would have considered entirely unsuitable for a woman.

Martin was not in the mood for helping Germans, not after all that he'd witnessed. He continued walking. He hated the Germans. They had spread misery across an entire continent. Perhaps they were the ones who should be eliminated, instead of the Jews. They had given Sonja her scar. He thought of Sonja. She was German. She was blamed for the actions of others, actions for which she took no part.

He thought of her kindness. He knew that in similar circumstances, she would not hesitate to stop and help. With a sigh, he walked back to where the cart still perched undecidedly on the edge of the ditch.

"Hello," he called down to her. A red face appeared around the side of the cart. She looked equal parts angry and startled and completely bedraggled.

Martin didn't wait for a response. It was for Sonja that he joined her down in the ditch. With both of them pushing, the cart was persuaded to return to the road. Climbing back onto the road, Martin spotted a wheel lying on its side, and he understood how the accident had occurred. He pointed at the wheel with his soggy boot, and lifted the corner of the cart. Without need for explanation, she grabbed the wheel and placed it on the axel, pushing it as far back as it would go.

Fortunately, the sides of the cart had prevented the bundles of early summer vegetables from sliding off into the ditch. She grabbed the cart handles and began pushing it towards the village. "Thank you," she mumbled without turning to look at Martin.

"You know English?"

She didn't respond or slow down.

Martin stood watching her, half amused and half frustrated. She was taking her vegetables to the village, in the direction opposite to where he was headed. He called after her. "That wheel will probably come off again. Do you want me to come with you in case it does?"

"No. Thank you." She didn't pause or glance back.

He stood, watching her progress. She covered the length of a football pitch when the wheel toppled once more, and the cart pitched sideways. Martin gave another sigh and jogged over to her. Again, he lifted the corner of the cart so she could replace the wheel.

"Thank you," she repeated as she set off once more, still not willing to look at him.

"I think I should follow you as far as the village, in case that happens again."

"No, not needed." She continued pushing the cart.

Martin decided to walk with her anyway. "How did you learn English?"

"Our school has teacher." She pushed on determinedly. She seemed nervous or perhaps frightened to have Martin walking beside her. Martin guessed she was about his age, or perhaps a little younger. She looked athletic, used to farm work.

When they reached the village, she turned and looked at Martin for the first time. "Thank you. Man in village will fix wagon." She gave a small smile. She seemed to relax more being around houses and people.

"May I know your name?"

She hesitated, before responding. "Johanna."

"Nice to meet you, Johanna. I'm Martin." He tipped his hat.

As he turned to head back out to the forest, the siren in his head returned. It was then that he realised that the sense of alarm had receded while he had been helping Johanna.

The following week, when Martin made his next visit to the forest, he kept watching for Johanna. But she was nowhere in sight. There being only a few farms between the village and the forest, he tried to guess which farm might be hers. Then on his way back to base, there she was, bending over a field of cabbages. As she straightened up, she saw him and gave a small wave of acknowledgement. She seemed to have decided that Martin was not a danger to her.

He said hello and walked over to her.

"Who else is here to help with the farm?"

"My mother and my sister only. Is much work for us."

"Where is your father?"

"He was made to fight, and my brother."

"Do you hear from them?"

"My brother sent letter four months. We not hear since. My father—we not hear long time." As she said this, she dug her hoe in savagely, as if the weeds were responsible for her missing family members. Then she looked up at Martin. "And your family?"

"My parents were killed in the bombing of London. My little sister lives with my grandmother. My brother is on his way home from a prisoner of war camp. We don't know anything about his condition. "

Johanna stopped her hoeing. "I am sorry you have loss." She looked straight at Martin.

"Thank you. I hope your brother and father return safe." Martin smiled and continued on his way back to camp.

The next time Martin passed their farm, Johanna called him over. She asked him to wait while she ran into the farmhouse. She returned carrying a small jar of honey from the hives they kept at the back of their farm. A thin red ribbon was wrapped around the jar and tied into a neat bow.

"My mother says thank you for the help."

Martin felt bad taking food from this family but knew they would be offended if he refused their gift. Over the next several weeks, Martin stopped often to check in on Johanna. He thought she might be finding excuses to work the plots of land nearest the road on the chance that they might see each other. Occasionally, Martin helped with small tasks that neither Johanna nor her mother were strong enough to do on their own.

Although Martin was elated when the orders came through to demobilise, he felt regret at not knowing if he would see Johanna or her family again. He asked her to write so that he could know the fate of her brother and her father. Martin felt he and Johanna shared a common bond, with their dead or missing family members.

CHAPTER 42

Weymouth, June 1945

LICE COULDN'T CONCENTRATE. DESPITE having stepped down from the Observer Corps, she wasn't making progress on her book. It was her stepson's fault. She still had misgivings about establishing connections with him. She gave up on her writing and went into the kitchen to start preparing their evening tea. It was Rosa's day off.

Lydia came in to the kitchen to see if she could help.

"Thanks, but I think I have things managed. I could use your help on another matter, however." Alice decided that Lydia might provide another helpful perspective, in addition to Helen's. While she worked on their supper and Lydia sat at the kitchen table, she relayed the entire story of how she had come to realise that James was her stepson.

"There is no fault from you or from James. Neither of you have anything to be ashamed of. You should do what suits you." Lydia's advice echoed that from Helen, which didn't surprise Alice. Perhaps she had asked simply to gain some additional encouragement with which to face the next hurdle, which was talking to Irene.

The next day when Irene returned from her volunteer hospital duty, she called her into the sitting room.

"Irene, dear, there's something I'd like to tell you." Alice sat in her favourite chair, and Irene took a seat directly across from her. She seemed to sense that this was serious.

"I want to let you know that your grandfather had another son, besides your father."

"Yeah, Martin told me about James and Lilly." She seemed disappointed that her grandmother didn't have anything new or interesting to tell her.

"No, there's someone else. Someone I found out about just recently."

"Who are you talking about?" Irene seemed impatient. She truly had hit adolescence. Alice decided she may as well be direct.

"Edgar had another family."

"You mean he had a first wife?"

"No. He had an affair. With a woman who worked with him at the courthouse. They had a son, and they kept everything hidden all these years."

"Oh." Irene took a moment to respond. "Grandfather had another woman?"

"Yes, dear." She had wanted to shield her grandchildren from all this. She wondered if this was a mistake, but it was too late now.

"How did you find out?"

"I've noticed their son around town. He looks a lot like your father did when he was younger. His name is James—named after your other uncle James who died. He hadn't wanted to intrude on our family, but I had recently heard a rumour and sought him out because I wanted to know the truth."

"So, you mean this man is my uncle?" Irene sat up straight. Alice worried that the news was coming as too much of a shock.

"Yes, he is your uncle."

"When can I meet him?"

That took Alice by surprise. "Do you want to meet him?"

"Of course! It's an uncle I never knew I had. Like a story out of a novel."

Alice exhaled and relaxed into her chair. She had anticipated feelings of shock and betrayal from Irene. Perhaps because that's how she herself felt. She had not anticipated excitement.

Alice decided not to try to explain the situation to Martin in a letter. The news could wait until Martin returned.

She and James met in a café near the Town Bridge. James appeared more settled than at their previous meeting on VE Day. Sitting across from him, Alice got straight to the point. "James, would you be interested in meeting the rest of the family?"

"I would very much. But not if it in any way places you in an awkward position."

"No, it does not. I've spoken to my granddaughter, Irene, and she's excited to meet you. My grandson, Martin, is still in service in Germany, but I'm sure he'll want to meet you as well when he's demobilised. My other grandson, Leo, has recently been liberated from a German prisoner of war camp and is on his way home. That's the extent of my family. My children have all passed on."

As Alice looked across the table, she saw in James that he had inherited Edgar's gravitas but without the pompous nonsense. He grew up in humble circumstances and had not been indoctrinated as to his own self-importance.

Alice told James about Lydia coming to stay with her and about her work with the Observer Corps during the war. James talked about growing up in Southampton and about his university studies where he completed a law degree. He hoped to become a solicitor, rather than a barrister.

It was time for Alice to return home. "James, I'd like to you to join us for tea one evening."

"I would like that."

All the way home, Alice thoughts were on James. Their meeting had only increased the bond she felt with him, that he belonged in their family. Yet, she couldn't escape the image of Elizabeth Chambers smiling smugly down on her. She would see to it that the news spread quickly, and then everyone in Weymouth would know their family secret. Whether it was going into town to shop, or worshiping at their parish, she would always be left wondering. While being outwardly polite, were her neighbours talking about her behind her back, looking down on her, judging her and her family.

Alice's thoughts were interrupted by Irene, who came running out to meet her.

"Leo is home!"

Thoughts of Elizabeth Chambers disappeared. Alice hurried up the front steps, through the entryway, and into the sitting room, where Leo rose from the sofa to greet her. As Alice embraced her grandson, she noticed how easily her arms encircled his thin frame, how little padding separated skin and bones. Holding him at arm's length, she looked into the sunken eyes, noted the pinched cheekbones and nose, the stretched grey skin. But he was alive, and he was home.

Leo sat down across from Alice but did not meet her eyes. Rosa brought through a tray with tea and biscuits and set them down, beaming at Leo.

"What will it be for tea tonight, Leo? You name it, and if we can get our hands on it, we'll fix it," Rosa asked.

"Whatever you're having will suit fine, thanks." He shifted in his chair, as if uncomfortable with being the focus of attention.

"I'll see what we can come up with. You'd think with the war done past a month, there'd be an end to the rationing." Rosa headed off to the kitchen.

Alice looked over at Leo. She wanted to hear about what he'd been through but sensed that an interrogation would not be welcome at this point. "What can I do to help you get settled? We have the blue room all set up for you. I thought we should keep Martin in Henry's old room once he's demobilised, since he's used to staying there."

"That will suit fine."

Leo got up and started across the room. That was when Alice noticed his limp. She made an effort to keep her response low key. "I see you're limping a little. Were you injured at some point?"

"It's nothing." Leo kept walking. He sounded impatient. "Lots of blokes got much worse."

***

In the midst of all the commotion around Leo's return, most of the household failed to notice the arrival of the day's post. But Lydia noticed. She had been watching anxiously every day for almost two months.

There was a letter addressed to her, posted from Chicago. Lydia tore it open. Anthony's mother explained that she found Lydia's letters among Anthony's things sent home to her. She apologised for taking more than a week before she could face writing to Lydia. She wasn't sure if Lydia had heard the news about Anthony. He had made the ultimate sacrifice for his country, had been courageous. Their all-negro regiment had been recognised for their bravery. She went on to describe war medals that meant nothing to Lydia.

The United States finally decided that negroes could be heroes. Lydia had not wanted him to be a hero. She had just wanted him to return alive.

With the focus on Leo, no one saw her, standing in the entry hall, reading the letter. Nor did they notice her escape upstairs. She threw herself onto her bed and sobbed until she had no tears left to give.

CHAPTER 43

The Midlands, September 1945

MARTIN DISEMBARKED AT THE St. Pancras Station to change trains. As he walked to the ticket booth, he passed an overflowing garbage bin. Something very foul was rotting in the depth of the bin. Suddenly he was back at Bergen-Belsen, surrounded by the dead and dying, the smell of their death and disease permeating everything. He found his way to the exit and leaned against an outside wall. The London air was not exactly fresh, but there was a breeze and a light rain which helped revive him. His breathing returned to normal, and the siren receded. Martin gathered his resolve, and re-entered the station, steering well clear of any bins.

Desperate as he was to get to Weymouth, there was a detour he needed to make. He reviewed a timetable, and purchased a ticket on a line heading northwest. The crowded train stopped at every town, and it was almost two hours before it reached his stop, a small-town station like hundreds of others scattered across England.

After consulting a map, he made his way on foot to where the homes were just starting to give way to dry, sweet-smelling fields heavy with corn and wheat. It was a small house—almost a cottage. A vegetable patch dominated the front garden, overflowing with beans, tomatoes, varieties of squash, and rhubarb. All along a white picket fence, anemones, sunflowers, lavender, and small pink climbing roses buzzed with pollinators.

He walked up to the neatly painted front door. Bright yellow window shutters were matched by the patterned curtains tied back from the windows on either side.

Mr. and Mrs. Walker answered Martin's knock. His first impression was that they were both small, like the house. Mr. Walker stepped forward and solemnly shook Martin's hand. He had wire-rimmed glasses, similar to Howard's. "You must be Martin. Thank you for coming."

Martin stepped inside. Mrs. Walker shook his hand with both of hers, clinging to it warmly as if she might glean just a touch of Howard channelled through Martin. In contrast to the bright garden, the sitting room was decorated in subdued browns and immaculately clean.

Martin sat down, and Mrs. Walker went into the kitchen to put the kettle on for tea. She returned and sat with her husband, across from Martin, smiling earnestly. "Howard told us so much about you—and Jack. We feel like we already know you. We can't think of how to properly thank you. It was such a relief to hear he had found such true friends. We worried so about his going into the army."

"Thanks, but I think Howard was being modest. He's the one who was a true friend. I wouldn't be alive if not for him." Martin felt wholly undeserving of their appreciation. But the Walkers continued to smile at him.

"He told us about how you saved him from drowning. His letters were full of 'Martin did this' and 'Jack said that'. I don't know what he would have done if it hadn't been for the two of you."

From the kitchen, the kettle started whistling. Mrs. Walker left and returned with a tray carrying teapot, cups and scones. Martin was feeling increasingly uncomfortable. Uncomfortable playing the hero. He now knew the hero was always and only Howard. Yet, he didn't feel he could set the record straight—that it was the men who pulled them both from the water who had saved Howard, not Martin. They wouldn't hear it. If Martin was diminished, their son's sacrifice in saving him would also be diminished.

"Would you like to see Howard's room?" Mr. Walker looked up at Martin. He could see how much this visit meant to them.

"Of course." Martin wasn't sure he did but couldn't possibly turn down these two people whose life had obviously revolved around their son.

Martin's father led the way down a short hall to a tiny bedroom. The furniture consisted of a bed, a dresser, and a simple long desk taking up most of one wall. The desk was filled with radios and other electronic gadgets in various states of disassembly. In the corner sat a large tray with compartments for screws, wires, and other small parts. A wooden tool box sat on the floor next to the desk.

The room looked as though it had been tidied up, except the desk, which appeared to have been left untouched since the day Howard departed for basic training. There was not much else to look at. Centred on top of the dresser was a framed photograph of the three Walkers. Martin guessed Howard would have been about ten years old. His face was rounder, but he recognised the large, angular nose. Howard had been a cute kid, smiling up at them from between his mother and father. This was before he had grown into his awkward, bony, angular frame.

Martin had thought he might stay for evening tea, if invited. Now he was eager to be away. He felt he was masquerading as the hero. But there was no way he would detract from the narrative Howard's parents were clinging to, as if now they were the ones drowning.

He found a train back to London. He would need to find a place to stay the night before continuing on to Weymouth. As the train bumped along, he could not stop thinking of Howard offering his life to save Martin's. He realised that this was more than just Howard's parents and the gaping hole in their lives that would never be filled. It changed how he viewed his own life. To waste his life would be a dishonour to his friend. His life was no longer fully his own. Howard claimed a part of it from his grave in the French countryside.

He also thought about Jack Green. Jack had sent word that he was demobilised back to Sunderland and hoped that Martin could pay a visit. Martin was eager to do that, but that trip would need to wait. Now, he was singularly focused on reaching Weymouth.

Partly, he wanted to see Leo. It had been over five years since they had made the trip to London to clear out what remained of their old household, and he had watched Leo march off towards the tube station on his way back to basic training. What had all those years of war and prison camp done to him?

But even more, he wanted to see Sonja. He had so much to tell her. His grandmother had written to let him know that Sonja had received confirmation that her parents had been murdered at Buchenwald. The news had shaken Martin. He wanted to be with her to share her grief and to support her. He had failed to do that before being enlisted. He wanted to make up for that now. He felt he understood her at last.

CHAPTER 44

Weymouth, September 1945

MARTIN WALKED UP FROM the Weymouth train station. His route took him within a block of the house where Lydia had grown up. Last he'd heard, she was still living with his grandmother. He passed Ellis's cottage. Was Ellis back in Weymouth? His grandmother had not mentioned him in any of her letters.

Elm House came into view. The walk from town had seemed a long trek, before he became a soldier. Now, it hardly qualified as a warm up. Elm House was now the closest thing he had to a home, and seeing it after two years away, it did feel more like home.

As he crossed the threshold and closed the door behind him, Martin noticed the quiet. The home's peacefulness brought to mind the forest in Germany. Except, of course, the grandfather clock ticking away. The calm contrasted sharply with the noises of London and the constant clatter of train travel. He poked his head into the sitting room, the dining room, and then into his grandfather's old study. Where was everyone? This was not the grand entrance he had envisioned.

He was hungry, so he ventured into the kitchen. Rosa turned from the counter she was working at, saw Martin and ran to greet him. "Good to have you back, Martin. You look as though you came through this in one piece."

"Thanks, Rosa." Martin had always liked Rosa, but he wanted to see his family. "Where'd everyone go?"

"Your grandmother is over at the neighbours. I'll run fetch her. She wanted to know the minute you got home. Lydia and Irene are at work at the hospital. I expect Leo's up in his room. That's where he spends his time these days." She wiped her hands on a dishrag. "You wait here. I'll fetch your grandmother." She dashed off.

Martin didn't have a chance to ask her what there was to eat. He snooped through the cupboards and was disappointed. Apparently, the news about the war being ended hadn't yet reached their kitchen. He found a crumbly loaf of wartime wheatmeal bread. This was not something he had missed, but he cut off a piece anyway and sliced up an apple from his grandmother's tree.

His grandmother came in through the back kitchen door, and Martin was enveloped in a hug. "It's so good to have you home." Martin thought she was close to tears. Rosa smiled at them. His grandmother turned to her. "Would you be so kind as to let Leo know that Martin's home?" They went into the sitting room, and Martin tried to answer his grandmother's questions through mouthfuls of bread and apple.

"Martin." Martin turned to see that Leo had entered the room. He could tell immediately that it was not the same Leo who had walked off to war on a London afternoon five years ago. Gaunt as a scarecrow, eyes vacant. Even his voice had become thin, diminished. Martin stood up and crossed over to Leo. He didn't know if he should hug his brother, as he stood there, unresponsive. He opted for a handshake, but Leo's hand was slack, the handshake empty.

As they went to sit down, Martin noticed Leo's limp. Leo asked him about his postings, and Martin talked about crossing to France, then marching and driving through the Netherlands, Belgium, and Germany. He didn't mention Bergen-Belsen. That was not something he wished to discuss. Other than in the days immediately following his visit, he had not shared that nightmare with anyone.

Martin asked Leo about his experiences. "We thought Africa was hell, but then we found out that no, hell was Italy." That's all he would say. Martin was curious about what it was like in the POW camp, but Leo deflected any talk of it.

The four of them were still sitting there as if at a funeral, when Lydia and Irene arrived home. Irene squealed and ran up to Martin, while Lydia smiled at him. Both Lydia and Irene overflowed with questions, and the gloom that had occupied the room lifted. Martin thought that his grandmother might have been the only other person to notice Leo quietly slipping out of the room. Rosa had already returned to the kitchen to finish preparations for evening tea.

Martin wanted to go straight to the sheep farm. He wanted to see Sonja. But it was already late, and he could not take himself away from his grandmother, sister, and brother, who had been anticipating his return. Sonja would have to wait until the morning.

The evening meal was lively, with Irene holding centre stage. Martin marvelled at her transformation. He left behind a sister who was unnaturally quiet and withdrawn and came home to one he wished would stop talking once in a while. The dark cloud that hung over the dining table was Leo. He finished his meal in silence and made an early departure, returning to his room.

The next morning, Martin was up early. His grandmother came downstairs as he was eating breakfast. "Where are you off to today?"

"Nathan's farm. I thought I'd pay Sonja a visit."

"Splendid idea." His grandmother put the kettle on for tea. "You might see Ellis as well."

"Ellis?" Martin looked up from his porridge.

"Yes. He was demobilised a couple months ago and has been working at the farm."

Martin didn't know what to think of that news. He woofed down the rest of his breakfast and headed to the back shed for his father's old bicycle. Pedalling hard, he felt a foreboding about what he would find.

Moss was the first to come out to greet Martin. The collie was slower, showing signs of arthritis. Then Nathan appeared from around the corner of the outbuilding. He gave Martin a scrutinizing look and wanted to know everything about his time at war. Martin tried to be polite, but he wanted to see Sonja.

"I was wondering if Sonja was about?" Martin finally found a break in the questioning.

"Yeah, she and Ellis are just in back. They'll be delighted to see you."

Martin walked around to the other side of the outbuilding. Sonja ran over to give Martin a hug. He was shocked once more by the prominence of her scar. He'd forgotten how noticeable it was. Ellis followed with a hearty handshake. They both smiled at him. Ellis had become very fit in the army. He looked perfectly suited to farm life.

"This is wonderful that you're back." Sonja's English had definitely improved. "We have news, and you can be the first to share it. Ellis has proposed, and I have accepted him."

Martin looked to Sonja and then to Ellis. He felt his head spin. They just smiled at him. Recovering himself, Martin did the only thing he could do. "Congratulations!" He shook Ellis's hand again.

"Thanks mate. We'd like you to be best man, if you're keen."

"Sure." This was so unexpected that Martin couldn't think of what else to say. It would have seemed churlish to say no.

Ellis suddenly turned serious. "Look mate, I never properly thanked you for going to the bobbies. Near enough the best thing to happen to me, 'cept finding Sonja." Again, this was not what Martin had been expecting. "It was your grandmother who talked to the judge. He and I had quite the discussion—told me about Sonja ending up in detention on account of my stupidity. Got me doing a whole lot of thinking about where my life was headed and what was I going to do about it."

Martin sensed the time had come to be straight with everyone. "I didn't want to suspect you. I kept putting it off. If I had acted sooner, Sonja wouldn't have ended up in detention." Implied but left unsaid was that she also would not have ended up with her scar.

Sonja smiled at him. "I do not blame you, and I do not blame Ellis. I will not let the hatred of others drive away those who have shown me kindness. Besides, that was how I came to know Ellis. He wrote to apologise for what had happened, and I answered his letter. He has been writing to me all through the war."

Nathan emerged around the corner of the outbuilding with a question for Sonja, and she went off to talk to him. Ellis turned to Martin. He wanted to know all about what Martin had been up to. And Martin found he had a thousand things to catch up on with Ellis. So much had happened to both of them since their enlistment. There was no space for Martin to absorb the news that just upended all of his half-formed dreams. But he realised that he couldn't hate Ellis for having won Sonja's affections. Their friendship seemed to pick up where it left off.

Sonja rejoined them. She looked over at Martin. "Will you walk with me?"

They passed through dry, golden fields set alight by the morning sun. The air buzzed with bees and wasps. Sonja waited until they reached the clifftop footpath with its views of rocky headlands and miles of ocean before turning to face Martin. "I'm sorry things didn't work out between you and me." Martin looked over at her, startled by her directness. "Forgive me. I didn't want to give you false hope, but I also didn't want you to feel left alone when you were off fighting for your country. I don't feel sure whether I did right by you, but I didn't know what else I should do."

While Martin struggled with how to respond to that, Sonja continued. "I think you are wonderful person, and you have great future ahead for you. But not with me. I don't think you ever got used to my scar." Martin was about to object, but she spared him from having to do that. "It's okay. But I need to be with someone who never hesitates to look at me. That person is Ellis. He has been good to me. The scar to him is no matter. I was always the same person when he looked at me. I hope you understand."

Martin thought perhaps he was beginning to understand. He had anticipated seeing Sonja because he had so much to tell her. Now he realised it was the other way around. She had already understood. She had wisdom still to impart to him.

"I'm sorry for the news about your parents." At this, Sonja turned to look out over the Channel. "Do you have any relatives left in Germany?"

She turned back to Martin. "No, they are all gone. I try to keep to mind that my mother and father did what they did so that I could live my life. That is the best way that I can remember them."

They walked on in silence. But it wasn't silence. The waves softly thundered on the beach below, while above them a hawk circled in the updraft.

CHAPTER 45

Weymouth, December 1945

OR NOW, ELM HOUSE was filled with a most extraordinary family. Alice decided it did feel like her home, at last.

Martin would head out in January to start at university. He had announced plans to study electrical engineering. She gathered that inspiration came from one of his army friends, one who would never have that opportunity.

He and Lydia seemed to have a friendly banter going. But she also noticed a steady stream of letters to and from a young lady in Germany. Alice asked him about his German friend, but his reply was non-committal. She considered it a healthy sign that he seemed in no hurry to form a serious attachment.

She was proud of Martin. After so many years of hesitancy, he had become a man who knew his own mind. In Alice's view, that was an achievement that many never attained.

She wondered if she should have prepared him for what she thought was happening between Sonja and Ellis. Perhaps warned him before he set out that day, the morning after his return from war. But in the end, she decided it would be better for them to settle things without her interference. Was that the wisest decision? Like so many things, she might never know. But they seemed to have worked it out and remained friends.

Ellis's and Sonja's wedding was a simple affair. Ellis's background was Church of England, and Sonja came from a Jewish family. So, they compromised by holding the ceremony at the farmhouse. Martin properly roasted Ellis in his speech as best man, and Irene was delighted to be a bridesmaid. It was a very small wedding, but Ellis's father and some of Ellis's mates from the army were there. Sonja, of course, had no relatives to see her married, but her former fellow Land Girls both attended. Nathan walked her down the short aisle between the two single rows of chairs set out in the farmhouse great room.

Lydia also planned to move out in January. In her case, to study nursing. She was back on civil terms with her parents, now that her relationship with Anthony had been tragically cut short. But her relationship with them was damaged beyond the point where it could be fully mended. At least, not with the tools Lydia's parents had cultivated during their lifetimes. Alice felt they lacked the requisite humility and compassion. Without those resources, they seemed destined to remain hurt and confused by the distance between themselves and their daughter. She had no desire to come between Lydia and her parents but was happy to continue her friendship with Lydia.

James, her adopted son, had recently taken up residence at Elm House while he worked towards establishing himself as a solicitor. It seemed a waste for him to pay for lodgings when an extra room sat empty, and the money he saved could go towards his new endeavour. For the moment, every bedroom at Elm House was occupied.

Leo remained a concern. He was slowly becoming more comfortable in the presence of others. He had taken up a friendship with James, of all people. James's personality was calm and unassuming. He fit seamlessly into the household. She guessed it was the type of friendship Leo needed. No pressure, no agendas. She hoped that over time, Leo would be able to share with James some of the horrors that had inflicted so much damage to his soul. She also hoped the day would come when Leo would be able to seek employment, and put his life back together. Most of the time, it felt like that day was still far into the future.

Irene had managed to negotiate the past six years and come through mostly unscathed. A bit like Alice's cat, Oscar, which had become Irene's cat. And, yes, Irene had suddenly realised there were boys. All of that craziness lay ahead of them.

Alice and Rosa were planning for a large gathering for Christmas tea—her family of misfits, plus Nathan, Sonja, Ellis, and Emil, home from university. The icing on the cake was that Peter Gurin had flown over from the States to retrace some of the places he visited as a serviceman. He was to join them for Christmas tea and was bringing a special friend. Alice looked forward to meeting him.

Alice still tried to find scraps of time to work on her book on the natural history of Dorset. Perhaps at some future date she would finish it. Or perhaps she wouldn't. At this point, anything was possible.

Also by William McClain:

The Risk in Crossing Borders

ACKNOWLEDGEMENTS

I benefited from a number of brilliant historical resources covering this most fascinating chapter of human history. In particular, the BBC archive of World War II memories preserves hundreds of first-hand accounts covering all aspects of the war, both from the battle front and the home front. The historical documentary *Wartime Farm*, which aired on BBC, delightfully illustrates life in rural England during the war. The Imperial War Museum provided a wealth of online information, background, and photographs.

Richard Samways of the Weymouth Museum kindly provided assistance to a complete stranger. In particular, he pointed me to the book *Weymouth and Portland at War* by Maureen Attwooll and Denise Harrison, which proved to be one of my most valued resources.

The characters in *Alice's War* are all fictional, as are Walbridge Manor, Elm House, and the Observation Corps lookout post used by Alice and Nathan. The closing of Weymouth Beach occurred later than depicted in the story. The aerial attacks on Weymouth and the major military operations portrayed in the book were based on real events. The scenes describing Bergen-Belsen were based as closely as possible on those first-hand accounts available to me.

I am indebted to a number of individuals who helped make this book possible. My editors, Nicky Lovick and Sinead Fitzgibbon provided many perceptive suggestions that accumulated to a substantial improvement in the final story. I'm grateful to beta readers David Gruenwald, Marlene Stutzman, Mary Kooistra, and Susan Evans for valued insights and encouragement. Rebecca Brown and Andrew Brown from Design for Writers did marvelous work with layout, design, and cover. Thanks also to the Edmonds Waterfront Center Writers Group for their helpful suggestions and encouragement. My greatest debt is to my wife, Carol McClain, who reviewed several drafts, but more importantly, willingly gave her support, advice, encouragement, and patience throughout the project.

Made in United States
Troutdale, OR
07/02/2023

10870668R10184